THE MIDNIGHT TAXI

THE MIDNIGHT TAXI

YOSHA GUNASEKERA

Berkley Mystery
New York

BERKLEY MYSTERY
Published by Berkley
An imprint of Penguin Random House LLC
1745 Broadway, New York, NY 10019
penguinrandomhouse.com

Book design by Nancy Resnick
Title page illustration by Bahau/Shutterstock

Library of Congress Cataloging-in-Publication Data

Names: Gunasekera, Yosha author
Title: The midnight taxi / Yosha Gunasekera.
Description: First edition. | New York: Berkley Mystery, 2026.
Identifiers: LCCN 2025032887 |
ISBN 9798217187539 trade paperback | ISBN 9798217187546 ebook
Subjects: LCGFT: Detective and mystery fiction | Thrillers (Fiction) | Novels | Fiction
Classification: LCC PS3607.U54724 M53 2026
LC record available at https://lccn.loc.gov/2025032887

First Edition: February 2026

Printed in the United States of America
2nd Printing

The authorized representative in the EU for product safety and compliance is Penguin Random House Ireland, Morrison Chambers, 32 Nassau Street, Dublin D02 YH68, Ireland, https://eu-contact.penguin.ie.

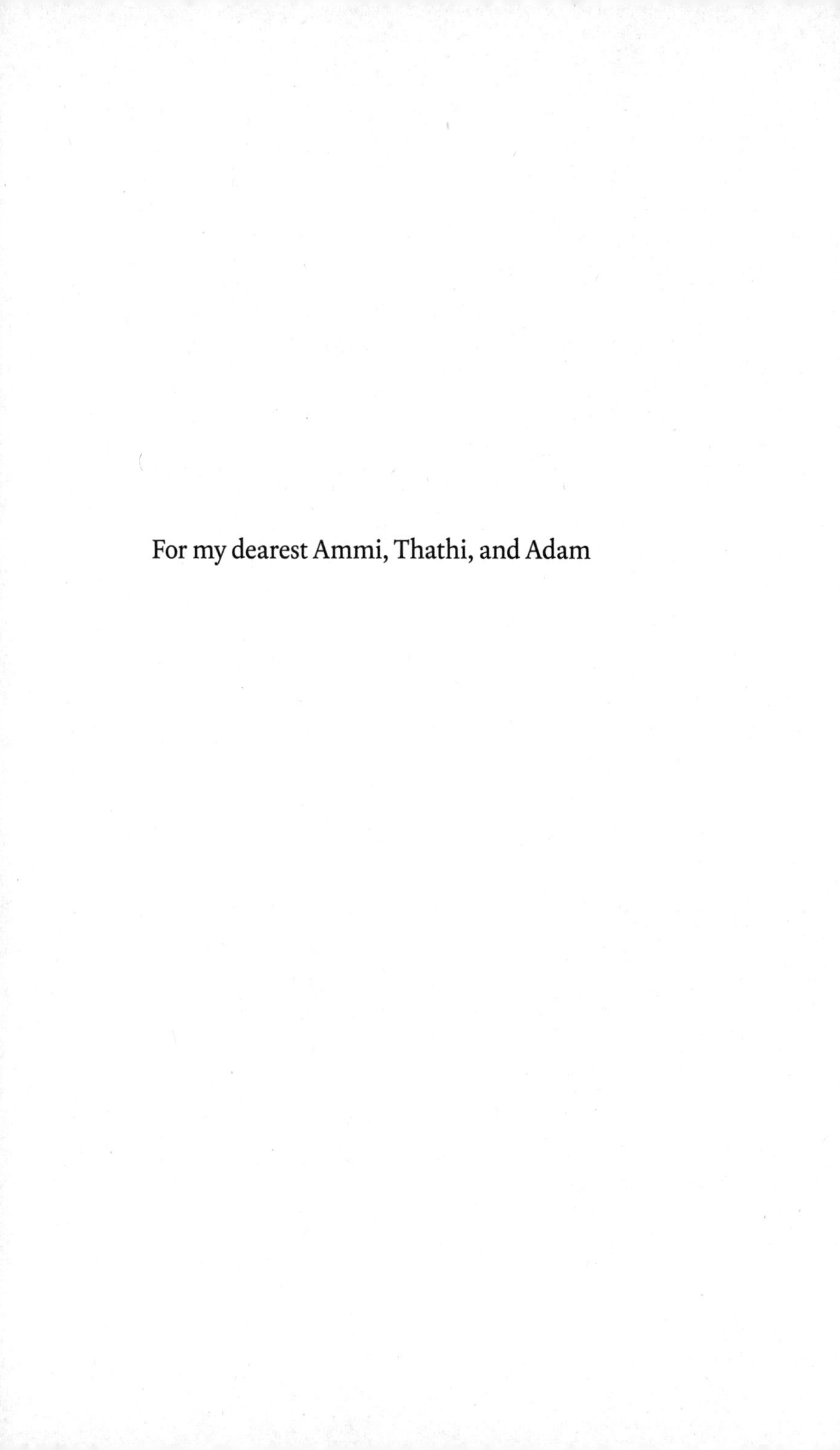

For my dearest Ammi, Thathi, and Adam

THE MIDNIGHT TAXI

CHAPTER 1

I spend most of my free time thinking about murder. The facts, means, motives, opportunity. My true crime podcasts are a lifeline to help me escape traffic, the passenger yelling at his wife who should surely divorce him, and the people who deem it appropriate to eat what appears to be a three-course meal in the back of my cab. Funny how murder is a tantalizing reprieve from my real life.

As I drive along the east side of Manhattan, I'm trying to figure out who really stabbed the Italian tourist seven times before the host does. This podcast is trying to throw me off the scent by suggesting a stranger did it. Like many true crime aficionados, I know 90 percent of murders are committed by people the victim knows. I'd almost be offended by this obvious red herring if I weren't so engrossed in the story. Instead of obsessing about a crime thousands of miles away, I should be focusing more on picking up passengers. The clock disapprovingly blinks midnight, taunting me for only completing eleven rides today, which is nearly an all-time low.

I look out on unobstructed views of the Brooklyn Bridge set

against the backdrop of the Brooklyn skyline. I remind myself that I'm not just a taxicab driver. I'm a New York City taxicab driver. My superpowers include weaving through bikes in rush hour, finding my way around the city without a navigation app, and silencing dudes in seconds with my resting bitch face when they have no manners. No, I don't want to go on a date with you, especially after seeing the tip you just left.

I take an exit off the highway and find myself close to Centre Street, where the criminal courthouse in Manhattan is located. There are often lawyers streaming in and out at all hours thanks to night court, which allows those arrested to see a judge even when it's late. It's usually a reliable spot to pick up a fare, and at times the people who enter my cab from court fill my incessant desire to learn more about those *New York Post* headlines. Is their "Groin Graffitier," charged with spray-painting all those penises on subway cars, going to get prison time? True crime podcasts are interesting, but it's best to hear the stories from the sources themselves. Sometimes I think I could be a lawyer, only to remember that my LSAT prep book has remained untouched for longer than the hair-waxing kit in the back of my bathroom cabinet. Ah yes, to be a twenty-eight-year-old woman who can grow a mustache to rival that of a pubescent boy.

I know I shouldn't try to talk to my passengers. Most people prefer to sit in silence, their pursed lips telling me that every word out of my mouth is one dollar less of a tip. I can almost hear my bank account whine in protest each time. Still, I'm nosy. I ask the person how they are doing, and depending on their response, I can quickly suss out whether they want to talk to me or tell me to shut up. Lucky for me, lawyers like to talk, especially about themselves and by extension, their work.

I slow my car outside the courthouse. I find the brutalist architecture a style more suitable for a bomb shelter than a bastion of justice. The quote etched in the stone facade declares EQUAL AND EXACT JUSTICE TO ALL MEN OF WHATEVER STATE OR PERSUASION. I laugh when I see that someone has added a *WO* in front of *MEN*. That's the type of graffiti I can support.

Scanning the steps of the courthouse, I see a man milling about before I spot a woman on the corner. She is shivering slightly. The late-night fall air certainly calls for a coat, yet she's without one. I hear Ammi tutting in my head. Even in 80-degree weather, my mother insists I keep a sweater around so I don't catch a cold.

The man waves me down just before she does, but if I have a choice, I'll take a female passenger any day.

The woman appears to be a lawyer, judging by her suit and high heels. Both of her bags are filled with files that are popping out the top. I make the snap judgment that she is a public defender. Most of the prosecutors I pick up are white men; she is some sort of Brown, like me, and while her suit is nice, it looks well-worn.

I try to avoid judging people on their appearances, because if driving a taxi for this long has taught me anything, it's that people are often more than they appear to be. Or less. Like the man in a tuxedo who clipped his toenails in my cab one time—when I asked him to stop, he pretended he couldn't hear me.

I pull over and the woman hops in, taking a second with her bags. The man who hailed my cab looks annoyed when he sees I've decided to pick up the woman, and he calls me something I can't quite hear but I'm positive isn't a compliment. I ignore him. If I had a dime for every lazy, sexist diss I've received, I'd be able to afford to see the Knicks courtside . . . well, maybe not courtside, but in great seats, and I wouldn't have to smuggle in my own snacks.

"Do you need help?" I ask the woman. Men always seem a little offended when I offer to load their bags into the car, but it's just part of the job. Fragile ego, bro?

"No, I'm fine," she says, settling in. "Bedford and Greene Ave. Brooklyn, please."

She immediately turns off the taxi television that plays the same loop of puff piece news stories. I'm grateful when people do that so I can better hear my podcasts, which I play at low volume on my phone—just loud enough to drone out an obnoxious guy in a suit complaining about the stock market but not loud enough for my passengers to think they hopped into the car with a cab-driving murderer. Less than 10 percent of serial killers are women, so I can't imagine I pose too much of a threat, but you never know. There are also very few women cabdrivers, yet here I am. Sometimes the taxi television plays interesting news stories though. The one last week about the goats at Riverside Park was entertaining the first and second time I heard it. However, by the end of the day, after hearing the story repeat over forty times I officially hated goats and sought out some goat curry for dinner.

She doesn't seem to want to talk; nevertheless, I ask my customary question. "How was your night?"

"Ugh, it was rough. *Rough*," she replies.

"I'm sorry to hear that. Why?" This seems like it may be my first real conversation of the day. People who don't want to talk simply say "fine" and take an urgent phone call where the phone suspiciously doesn't manage to ring. Not sure if I can blame them. I'm just a mode of transportation after all.

"My last guy got held in on five hundred dollars' bail. He's homeless; how is he going to afford that? Bail for trespassing," she says, an air of sarcasm in her voice. "He was evicted from his own home, didn't leave it instantly, so they arrested him. It's barbaric."

That all but confirms she's a public defender, and I congratulate myself on my successful assessment.

"It's very cold outside," I say as I pass yet another cardboard-box house on the street. Even though I can't really afford it, I've given more than a few free rides to those in need. It seems like basic decency. My Venmo balance would suggest otherwise.

I notice how candid she is as she continues discussing her day. It's a degree of honesty that I frequently see in my cab. People revealing their most real, raw selves to someone they will never see again, also known as free therapy!

I look in my rearview mirror but can't really tell what she looks like because my plastic divider, graying with age, gives everyone a murky appearance. The dark night further distorts my view. As soon as I save enough money, a new divider will be the first improvement for my taxi. Not being able to see what people are doing in my back seat, especially at night, is a constant source of anxiety. I've been avoiding the 2 a.m. bar crowd for this reason, but with my passenger numbers so low, I may risk the occasional surprise puke—or worse—in the back seat. We need the money.

The woman is speaking animatedly, and her voice is pleasant. It rises a little when she makes her important points and grows just a note deeper when she seems irked. It's a wide range for just a few seconds of conversation.

"Sounds like you've been through it tonight." I want to offer something more profound, though nothing comes to mind. I'm starved for conversation, yet I can't think of anything to say.

"Thanks, that's nice of you. Anyways, how is your night going?"

I startle a bit at the question, not remembering the last time someone asked me about my day.

"It's going okay, I . . ." I mumble, unsure what to say next. I think about the question. How am I? Goose bumps form on my skin, and a familiar ache fills my heart. I'm certainly not going to reveal how I genuinely feel to a perfect stranger . . . or to anyone for that matter. Imagine the type of tip that would result in if I poured my heart out to her. She might ask me to pay for her time.

"Wait, wait . . . are you Sri Lankan?" the public defender asks, not waiting for me to expand on my answer to her previous question.

What? How does she know? Just as I can't see her, there's no way she could see my face through the divider.

As if she can read my mind and silence, she says, "I can see your name, Siriwathi Perera, on the taxi license!" I had forgotten all about that small, unflattering passport-type photo paired with my name and license number, which is displayed prominently in the rear of my taxi. You're not supposed to smile, so instead I look like I'm either suppressing a fart or slightly pissed off, so basically just a *gorgeous* headshot. Should anyone lose anything or have complaints, they know whom to blame. I'm proud to say that I've never received a single formal complaint, though I have been cursed out plenty in the car.

"I am Sri Lankan," I say, impressed that she didn't automatically assume I was Indian, the default assumption of most everyone.

"I'm Sri Lankan too," the woman replies excitedly. "I'm

Amaya Fernando. I almost never meet other Sri Lankans. And you have a beautiful name. Siriwathi." She says it slowly and pronounces it perfectly.

"Uh, thank you!" I respond, my excitement rising at meeting another Sri Lankan. "Most people just call me Siri." Ammi said that in America I had to make it easier for people to pronounce my name. Easier to blend in was more like it.

"Hi, Amaya. How can I help you?" a robotic voice sounds out of seemingly nowhere.

"Oh, shut up, Siri . . . Not you, Siriwathi . . . it's just my stupid phone . . ." Amaya mumbles as she clicks her phone off.

"It happens all the time," I respond. "Don't worry about it." I've finally trained myself to not respond to my own name in my own car.

"You should go by your full name, it's incredible. And you wouldn't have Apple products harassing you either . . ."

I rarely hear anyone outside my family call me by my full name. In America, I've always been Siri.

"That's a good idea, maybe I will." I haven't even seen Amaya's face. But, somehow, I just know I'd like her.

"Have you managed to have any good Sri Lankan food in the city?" Amaya asks.

"Uh . . . there are a couple of places in Staten Island that are great," I say. While the city is full of excellent Indian restaurants, there is only one Sri Lankan restaurant in all of Manhattan.

"There's a new place that just opened in Manhattan! You seen it?"

"Really? I haven't heard of it!" I respond with genuine excitement.

"Yep, Fifteenth and Irving. I'm planning to get a big group together to go. Least I can do is try to support Brown-owned businesses. To support people like us."

People like us. I smile thinking of a big group of friends at a Sri Lankan restaurant, clinking glasses over chicken curry that tastes like my ammi's. I try to remember the last time I went anywhere with a big group of friends. I just hang with Alex, my best and only friend. I used to have more, but friendships fade if you're not constantly tending to them. And I'm either driving my taxi all the time or, as of late, moping around as my friends move forward with their lives.

I see my old group of friends that I've lost touch with on social media. At one point in my life, it seemed as if we went everywhere together. Now, one is getting married, another just received her PhD, and a third is moving abroad. Everyone is doing incredible things, and I still feel stuck. I heart the photos but feel too far removed from those friendships to even comment on them. These used to be my people—the four of us would make microwave nachos while we binged *Law & Order: SVU*, drank wine out of a bag, and marveled at life's biggest question at the time: *Will our crushes text us back and when?* Now, we've all gone our separate ways—friendships that weren't meant for the ages. I'm left with Alex, whom I adore more than anything, but who also still burps the alphabet and gawks at me awkwardly when I cry about a hard day at work or a recent breakup.

I wish I could have found friends at work, but driving a New York City taxi is a boys' club. One driver asked me who was feeding my husband and taking care of my kids while I worked. Thankfully, most of the cabdrivers mean no ill will and just ignore me. They have their own friends. Their own routines. Not to mention, most of the cabdrivers at the stand are decades older and literal grandpas.

"A big group dinner at a Sri Lankan restaurant sounds incredible, wow." I pause, thinking of what to say next, desperately wanting to keep the conversation going. It's in this moment I realize how lonely I truly am. "Your parents must be so proud," I blurt out awkwardly, wishing I could say the same for myself. My parents are not happy I've chosen this life. It's a constant barrage of them telling me it's too dangerous, too hard, and that I should be settling down. Twenty-eight is apparently the start of almost certain spinsterhood.

"Most people consider my work crazy. I think my parents would have loved it if I had gotten one of those prestigious jobs working at some big law firm downtown instead. At this job, I barely get paid anything. It's not glamorous. Frequently thankless. Somehow, I love it."

"Wow, that's amazing. The work you do . . . it's . . . important." I struggle for the right words again. I want to tell her she is special because she is one of only about ten thousand public defenders in the country out of 1.3 million lawyers—I heard that on a podcast yesterday. Apparently, I'm a repository for exceedingly useless information. Finally I manage, "Everyone needs a lawyer. Everyone needs a voice in the system."

"Thanks. People need advocates. This system can eat people up," Amaya says.

I can't help thinking about the one time I was stopped by police for no reason other than for being Brown. It is the only reasonable explanation, since I did not run a red light or double-park or break any of the myriad of other traffic laws. I've never been arrested, but I remember the sheer fear that coursed through my body every time an officer approached my car. Would a sudden movement make the officer skittish and draw his weapon? I try to force these unpleasant memories out of my head and focus on this conversation with Amaya, who is one of the people providing that "equal and exact justice to all (wo)men."

"Everyone is doing important work," she says. "You're doing me a solid, driving me home tonight. It's dark, cold, and I really didn't wanna take the subway."

I want to be Amaya's friend, but she probably has her own large group of fabulous, interesting friends. I think of Alex and me scarfing down the McDonald's we ordered to his apartment, and sadly, I don't think I'd be a value add to her successful group of friends. I still can't help but want a group of women to talk to about things that Alex can't fully appreciate.

My cab stops at her apartment. I unlock the door for her, as my NYC taxicab automatically locks when I go above five miles per hour. Another unintended benefit is that people can't run out before paying.

"Paying in cash, keep the change," she says as she gets out.

I don't really care if she shortchanges me. I look out my passenger-side window and can finally see her clearly, illuminated perfectly by the streetlight. She has dark wavy hair, dark brown eyes, and the expression of a reluctant smile as she walks toward an old, worn brick brownstone covered in ivy. I wait for her to open the gate and her front door and enter safely inside.

I grab the cash and begin to count it. In between the bills is a business card.

Amaya Fernando
LEGAL AID OF MANHATTAN
Public Defender

Below these lines are her fax number, email address, and work cell number. On the back side is a note: *If you ever wanna grab Sri Lankan food with my friends, we'd love to have you!*

I smile widely and I can feel my heart beating out of my chest like someone has just handed me a steaming bowl of chicken curry. I take the card and place it in my pocket along with her generous tip.

CHAPTER 2

After I drop off Amaya, I drive around Brooklyn, past my familiar corners, noticing that everyone in the bustling streets seems to be staring at their phones—the glare giving their faces an eerie zombie-like glow. I guess I'm predisposed to see them in a negative light, as they are probably waiting for their Ubers to arrive. I want to yell, "No surge pricing with yellow cabs!" from my open window, but I'm still on a high from meeting Amaya and am now less stressed about the lack of fares this evening than I normally would be.

The fog and exhaustion that seem to constantly bathe my brain are temporarily lifted. I am buoyed by the idea of a new friendship. Had she seen my tangled curls and unibrow that Ammi tries to brazenly pick at with her tweezers while I watch TV on the couch, she'd probably think twice about inviting me to dinner. After seeing Amaya, a small part of me thinks that maybe I could put a little more effort into my life. I should be living my life intentionally instead of just going through the motions.

I pull up to a bodega, a hallmark of New York City. I make a beeline toward the drink section, seeing every snack I can think of crammed onto shelves as I go. *Tell me you're having a bad day after you've had some Takis*, I think to myself as I grab a bag.

I once read that there are an estimated thirteen thousand bodegas sprinkled throughout New York City. Many are open 24/7, so I can depend on them for my reliable cup of coffee even in the middle of the night. It isn't a stretch to say these corner stores are a lifeline for me with my odd hours. Almost all of them are run by immigrants or people of color, yet, as the city expands with fancy luxury office buildings and skyscrapers, I worry the bodegas will be bought out to make way for a sanitized corporate version.

I feel something at my feet and look down and see a black cat staring at me. Most bodegas have a resident cat that can be seen making itself at home among the boxes, bags of chips, and toilet paper. Corporate stores certainly wouldn't allow for these delightful surprises. Instead, they'd probably replace my diet Dr. Brown's cream soda with some green juice that both tasted awful and I couldn't afford. I reach down to scratch its head, and it purrs in satisfaction. Black cats are seen as bad omens, harbingers of bad luck, but I can't understand why as I peer into the cat's face and take in its tiny fuzzy ears and little paws.

I pay for the Takis and soda and consume both while leaning against my cab door studying the tarot card reader sign across the street. **COME LEARN YOUR FUTURE NOW**, the sign promises. I think I already know what my future looks like, though I try to remind myself it isn't as bad as some people have it. For now, I have a roof over my head and food in my stomach. I take a moment to wipe down my cab. I hate the dirt and grime that build up when people think it's appropriate to eat—say, an entire steak dinner—in the back seat. I carefully wipe down the handles, the seats, and the credit card machine.

I get back into my taxi when I get a ping from the Curb app. Someone needs to be picked up. For yellow cabs to be competitive with other rideshares, the Taxi and Limousine Commission made it so you can also call one from an app. I drive five minutes to pick up my passenger. And I wait. We're only supposed to wait for two minutes, but I linger.

Out of the corner of my eye, I notice a man carrying an odd oblong case with holes along the sides and top. I wonder what could be in there, but I don't stare long. Staring at the wrong person in New York City could merit a punch in the face. Besides, if I took in everything that was truly strange in this city, I'd never get any work done.

I wait for a few minutes longer. I need this fare. I'm contemplating calling Alex to return his numerous missed calls over the past few days when the Curb app pings. We never go more than a few days without talking, and I'm about to reach the point where he'll send a search party after me if I don't respond soon. The Curb notification shows a cancellation. I curse a little under my breath. I'm about to drive off when a man dressed in a hoodie and sweatpants with thick-rimmed glasses approaches my window. It's the man who had the odd oblong case. Now that's gone.

"Are you working?" the man demands. He's shouting through gritted teeth. Yelling and still expecting good service is typical entitled male behavior. Upon reflection I figure he is probably in a hurry. It is late at night, cold, and unsurprisingly, the man isn't dressed properly for the weather.

"Yes." I unlock the door, and when the man slides in, I ask, "Where are you going?" I lock the door again.

"JFK Airport."

"Which terminal?"

"Uh, Air France. Wherever Air France is at."

"Terminal one." I memorized all the airlines and their corresponding terminals long ago. Schlepping bags between terminals is a nightmare that I'd like to spare my passengers from. It's very considerate of me, I know.

I glance back at the man, realizing I didn't pop the trunk. "Any bags?" I ask.

"Nope," he responds, patting the small orange-and-black backpack with a logo and initials emblazoned on it next to him. I ponder for a second where that other case he had with him could have gone. As usual I'm overthinking, assuming that everything is a puzzle to be solved like the murders in my podcast. I really should be better at minding my own business.

I immediately ignore my own mandate and ask, "How are you doing?" I can't help myself, though I'm pretty sure he won't answer.

"I just need to make it on my flight," the man huffs.

So I was right. He is worried about missing his flight. I am two for two on reading people tonight. He is rude enough that I contemplate driving extra slowly, but that's a little too petty even for me.

"When is your flight?"

"Five a.m."

I look at the time. Only half past one.

"I think you'll have plenty of time," I reply. Maybe he has access to one of those fancy airport lounges and is trying to take advantage of all that free food. Free food always tastes better. One time Alex took me to a work party where waiters in tuxedos passed around all sorts of delicious foods in miniature format. I ate as much as I could and—to Alex's extreme embarrassment—

even packed a few to-go snacks in my purse. Trying to transport shrimp cocktail without a lidded container wasn't my best idea.

The man rolls down the window despite the chilly outdoor temperatures, and the smack of cold air brings me back to the present. It's a little annoying at first, but it does sort of wake me up. Besides, the customer is always right, even when he's wrong. A lesson I've had to learn the hard way. *Arguing isn't going to get you a better tip, Siriwathi,* Ammi's voice annoyingly rings in my head. Sadly, I've never had the easy charm of my big brother.

After a few seconds of silence, I think I can hear the consistent, rhythmic breathing of someone who has passed out cold, so I turn one of my true crime podcasts, realizing I left this one off at a very dramatic point. It blares louder than I anticipate, and I quickly turn the volume down a little bit. Luckily, the man appears to still be sleeping, so it plays loud enough to drown out the city sounds. Was the podcaster finally about to uncover that it was the tourist's friend all along? My hands clench the steering wheel in anticipation as if I'm somehow personally invested in this drama. I'm certain my passenger can't hear it over the din of the taxi television blaring in the back, which he makes no effort to turn off.

I cruise through Brooklyn. The main roads are crowded as usual with late-night revelers and cars. Some bros stumble out of bars as they begin to make their last calls. I eye several people wobbling like toddlers who just learned to walk, and I'm pretty sure they are about to puke. I mentally send thoughts of camaraderie and strength to whichever rideshare service picks those people up. It might be me tomorrow.

I hear a ping and look down. It's a text from Alex. Let's catch up.

My guilt gnaws at me. He's been checking on me consistently since the worst day of my life, and I can't even return his calls in a timely manner. Alex and I couldn't be more different, and if we met today, I'm positive we'd hate each other. Good thing we met almost twenty years ago, when merciless bullying drove us together, and now we're trauma bonded for life. It's also given me plenty of time to get used to his inability to make proper plans and his insistence that women love receiving shirtless photos of him.

I slow at a red light, and a group of dangerously drunk people begin to moon and flash us. I look back at my customer, who doesn't stir. I look back in time to see one man even boldly reach through the open window of the taxi and grab at my passenger in the back.

"Stop!" I yell, preparing to get out. I've practiced an authoritative voice that's one octave lower than my normal speaking voice for just these instances. The drunk man simply runs away. *This is why I like my windows up*, I think to myself with a smug satisfaction. Customer's always right, my ass. I look through the murky divider.

"Are you okay?"

The man doesn't respond, and I'm grateful that he's a deep sleeper.

I continue to drive, and at the next intersection, a motorcycle slides up next to the taxi as I stop at a red light. Whoever is riding it is revving the engine, and I look away in annoyance. Tell me you're trying to compensate for something without telling me . . . I turn up my podcast even louder to drown it out and am lost in it for a few seconds before the light turns green. Instead of traffic moving, there's some commotion up ahead, and despite the late hour, no one has any qualms about laying on their horns. I stick my head outside the window to see what's going on, and a few seconds later the traffic starts again.

I turn onto a quiet residential street where there are barely any cars. Driving past the rows of houses, almost all with their lights off, I try to imagine the people inside. I sometimes imagine myself inside, with a husband and children, all of us having dinner together and talking about our days. Maybe my brother is visiting with his family. A long-lost rich uncle is there, too, about to bequeath me millions of dollars . . .

I look back to the road in time to observe the four-way intersection just ahead. I have a green light, but a woman stumbles onto the crosswalk right ahead of me.

I hit my brakes hard and slam on my horn even louder. In New York City, it's illegal to honk your car horn unless you're warning others of an immediate danger. This situation qualifies. *Jump out of the way*, the voice inside of me screams. I watch in horror as my car stops within inches of hitting the woman. Is she maybe drunk? Didn't she see me? Didn't she even hear the screeching tires? She suddenly falls down as I stop in front of her.

Oh my God, I scream to myself. I don't think I hit her, but I throw open my car door to check on the woman as if I did. I walk several feet toward her, half expecting to see my first dead body.

"Are you okay?"

I help her up, but once I do, she runs away as quickly as her stumbling legs will allow her, the shock of almost getting hit jolting her from her slow walk. Despite only seeing her for a second, I don't think I can ever forget the face of someone I nearly ran over. I stand for a moment in the intersection and try to slow my breathing as my brother taught me years ago. My hands are shaking as I walk toward my car. "It's okay. It's okay," I repeat to myself as I take a deep breath. Despite my years of driving, I've never had such a close call.

Death still feels so close to me. I wipe my eyes on the back of my hand as I try to steady myself. *Come on!* I chide myself. I'm stronger than this. I dig my nails, badly in need of a manicure, into my palm. Climbing into my taxi, I then remember the man in the back seat of my vehicle. From his outline through the dirty partition, it seems he is still sleeping soundly despite all the commotion.

"I'm sorry about that," I call out to the man, just in case he saw it all transpire or hurt himself from the sudden stop. Hearing no response, I slowly make my way toward JFK and focus on steadying my breathing and looking, wide-eyed, at every intersection with intense scrutiny. I sincerely hope he hasn't popped a sleeping pill this early. He needs to wait to do that until he's actually on the plane. I drive at a snail's pace, knowing my passenger has hours to spare before his flight. At least this man won't be able to leave me a one-star review like I'm a hotel where he got bedbugs.

The man turned off the taxi television at some point, so I drive in silence, which I hate. Being left with my own thoughts isn't something I want. But I'm also unwilling to restart my podcast for fear it will divert my attention from the road. Despite my best efforts, my breathing is still rapid, and my knuckles are pale from squeezing the steering wheel so tightly.

I pull toward the bright lights of JFK. It is nearly quarter past two, but there are still a few cars dropping off and picking up passengers. After what happened, I decide that this is my last ride of the day. I need to go home. As we approach the terminal, I look in my rearview mirror, hoping the man is starting to get ready to leave, with the lights of the terminal signaling the arrival at his destination. He doesn't move.

"Sir, we are nearly there." I find that waking sleeping passengers up a few moments before I drop them off makes them better able to orient themselves than doing so the second we arrive. It also makes it easier for them to calculate a fair tip.

The man still doesn't stir.

"SIR!" I shout now, having had a few passengers before who were in such a deep sleep they practically needed to be shaken awake. I'll do everything before I have to physically touch this man to wake him.

"We're here!" I yell, my voice growing louder than maybe it's ever been. The man still doesn't stir. I wonder if he actually took that sleeping pill too early? People always think those pills take a while to kick in . . . I pull my cab over and stop directly in front of Air France. I get out and open the back seat door, preparing myself to project like the sports announcer at a Mets game.

But I don't need my booming voice. I blink my eyes, certain the drowsiness of the day is catching up to me and that I'm not seeing clearly. I squeeze my eyes shut and slow my breathing. When I open my eyes again, the man is seated, slightly slouched, his hand on a silver knife that is sticking out of his chest.

CHAPTER 3

I rub my eyes, sure that once I do, the man will be very much alive and well without a knife sticking out of his chest. I've got to stop listening to so many true crime podcasts. I close my eyes and open them. I see the blood. A thick trickle from the wound. I reach over to check his pulse, which confirms what I already know but can't understand. This man is dead.

Bile rises in my throat. The descriptions of dead bodies on the true crime podcasts gross me out, but to see it in person is something else entirely. In just hours, the man's body will start to stiffen, a fact I wish I didn't know right now. I think I'm going to puke.

How did this happen? We were in a locked, moving vehicle. He was breathing when he got into the taxi. Did he kill himself? Stabbing yourself in the heart in a taxi seems like an awful way to go. Was he somehow holding a knife and stabbed himself when I braked suddenly to avoid hitting that woman? No, that seems impossible. Right? *Right?* Out of the corner of my eye, I see a police officer approaching, and my stomach lurches in that uncomfortable way like when the doctor asks me if I'm exercising and eating healthy. How can I explain this? There is no explanation, at least not one that makes sense.

I look around the car. Other than the dead body in the back seat, I don't notice anything . . . except, wait—the man's backpack is gone.

As the officer moves closer, I think again about the time I was stopped by the police for a supposed minor traffic infraction that hadn't really occurred. My pulse hammers away, and my breath becomes quick and shallow. They didn't give me the benefit of the doubt then, and they certainly won't do it now with a dead body in my back seat.

I look down at my hands, realizing they feel sticky and warm. I *literally* have blood on my hands. *How did that get there?* I shut the door and clench my fists to hide the blood, readying myself for what is to come.

"EXCUSE ME," the officer yells as he walks toward me. The officer looks angry, ready to arrest me . . . or worse. Is the officer reaching toward his gun? Should I put up my hands and yell, "Don't shoot"? Would that even matter, as it hasn't on so many occasions for others before? I can't even speak as panic courses through every part of my body. I speak English very well, but I can only think in my native tongue of Sinhalese.

The officer continues to advance toward me, and yet I cannot move.

"Sir . . . I mean, ma'am!" The police officer seems momentarily stunned that I'm a female cabbie. "You can't park here. Even if you drive a yellow cab. The taxi stand is up there for new passengers. MOVE!"

I look at the officer open-mouthed, trying to form something to say in response. With all the might I can muster, I force my feet to move and quickly get into the front seat. I glance at the back seat, hoping the man is no longer there. Somehow my hallucinating the whole thing is still a better scenario than reality.

My mind is racing with thoughts of what to do next as I drive off before pulling into the short-term parking lot, taking up two parking spots in my haste. I am on my way to a full-blown panic attack as I circle my car. I try to steady my breathing again, and I squeeze my eyes shut. I think of my brother, and my breaths and heartbeat slow enough that I am out of cardiac arrest territory and can think a little more clearly.

I put my hand inside my pocket to grab my phone and call the police, when I feel it. Her business card. Amaya Fernando. The lawyer. The criminal defense lawyer. I quickly dial her number, saying a prayer that she answers her phone at this hour.

CHAPTER 4

OH MY GOD!" Amaya screams as she opens the back door to my cab. She's just gotten out of her own taxi. Maybe the last one she'll ever take after seeing this. She curses under her breath in Sinhalese.

I couldn't muster the words to tell her everything on the phone. I merely said something bad happened and that I needed a lawyer quickly, like I was a very shady criminal defendant on an episode of *Law & Order*.

I was prepared to give Amaya all the reasons she needed to leave the comfort of her warm bed at 3 a.m. and travel across the city for some random person. Despite my vague pleading, to my surprise, she simply replied, "Okay," and the line went dead. Now here she is. I consider asking her why she'd show up for a virtual stranger (who very well could be a killer), but I'm not trying to push my luck.

"Why did you kill him? Did he attack you? Was it self-defense?" Amaya quizzes me as she backs away from both the body and, understandably, me. She'd make a great police detective on one of my podcasts. Her interrogation style is scary to say the least. I wonder if she'll pull out a flashlight and shine it in my face next.

"I didn't do it; I *swear* I didn't." How original, I think, but it is the truth.

Amaya looks at me and must see a super-freaked-out girl in front of her, because her face instantly softens.

"I'm sorry, I didn't mean to grill you. It's sort of second nature—me trying to get to the bottom of whatever crazy situation I've been dealt."

This is a crazy situation. There is a dead body in the back of my taxicab. The man was alive when I picked him up and dead on arrival? Who else could have done it? I can't think about anything right now other than the dead man in my back seat. The feel of the dried blood on my hands. The gut-turning dread. This is a circumstance where a normal person would probably cry, but I have a rule about crying in public. Don't do it.

Amaya puts a hand on my shoulder and says with enough sincerity I can almost believe it, "You're going to be okay. I'm here."

The tension in my shoulders releases just slightly, before a fresh wave of dread washes over me. Someone is dead. I have broken the most basic duty of my job—get my passengers to their destination safely. It isn't a complicated mandate.

I look at Amaya and wait for her to walk away. Why would she help me? This isn't her problem.

"Okay. Okay. Calm down." Is she saying that to me or to herself? Both would be valid. "The first thing that we need to do is to call the police. You should have called when you saw him initially."

"I was panicked, scared, I don't know." As the ability to think clearly starts to come back to me, I realize the delay will cast further suspicion on me. I already have the means and opportunity. If this were a podcast, I'd be the prime suspect.

"It's okay. Panicked and scared, it's totally normal." Again, I'm not sure if she's saying that to me or herself. "Second, after I call the police, I will go to the precinct with you. At some point, they will separate us to process you. You will go through central booking. They will ask details about yourself. You must not, and let me repeat, you must *not* talk about any of this. You can give them your name, basic details, but don't say anything about *this*," Amaya says, gesturing toward the dead body.

"I . . . I didn't do anything. Not saying anything is going to make me look even more suspicious, won't it?" The people who lawyered up on my podcasts always ended up being guilty of something.

"I know it seems like you can tell the truth, but given the situation, they probably won't believe you. They will arrest you no matter what you say. And, as you've probably heard, anything you say *will* be used against you. You have an attorney. You don't need to say anything."

If anyone looked at the podcasts I listen to, they'd be convinced I'd know how to get away with the perfect murder and assume I'd just botched it really, really badly this time. I look so obviously guilty I might as well have googled "how to murder a passenger in a moving taxi" for the police to find in my search history.

I'll take Amaya's advice and won't talk to the police. I push down the sinking feeling that it makes me look so guilty, and it heightens my anxiety even more. I focus on the fact that someone is in my corner. And this someone clearly knows what she is doing.

"I've got to call the police. They *will* arrest you. I hope they won't be rough with you since I'm here to witness, but they don't particularly like public defenders either. They will process you, and I will see you when you're ready for your court arraignment. I'll explain more of how this all works then." Amaya sounds flustered. She is talking fast and buttoning and unbuttoning her coat over and over again. She seems nervous, the opposite of all the smarmy defense attorneys on my legal shows.

Amaya takes out her phone and explains the situation to a probably bewildered police officer on the other end. As I watch her speak into the phone, I think about donning that blond wig I bought when I dressed up as Courtney Love one Halloween (with not a single person guessing my outfit!) and heading out of town. Immediately, a memory surfaces of my brother telling me I have to face my problems rather than run away from them. Ever the responsible and practical older brother. Most irritatingly, his almost unfailingly correct advice always bubbles up when I want to hear it the least.

I've never been in serious legal trouble before. I did get busted once for smoking a joint with Alex before weed was legalized. Despite the cops rolling their eyes about me proclaiming it was my first time, it was in fact my first time. Thank God for Alex's charms, because they didn't end up arresting us, in what I originally thought was a phenomenal stroke of luck, but then realized also may have had something to do with the fact we were smoking in his brand-new Mercedes outside his Upper East Side penthouse.

I always remember what my parents said to me about behaving as an immigrant in this country. My parents remind me, not infrequently, that I will be the first to be targeted and have the most to lose. I'm lost in spiraling thoughts when Amaya gets off the phone and walks back to me. Do I detect nervousness in her eyes?

"They'll be here very soon."

"My parents. Will you call them? If you could just . . ."

"I understand. I have Sri Lankan parents too. I'll be as careful as I can and do whatever I can to calm their nerves. I'll try not to worry them, but, Siriwathi, this is bad. This is *really* bad."

I nod as the sirens in the distance get louder.

CHAPTER 5

The police come for me in the short-term parking lot, and I raise my arms in the air as instructed. At first, they look to me and Amaya with confusion on their faces. I'm not sure what they expected to see, but it's certainly not me in an outfit I cobbled together from the H&M clearance section that consists of leopard-print pants and a pilling black sweater and Amaya in pj's and a puffer jacket.

After a few seconds of staring, though, about half a dozen cops point their guns at our heads. At that point, I am sure we'll be shot dead. They gloss over these parts in my podcasts. Or maybe I'm too busy rooting for the murderer to get caught.

"Get down on the ground," the police instruct both of us. Amaya does as she is told, terror in her eyes.

"I'm a lawyer," she says repeatedly, though they don't seem to care—possibly not believing real lawyers wear glittery pink UGGs. She explains that she had called them. Finally, they ask for identification, and she pulls it out as guns continue to point at her head. After reading it, they holster their guns around her, allowing her to stand up, dirt and dust coating the front of her outfit. They've determined she's not a threat. She pleads with them to be careful with me. "She is turning herself in. She is willing to do this all the right way. She will cooperate."

"We will be careful," they say. They didn't want Amaya riding with us, so they told her to meet us at the precinct.

As they gently guide me into the police car, I think I am in good hands.

When we're on the move, away from Amaya's gaze, the police officers sneer at me in the back seat of the car. When I mention I am innocent, they inform me that I am going to jail for the rest of my life. They speak slowly like I can't understand English, though I'm positive I enunciate my words more clearly than this cop speaking with his mouth full. I try not to imagine him eating a doughnut, because I refuse to stereotype him like he is doing to me right now. The cop tells me that I'm very "goblity," by which I assume he means guilty, and thanks me for making it such an easy job for them to solve this . . . murder? Case? He finishes whatever he was eating and starts on something crunchy.

"What dumbass kills a guy in the back of her own cab? Thought you could get away with it 'cause you're a woman?" His words are a sharp contradiction of how they spoke to me in front of Amaya. Or how the cops speak to the suspects on my podcast when they know they're being recorded.

They were careful with me in front of Amaya, conscious that she is a lawyer documenting my treatment. Conscious that they could get sued by the city for mishandling me. Unlike so many times before, this time there was a witness to this arrest. An authoritative one the city will listen to.

I am dragged out of the car and shoved up the steps to the police precinct. The walls inside are gray, and officers shuffle in and out past me. The light above, fluorescent and unflattering, flickers every few seconds. There is a poster on the wall that reads **If you see something, say something** with a person who looks remarkably like me committing a crime. I catch myself in a mirror of the precinct. My curly hair is even more unruly than normal, and dark circles have formed around my eyes. I've managed to fit their description of what a deranged killer would look like without even trying.

My cuffs are too tight and dig painfully into my skin. I try to catch the eye of the officer who only seems to want to look at my chest.

"Can you loosen these?" I ask politely but assertively. Men often mistake a woman's confidence for bitchiness, and I don't need these cops to hate me any more than they already do.

The officer shoots me a disgusted look but doesn't further acknowledge what I've said. My mouth is dry, but given the last response, I don't dare ask for water. For once, I'm following my parents' advice. Blend in and don't cause a stir. It's the mantra my parents always taught me as immigrants, even though all of us are now full-fledged citizens.

Finally, another officer comes in. He looks friendlier than those before him, and he appraises me with a neutral look, which is decidedly better than the frowns and creepy stares I had been getting. Maybe his arrival indicates that the booking process will begin. The sooner it does, the sooner this whole ordeal at the police station will be almost over and I can talk to my lawyer and eventually leave. I am confident that this will happen, because though I may not be a lawyer, I know it's happened in many,

many podcasts. It's protocol. It's the law. As I don't plan to give a statement as per the orders of Amaya, I wonder if I'll just go straight from the station to the courthouse. Police have to stop questioning me when I invoke my right to an attorney.

"Name?"

"Siriwathi Perera."

"Occupation?"

"Cabdriver."

The police officers raise their eyebrows in surprise . . . even though they are the ones who are booking me for the murder of someone in the back seat of *my* taxi. I want to protest and say women can be cabdrivers and murderers, too, but this isn't the time.

"Address?"

These questions go on for a while. I answer them truthfully and succinctly, as Amaya instructed. Pedigree questions about my background and who I am—my answers reveal nothing beyond my being an entirely ordinary and unremarkable person, which is exactly what I am. If they ask me any other questions, specifics about the case, I will exercise my right to remain silent, like I've seen and heard people do hundreds of times on TV and on my podcasts. However, the prospect of remaining silent makes me worry. Were this a show or one of my podcasts, and I were witnessing myself being questioned, I would think that I am guilty. Who doesn't defend themselves?

A different group of men come in and swab my hands for blood residue. They start to examine the rest of my body for droplets of blood. I inquire if a female officer can do this part, and they just stare at me blankly.

Others take my hands and roughly roll them in ink, as if

touching my hands even with gloves on is an offensive act. Next, they take me into a small room. I look up at the mirror, and though I only see myself, I know that there are cops on the other side watching—likely with a mix of revulsion and curiosity. I cross my arms over my chest, feeling so exposed and vulnerable, wishing my sweater were bigger so I could just hide. I want to make myself smaller. I want to disappear.

Two detectives, both white with closely cropped hair and Long Island accents, arrive and sit across from me. For a second, I think I am on one of my shows, and these two guys are paid actors. I try to dissociate from reality, but sweat still forms on my brow. When I realize this must make me look guilty, I perspire more.

At first they ask me softball questions. How am I doing? Do I like to bake? Which makes me wonder if these cops has watched too many tradwife TikToks. I answer them through gritted teeth. Maybe this won't be so bad. Then they ask the real questions they came here for.

"Why did you kill the guy? Maybe there's a good reason? Did he try and rape you or something? You can trust us—we believe women in this precinct." The detective on the right is trying to play it nice, but I detect a hint of sarcasm in his tone. He's a bit taller and bulkier than the detective on the left, but otherwise I can't discern a difference between the two.

"I'm sorry. I can't answer your questions. I cannot speak without my lawyer present."

I hope this ends the questioning and I can be made ready for my criminal arraignment in the courthouse downtown. I know that police can't keep talking to me after I've invoked my right to counsel and my right to remain silent. It foiled police, temporarily, in a *Dateline* podcast once.

"You got somewhere to be?" the smaller detective demands. He is certainly no kind, strong, and independent detective, like Olivia Benson.

The detectives look at each other, communicating by some silent language that must have developed over years of being partners. One of them furrows his brow and clenches his fist. That's when I know the next questions will be aggressive and angry. As a taxi driver, I know it's easier to yell at someone you'll never see again, someone whom you don't have accountability to. Unlike in my taxi, the police officers here have more power than just determining my tip.

"Why did you kill him?" the detective demands, his voice lowering into a growl. When I remain silent, he continues. "How did you know him? Were you just trying to rob him and then it got out of hand? It's okay, you can tell us. We know you did it. We may even be able to help you if you cooperate. Besides, they'll probably go easier on you because you're a woman."

I am tough, I try to convince myself. This interrogation has nothing on Ammi questioning me after coming home from a party with the faint scent of beer on my breath, even after I turned twenty-one. When she announced my full name, including my middle one, which she never uses, I knew I was in trouble. At least, this is what I tell myself. But my heart thrumming so loudly reveals my fear.

"I'd like to speak to my lawyer," I tell the cops again. This statement must feel like a challenge to them, because the detective questions me even more aggressively. I jump when the detective bangs his fist on the metal table bolted to the ground. I start to anticipate it as it happens more and more, to the point that I don't physically jump, though I do rattle all the same.

The other detective steps in. The one who so far has been silent.

"You'll get life in prison. We can help you avoid that," he promises. "If you want us to help you, you have to help us."

This isn't true. Detective Benson frequently argued with ADA Cabot over charges on *Law & Order*, because it's police who gather evidence and the assistant district attorney who decides the charges.

"We want to help you, sweetie," he says slowly and with a smile, as if I couldn't understand or hear him the first time. "We understand how hard the life of a cabdriver can be. It must be doubly hard as a woman. Strange men hitting on you. Did this man make advances? Was this self-defense? It would be understandable if you stabbed him because he was getting fresh." As though on instinct, both cops immediately eye my chest as if to decide whether it's worthy of being assaulted over. I remain silent, so the detective continues. "How frustrating it is to shuttle rich people around when you're barely making ends meet. I get it. I'm the son of an immigrant. I understand the struggle."

I look at the man who, outwardly at least, seems to have the highest privileges society can bestow upon him.

"Thank you for offering to help," I reply. I know my insincerity is rolling off me in waves, but I can't even fake politeness anymore. "I wish I could give you information that would be helpful, but I am innocent and I can't."

Perhaps it is my stubborn silence that is annoying them. This explanation, though unsatisfying to them, is the best I can give, and maybe it works, because they leave the room. They come back a few minutes later holding a USB thumb drive.

"We have footage of you from a street camera doing it. We just got it back. It's you clear as day. We know you did it," the angry detective says.

And for a second, in my sleep-deprived, dehydrated haze, I wonder if I did do it. If I blacked out and just don't remember it. *No.*

"I didn't do it," I mumble, wondering what else I can say, forgetting Amaya's advice to stay silent. I try to sound confident, but truthfully, I'm so scared. This isn't another case of me just trying to get a drunk dude out of my cab. The police are no longer following the rules. Are they going to keep me here unless I confess to something I didn't do?

I lose track of how long they question me. I need water and want to pee. Initially I tried not to ask for these things as I assumed I'd be let go soon, but I reached a point I needed to. Yet each time I make a request, I am refused. Until finally when I prepare myself to pee right there in my pants, they say that I can go to the bathroom, and I am spared at least one indignity.

Afterward, they continue to question me, and I continue to tell them I'd like my lawyer.

I read somewhere the definition of insanity is doing the same thing and expecting a different response. I wonder if they think the humiliation of this situation will erode me over time. I think, eventually, even an innocent person would confess under these circumstances. Is this why innocent people end up in prison? They break under the weight of questioning and think it's easier to confess?

Finally, after many hours that felt like days, the detectives give up trying.

"You're done," someone says from the corner of the room.

I don't bother to even look up, and it feels like an anticlimactic end to the torture. "You'll go to court now," the same voice informs me, "but not before we take your clothes."

For a second, I grip my clothes tightly to myself. But resistance is futile. They shove what looks like a white hazmat suit at me, and I change in the corner of the room as the detectives step out, fully aware they've only given me the illusion of privacy. They can watch me on the other side of the two-way mirror.

I would do anything to go back to the moment I picked up the dead man. He would tap on my window and I would drive away as fast as I could. I would appreciate the things that I had, that now seemed like they would be gone forever.

CHAPTER 6

I own an old legal textbook I found outside on the stoop of someone's front stairwell, discarded and waiting for a new home. It's standard New York City practice to leave unwanted items outside, and more often than not someone's trash is another's treasure. I count several stoop finds, including an old Van Halen tee, as treasured possessions. I've read the unwieldy book, stained with something I sincerely hope is coffee, cover to cover at least three times, and in it I learned that New York City is one of the only places in the country that process criminal defendants until 1 a.m. In New York, criminal defendants have a right to see the judge within twenty-four hours of their arrest and formally learn the charges against them. The twenty-four-hour period is one of the quickest turnarounds in the country, and thus New York City's courts are staffed 365 days a year until the early hours of the morning.

After processing me and questioning me for what felt like days at the precinct, the police dump me in a cell in the back of the courthouse while I await my lawyer. I feel like the deflated bags of trash that mark so many city streets. Smelly and only welcomed by rats. The cell is connected to interview booths where people talk in a semi-private manner to their attorneys, before being hauled off toward a door that opens to a bright space—a courtroom, I assume. I watch the corrections officers with the sort of anticipation I have waiting for a pizza slice to warm up in the oven. I'd kill for some pizza right now. *Wrong choice of words*, I think immediately after. Any small movement gives me hope that I will be ushered into an attorney booth to speak to someone. Hopefully Amaya.

There are a half dozen other women in various states, all waiting to speak to their court-appointed attorney. One woman is clearly not well. She is curled in the fetal position and has been sick—from both ends—twice already in the small toilet we all share. There's not even a door for privacy. Soon, the cell is filled with a stench so foul, I think I'm going to be sick myself, but I realize that would only add to the aroma. I ask the guards if they can get the woman some medical treatment. Upon closer inspection, I'm positive she is going into severe drug withdrawal. No one seems to care. I've seen this before. Most people have on the subway or sidewalk; a few times, I've seen it up close in my cab. I've rushed a number of people to the hospital, and when I asked one why he didn't call an ambulance, the man said he had no insurance and couldn't afford the costs.

"She may die," I try to protest. It's the most inflammatory thing I can think of to say to the officer to get the woman aid. Surely, this has to provoke some reaction. The officers still do not acknowledge me. In fact, they don't bother to look up from their phones, as if they are practiced in tuning out the complaints of the people they are supposedly in charge of.

I say it again, and this time the officer looks up. "No more tampons, we're out," he says. I'm momentarily confused, and then I realize he isn't listening to a word I'm saying and instead providing some canned response to a frequently asked question.

The other women in the cell, contrary to what I'd thought and been told by the police, are leaving me alone for now. Everyone is in such a sorry state, they only have enough energy to worry about their own problems, and sometimes not even the energy for that. No one seems to acknowledge or notice me.

The cell itself is incredibly dirty. A half-eaten apple has rolled to a stop in the middle of the floor. A few hard benches line the walls, and there's one pay phone in the corner. No matter what you are charged with, this feels inhumane.

Time moves at a glacial pace when there are no clocks around. How long have I been here now? To get my mind off being both cold and hungry, I try to think of my stupid, silly, wonderful older brother and all the adventures we had across the city. But, when I think of him, I only remember my last words to him. The argument we had. The memory whizzes through my mind before a voice brings me back to my sobering reality.

"Siriwathi!"

I immediately rise with strength and gusto, grateful to be broken out of my reverie. I know at once it is Amaya from the lilt of her voice. She did not abandon me, though I could have forgiven her if she had. The cell spills directly into interview booths, and I wander toward her voice. I sit down in the chair across from the clear piece of plastic that separates us, smudged by months—even years—of fingerprints.

"Hello." A little bit of my exhaustion and fear fades when I see her face.

"Are you okay?" she asks, her lips contorted into a pained position, her face filled with empathy. "I'm sorry that I couldn't be there at the precinct. I kept demanding that I be able to see you, but they didn't care. I told them it was illegal to hold you for so long."

"I'm okay," I say. While I feel far from okay, I don't want to worry her. Besides, I feel pretty stupid complaining as I look at the other women just behind me. I think of the woman going through withdrawal, suffering despite my attempts to get her medical help.

The time that follows is a blur, with Amaya asking rapid-fire questions, not only about what happened that night, but about my life, my family, and my job. The personal questions, she explains, are for my bail application. A bail application contains all the reasons that I should be released and why I won't flee. It's the CliffsNotes version of my life. All the poetry and nuance is gone. It's only the sterile facts.

"They are asking for bail," Amaya explained. "This means that there will be a certain amount of money that you or your family has to put up to get you out."

"We don't have any money," I say, looking down at my feet, feeling like my poverty is something to be ashamed of and certainly not something I want to discuss with Amaya. "What happens then?"

I know what comes next, I just hope somehow I am mistaken. I hope Amaya won't say it.

"If you can't pay, you get sent to Rikers Island."

My hope is dashed.

CHAPTER 7

I stand next to Amaya, trembling. Despite my best efforts, my body cannot stop shaking. Thinking of what will happen to me if I'm sent off to jail twists my stomach into knots. I've heard about the brazen violence, abuse, and isolation that happen on Rikers Island. I've seen people beaten for just talking back to the guards. The darkness of the cells has given way to the brightness of the courtroom, and I blink to adjust my eyes. The dank smell has been transformed into a neutral, almost disinfectant, scent. I notice the many people staring at me, all with looks of disdain, including the judge, a white man in a black robe sitting on his raised pulpit.

The court officers, beefy in a way that makes me think they drink protein shakes with a side of steroids all day, stand close as if at any moment I will try to run. The prosecutor, at least twelve feet away, shifts in his seat like he's trying to get even farther from me, with a face upturned in disgust as if I just spent the last hour mouth-breathing on him post-coffee.

Amaya faces the judge, knuckles white from her grip on the lectern.

"Court is back in session," a voice I can't place rings out. Whether it's the bright lights or my dehydration, I'm developing an intense headache.

"Okay, this is the case of *People versus Siriwathi Perera*. Ms. Perera, you have been charged with murder in the second degree."

"My client is pleading not guilty," Amaya replies with conviction almost before the judge finishes. Amaya glances over at me with a look that feels familiar. It's the same one my brother used to give me when he was worried about me. It provokes a mix of warm feelings because someone cares, but also dread because she's worried. About me? About the outcome of this bail hearing? About me being trapped at Rikers Island? My spiraling anxiety is off to the races.

"Very well, let's get on to the arraignment," the judge directs, while looking at his phone. I wait for someone to tell him to stop looking at it. When no one does, I realize this is his courtroom. No one tells the judge what to do.

The arraignment, Amaya explained a few moments earlier when we were still in the dark cell behind the courtroom, is when I am formally charged with a crime. The prosecutor reads out the version of what they believe happened.

"On October second, at 1:20 a.m., Siriwathi Perera stabbed her passenger in her taxicab, fatally injuring him . . ."

No, no, I think to myself. I am horrified to be associated with this. I want to interrupt the prosecutor and deny the charges, but Amaya tells me I cannot speak during this time. To do so would make the judge mad, and an angry judge sets high bail. I pray that whatever has him glued to his phone is going to put him in a good mood. I try desperately to slow my breathing, which seems to quicken with every new word uttered by the prosecutor. They got the wrong person. But who is the right one? How did someone kill a passenger in my moving, locked vehicle? So many questions are floating in my head all while I need to focus on what they are saying. I peek behind me, and there I see my parents huddled together on the bench. I can tell my mother has been crying. My father looks exhausted, and the bags under his eyes are deep set. My stomach tightens at the scene. It must be breaking their hearts to see me in handcuffs. Amaya must have called them. She said family support is a factor in how high a judge may set bail.

The beefy court officer yanks my arm, forcing me to face forward again.

The prosecutor continues. “Despite the fact that this is the defendant’s first arrest, we believe that the defendant is a flight risk because she was born in India and has significant ties to the country . . .”

This, I know, is the bail argument. The prosecutor is arguing why bail should be set, why I am a flight risk and a criminal who needs to spend the days until my trial in jail. But I have never been to India. Surely the assistant district attorney is talking about Sri Lanka and confused the two. And even if he had the right country, I haven’t been back there in years. I couldn’t afford the ticket even if I wanted to run. And, perhaps most importantly, I am innocent. I don’t want to run. I want to clear my name. I pinch myself under the flimsy illusion that this is just a dream. I suddenly feel awful that only yesterday I was rooting for bail to be set on a suspect in my podcast—that man, like me, is innocent until proven guilty.

"The defendant committed a grievous crime. Her bail should be set at one million dollars."

For a second, I wait for the ground to open up and swallow me whole. *One million dollars* and my name should never be uttered in the same sentence, unless Ammi finally wins one of the lotteries she enters weekly. Amaya explained I will have to pay 10 percent up front. That's $100,000. Amaya told me the judge will probably set some sort of bail; given the grave nature of the case and the evidence against me—mainly the dead body found in the cab I was driving—it will likely be high. I wasn't expecting a million dollars. If bail will be set this high regardless of my past, this exercise seems entirely pointless. She said if she can argue for it to be lowered, set at a more reasonable amount, someone may be able to pay. I didn't bother to repeat what I'd already told her, that my parents don't have that kind of money.

Suddenly, Amaya is speaking. Standing next to her, I feel as if she is vibrating with adrenaline.

"Your Honor, my client Siriwathi Perera has lived in New York City for almost twenty-five years. It is the only home she has known for a very long time. She is a United States citizen. While it's true she was born in *Sri Lanka*"—I hear Amaya emphasize the words and see her shoot a nasty look at the prosecutor for confusing the two countries—"she would never flee the country while this case is pending. She hasn't been back to Sri Lanka for many years."

I sneak a quick peek at the judge, but he is still looking at his phone. Is he googling where Sri Lanka is in relation to India? I bet he'll think they're the same place like the prosecutor.

"Siriwathi has been gainfully employed as a taxi cabdriver for nearly five years. She lives with her parents and cares for them in their home in Queens. Unfortunately, her family does not have the financial means to post such an incredibly high bail, and setting it so high would mean that Siriwathi would likely spend the duration of this case in jail, on Rikers Island. Siriwathi is an active community member . . ."

Suddenly, I hear the snap of cameras and notice the judge stand to attention. The clicking is rapid-fire. I turn my head just in time to see the bright flash of light coming from men with press badges dangling from their necks. They are sitting in the audience behind me. Were they waiting for my case to be called? They are not in the actual space where I stand and the judge presides, but they are close enough to take clear photos. The thought of my exhausted face splashed across the front page of my local newspaper, which in NYC means a national headline, makes me feel like the walls are closing in fast.

"After listening to both arguments and carefully considering," the judge growls, as if trying to look even more formidable for the cameras that are still clicking away, "I've decided to set bail at five hundred thousand dollars. Next case."

I'm not sure how the judge could have carefully considered everything, given his immediate decision. I soon realize the judge made up his mind far before the arguments. It didn't matter that I have an otherwise spotless record, volunteer in my community, and work as a cabdriver. None of that matters if you are accused of murder.

In just a sentence, my life is changed forever. Bail is set. The lights of the courtroom start to swirl. My breath quickens, and I wonder if I'm about to faint or have a heart attack. I'd thought being innocent of this crime would keep me safe, and my naivete fills me with utter embarrassment. I'll be going to Rikers. I remember the police saying that people like me won't do well there. I shudder at the possibilities of what they truly meant. At this moment, for the first time in a long time, I just want to hug my parents, but the officers are already dragging me away. I look around to find Amaya, hoping there is something she can do to help me.

I see her across the courtroom speaking to a court officer. She turns and faces me with a smile for the first time. Her smile, in the midst of such bad news, feels like she's in on something that I don't understand. I'm so confused. Have I been wrong to trust her? Is she joking around when this is my life?

"Just hold on," she shouts as they continue to drag me away to my cell. "It's going to be okay."

I ready myself for the stench of the cells, something my nose had grown accustomed to when I was back there but will have to adjust to again after the open air of the courtroom.

I assume I will be waiting and readying myself to get on a bus, handcuffs placed even tighter than they are now. My wrists scream in agony at the thought. I wonder if my legs will be shackled, too, or what other restraints will be forced upon me. Will I have to bend and spread, the last shred of my dignity evaporating? I try to steady my breathing, knowing this is a terrible place to faint. The officer yanks me back toward the darkness of the cells. The cameras continue to click as I leave the room.

Without warning, tears prick my eyes. I dig my fingernails into my hands, but the tears still flow. I've managed to avoid crying even when threatened with a punch to the face in my cab, but I can't keep it together now. I'm mad at myself for showing my vulnerability when I need my tough facade most. The tears run down my face, and because I'm cuffed with my hands behind my back, they flow freely, hitting the ground as I walk.

The thought of handling what lies ahead in the next day—no, in the next *hour*—feels daunting to me. I bargain with a God that I haven't believed in for a long time to give me just one chance to find the person who did this, to make this right and clear my name. I can't bring back my dead passenger, but I can give him justice.

I am led into a back room and am told to turn around. The officer fumbles with the cuffs, and I almost want to scream at him to get on with it so I can be left to cry without his prying eyes. He looks like he feels sorry for me, but I don't want his pity. He grabs the cuffs and I hear a click. They feel looser, not tighter, until they are off completely.

Suddenly, I hear the words I didn't expect to ever hear. "You're free to go."

CHAPTER 8

I can go?"

Surely there is some mistake. The officer shrugs as he twirls the cuffs in his hand, not offering me any answers. He's just following someone else's orders.

After changing back into my clothes, I walk out through the courtroom, past the judge, the same way I was previously paraded in front of the cameras. The judge doesn't look at me, engrossed as he is on his cell phone, occasionally looking up at the prosecutor or defense attorney discussing the case before him. I am grateful to be walking out, though I can't fully accept that I'm free, worried that at any second I'll be told there's been a mistake and I'll be promptly handcuffed again and dragged away.

Innocent until proven guilty is a farce. All the times I watched the news and, by simply seeing someone in handcuffs, I came to my own—possibly very wrong—conclusions. People will absolutely assume I'm the Taxicab Killer, or whatever nickname the *New York Post* will surely give me. Trying to convince them I haven't killed anyone will be a fruitless endeavor. I will deal with all of that later. For now, for just a minute, I will try to enjoy my liberty.

I walk out the double doors to the street while looking for my parents; instead, I see Amaya. My stomach unclenches a little at finally being out of the courtroom and seeing a friend. Well, more than a friend. The person responsible for my freedom. I hadn't been able to see Amaya in the light of day, or really focus on her appearance while my head spun in the dark of the short-term parking. I was too busy focusing on getting out amid the grime of the cell and too nervous to look at her when I stood in the courtroom as she argued for my freedom. Now, I can see the details of her appearance clearly. She has jet-black hair, thick eyebrows, and large, beautiful eyes.

She looks both familiar and different, like me but also so completely unlike me. To see Sri Lankans outside of Sri Lanka is almost always a unique occurrence. She is wearing minimal makeup, and her hair is pulled back away from her face in a loose bun. She looks put together in a way I never could. Probably because I never try anymore. It's an effortless look, but even that requires a fair amount of work as I've learned from those "Look Like You're Wearing No Makeup" YouTube tutorials.

She begins quickly, passing by any pleasantries one may expect at a moment like this. "Okay, so I sent your parents home because they were exhausted. However, I told them I would wait for you. I know they took your wallet and whatnot, so I have a MetroCard for you to get home. I need to start the investigation."

My mind is swimming, and I'm slowly drowning in everything Amaya is telling me in what seems to be her trademark rapid-fire fashion. She speaks as if she is about to run out of air, as if everything has to be said before the clock runs out. I think about the numerous other cases she probably has on her plate and the limited amount of time she can spend on each one.

Then I see another familiar face. Alex. Relief washes over me when I see him. Seeing Alex is like a cup of hot cocoa (maybe spiked with booze) on a cold day—warm, comforting, and takes the edge off of any bad situation. Alex and I became friends because of a common enemy—a motley gang of kids who used good old-fashioned burn books and other means to terrorize us—but remained friends through a shared love of Food Network, board games that took a minimum of three hours to finish, and my mother's rice and curry. My mother would never turn away a hungry mouth—especially one that was so complimentary of her chicken curry. Before I knew it, Alex was showing up at my house all the time. He would be at most weeknight dinners that would turn into nights too late for my mother to allow him to trek back into Manhattan alone—so he'd sleep over in my brother's bedroom.

Alex won the genetic lottery. He's grown into the features that he always resented as a child. He could be on the cover of one of those romance novels I've seen Ammi read when she thinks no one is looking. He has an angular jaw, wavy brown hair, and a tall stature. I can't even imagine being attracted to him though. He's basically another brother.

"God, the bail payment system here is so archaic. I had to go get a cashier's check. I don't think I've ever paid for anything with a cashier's check . . ." Alex says as he wraps his arms around me. As we hug, I realize how good Alex smells and how bad I do. Alex doesn't pull away. What I wouldn't do for a shower and an endless supply of deodorant right now.

"Y-You paid my bail?" I stutter.

"Of course," Alex responds casually, as if he's used to dropping thousands of dollars in mere seconds. Alex could have been a stereotypical rich asshole, but—partially through a combination of being mostly raised by his extremely polite and kind German nanny and my mother—he's always had a heart of gold, to me, at least.

"Along with some of your family friends and members of the South Asian community . . ." Amaya adds.

"They don't have that kind of money." My community is rich in many ways. Monetarily isn't one of them.

"A lot of people chipped in what they could and gave it to your parents. Some people only had fifty dollars or one hundred dollars. Everyone mobilized quickly. But Alex paid the lion's share. You're clearly very loved by a lot of people, Siriwathi."

"Thank you, Alex." His generosity is overwhelming. For nearly our whole lives, Alex and I have had each other's backs, including my honestly vouching for him as a genuinely good guy to women he's interested in—a statement he continues to prove true. I'm not sure I'll ever be able to top this.

I feel heat rise in my face and slowly reach every part of my body like I am still engulfed in Alex's tight hug. As long as I come back to court, everyone will get their money back. There will be no running away, despite nearly every fiber of my being screaming that now is the time to become one of those expats in Bali never to return to America again. In fact, does Bali have an extradition? . . . No. I have to face this situation. If I run, Alex and my community are on the hook for the rest of the $500,000. While they only had to pay 10 percent up front, they're on the hook for the entire amount if I don't show up to my court dates.

I want to say something more poignant to express my immense gratitude, only yet again I don't have the words. Instead, I ask another question. "You said an investigation?"

"Yes, we just have five days before the grand jury presentation. The prosecutor will present your case to determine if it can move forward. I can't even be there, unfair as it is; it's done under seal and in secret proceedings."

I didn't realize such secrecy existed in a court of law, which I've always viewed as open to the public. Open courtrooms are a hallmark of the court system. I'm again finding the disconnect in how the legal system really works from how I've seen it presented. This isn't how it played out on *Law & Order*, and I feel like I'm about to channel some of Detective Stabler's rage.

Amaya goes on, "If there is enough evidence—it doesn't have to be much—your case will move forward. If the grand jury votes to indict you, bail could be increased at a subsequent court date. The grand jury is a critical moment in the case. If we can find something before then that proves your innocence, we can get the case dismissed. However, time is of the essence."

I consider myself more versed in the law than the average person, but I'm still a little confused. One thing stands out.

"Only five days?" I ask, bewildered. Didn't court proceedings drag on for years or more?

"Look, there has to be a way to get more time for this," Alex says, looking genuinely concerned.

Amaya ignores him. "Technically, six days from when you are arrested. You've been in police custody for over twenty-four hours though."

So what felt like an eternity in police custody had been just over twenty-four hours.

"Is there an investigator available? What's their plan?" I ask quickly.

"There should be an investigator doing this, but we lost more funding this year. So there aren't a lot of investigators to help us with something so time sensitive. I'm going to do the investigation myself."

"We can hire the best investigator," Alex announces. "I know a guy—"

I interrupt Alex. "No. I cannot take any more of your money. You've already been so generous." I didn't have a say in whether Alex paid my bail, but I have say now. Maybe it's my pride, but I'm reluctant to keep taking handouts. I'm already in so much debt to him. Instead, I make an offer to Amaya. "I can help you. I can investigate my case." I've listened to dozens of podcasts of real cases, haven't I? Sure, it's not proven helpful just yet, but I'm certain it will help with investigations.

Amaya is firm. "No. You're exhausted and I'll be able to do it." Her slight frown immediately conveys the opposite. She looks overwhelmed. The task before her is daunting.

If anything, my podcasts have taught me it's the days immediately after a crime that are the most important. I can't drive my taxi, which is now soiled with that poor dude's blood and in a police impound somewhere, so I don't have much else to do beyond wallowing in despair or assisting in investigating my own case. Although the first might be the easiest option, it isn't the one I want to take.

"I can help," I assert more confidently than I feel. Fake it till you make it, I guess. "I can take you back to where I picked up the man, try to remember all the details from that night. What streets we took, what lights we stopped at. Besides, I'm a taxi driver, and I know how to get around this city." I should go see my parents and comfort them, except I need to feel as if I am doing something—anything—to fight these charges. And I'm not ready to face my parents yet. Their disappointment in me will almost be too much to take.

"I don't think that's a good idea. It's not really protocol for someone to investigate their own case; it's too personal for them," Amaya responds. "You could even be accused of witness intimidation or—"

"We're a package deal. I can help too . . . I mean, how hard can it be?" Alex interrupts.

Amaya glowers at him. "Alex. Absolutely not. Go home."

I feel instantly defensive of Alex, although I know Amaya is right.

"Thank you for paying bail, Alex. There's something called attorney-client privilege. It means what I say to Siriwathi is protected as long as what I say stays between the two of us." Amaya takes what I imagine is a rare conciliatory tone. She still sounds like a schoolteacher about to put a misbehaving student in time-out.

"Siri . . ." Alex begins to protest.

"Alex. Thank you for everything. I love you. Go home and get sleep. You've done more than enough," I respond.

"Fine. Okay. Keep me updated on everything. On every part of the investigation. Do you know who could have done this?" Alex asks.

If I were in Alex's shoes, I'd be asking the same questions, only it annoys me still. "If I knew, I probably wouldn't be here."

"No leads at all?" he asks gently, concern etched on his face.

"No, Alex. I promise to keep you updated." Instantly, I soften again. I'm so lucky to have someone who cares about me this much. It reminds me of the times he'd always take the blame when we got in trouble with my parents, because he knew they'd never yell at him . . . only at me.

Alex shuffles out the door, and once it closes, I turn to Amaya.

"I can still help you investigate." I realize how desperate I must sound, but I don't care.

"Fine. Just for today. And only because you have important information. I lead the investigation, you'll have to follow my lead," Amaya says firmly.

"Okay. I got it."

She looks at me now with a furrowed brow, and I prepare myself for another set of instructions and commands to stay quiet. Little does she know how good I am at fading into the background.

Instead she asks, "So, how was a man killed in a locked and moving taxi?"

CHAPTER 9

Although I suggest that we take the subway to save money, Amaya disagrees. Despite everything I've been through in the past day or so, I think practically, something ingrained in me since childhood. When you're living paycheck to paycheck, every dollar counts. Yet if I end up in prison, the twenty bucks I save riding on the subway will not matter anymore. Nothing will matter anymore. Amaya reminds me of the little time we have to properly investigate. We have a little under five days before the grand jury presentation, and we need all the time we can scrounge. My insides gurgle like after I've eaten a double scoop of ube and pandan ice cream at Chinatown Ice Cream Factory. Over 90 percent of us Asians are lactose intolerant, yet I still persist in saying that I eat dairy just fine, often with disastrous consequences.

I also figure Amaya has other cases to handle. I think again of all the other people sitting in that cramped cell, some in pain and not receiving medical attention. They need help, too, and I'm not more important than them.

"Where do you think this guy was stabbed?" Amaya asks as

we walk outside the courthouse. I'm not yet sure we even know where we're going. She crosses her arms as if she's guarding herself against my bullshit answer.

"I don't know, I thought he was alive until I got to JFK," I say truthfully. "The cab wasn't always moving. I mean, I did get out once. That could have been the time to . . . have done it." My passenger's dead body flashes into my mind like one of those dreaded Times Square billboards.

"Where?" Amaya gets her phone out.

"The intersection of Eastern Parkway and Utica Avenue. There was a woman stumbling and I . . ."

"Maybe there'll be security camera footage," she remarks excitedly. She taps the information on her phone.

"Should we start there?" I ask.

"Is there another place where he could have been stabbed?" Amaya asks. She looks worried, and I can't tell if it's directed toward me, or because she thinks this case is going to be impossible to investigate.

I think of the late-night revelers.

"I'm pretty sure that someone may have reached into the cab's open window. These guys were drunk and trying to moon us, and it was distracting. I didn't think they were knife-wielding killers." I was too distracted by the man's bare bum. I haven't seen one of those in a long time . . . and this one wasn't even particularly nice. I try to think of my last romantic encounter, and I'm taken back to two years ago to my cheating ex, who annoyingly has a perfect butt.

"Where was that?"

I try to think back. "I don't remember."

"You don't remember?" She sounds incredulous.

"Well, it was a long drive to the airport. At least forty minutes. I was listening to my podcast. I wasn't paying attention. I didn't think this night might be the one night where someone was murdered in my back seat." I silently curse my constant need to escape the thoughts in my head through *Dateline* podcasts.

There was a bar on the corner, although there could be at least two dozen blocks that qualify based on that description alone. It was also dark . . . my mind elsewhere.

"We can trace the route and look for footage?" I suggest, hopefully trying to prove myself to be an asset. This was how one case in rural Kansas was solved on my favorite true crime podcast.

"Siriwathi, there are a million cameras even in one city block. You need to know the exact location. We don't have the time!"

"What about looking for signs of struggle? We could follow the route I drove and look for blood." I feel confident that this is some sort of solution. It's at least something to get us going. The killer must have left something behind. They always do . . . at least according to my podcasts, which thus far have not been helpful.

"Think about NYC streets. The struggle happened over a day ago now. Blood that's dried, been run over a million times, probably thrown up on by this point, isn't going to stand out. Besides, the guy was stabbed. Blood wasn't spraying out everywhere—you saw the body. There was just one trickle of blood out of the wound. There wouldn't be any in the road," Amaya explains to me more patiently than I probably deserve. I'm waiting for her to sarcastically ask me if I have any more bright ideas, but instead she looks deep in thought.

So much for my podcasts . . . I rack my brain to remember anything important.

"Wait!"

"Yes?" Amaya looks at me expectantly.

"There was a backpack that looked Halloween themed because it was orange and black. It wasn't in the taxi after the stabbing. The killer must have taken it."

"Okay," Amaya says. From the look on her face, I can see it's not the brilliant observation I had thought it was.

"So where does that leave us?" I ask, nervous that the investigation has ended before it began.

Amaya is texting away, and I assume she can't hear me. I'm about to ask her again, when she replies.

"Okay, well, my colleague owes me a favor, so she's picking up the video footage from the intersection."

At least I've been a little helpful? I'm lying to myself, like I do when I convince myself that I won't be a taxi driver forever.

"We need it ASAP before it's deleted, and she lives around there." Amaya continues. "Where did you pick up the dead guy?"

I try to wave down a cab, but I'm ignored. Amaya, hand in the air, causes the next cab to screech to a stop, and I try to hide my embarrassment as we pile in. I look through the clean plastic at the driver, grateful I don't know him and can remain anonymous for now. If I had known him, I'm not sure how that conversation would have gone. *How am I doing? Well, I was just arrested for murder. You? Wife and kids good?* The press will be bad, merciless even, Amaya cautioned me wearily.

The cabdriver doesn't make any conversation with us, other than to ask where we are going. I've turned into one of those people who don't want to talk in the taxi, and for once, I can appreciate their position. I tell him the cross streets, not just a specific address like out-of-towners do. People think I have some sort of encyclopedic knowledge of every individual address in the city, and they get mad at me when I inquire a little further.

We cross into Brooklyn on the Manhattan Bridge with a direct and beautiful view of the Statue of Liberty and the downtown Manhattan skyline, with One World Trade Center rising above all the other buildings. Suddenly, my mind takes me back to Sri Lanka, where I'm sitting in a cold, dark theater, a reprieve from the hot summer. I'm eating peanuts and spicy cashews—I wasn't introduced to the greasy deliciousness of popcorn until I moved here—waiting for the screen to fill with a dramatic bird's-eye view of the Empire State Building. I leave the theater with the distinct feeling that dreams come true in New York City, if you just work hard enough. That was, of course, before I moved here and realized my wide-eyed optimism needed to be met with grit if I was going to survive in a city where jaywalking was a competitive sport.

"You said you picked him up where?" Amaya asks, confusion on her face.

Truth is, I don't remember exactly where I picked him up. He carried an oblong box with holes. Why would a box have holes? Maybe it was a pet carrier. I remember seeing a vet office in the area. I pray he was coming from there.

"I picked him up around the vet office . . . or animal hospital or something . . ." I say, hoping this little white lie turns out to be true. If I can't help out, I won't get to keep investigating.

"Okay, great. Animal hospital . . . that would be open twenty-four hours a day . . ." Amaya looks lost in thought. "Could he have committed suicide?" The skepticism that coats her voice seems to answer her own question.

"It's an odd way to go, stabbing yourself." I shudder at the thought. "How could we prove that?"

"Forensics will be helpful. DNA. Fingerprints. All that should help clear your name but may take a few weeks or even months to get back to us. You said you didn't touch the knife, right?"

"Right." I nod. *True crime rule number one: Never touch potential evidence at the crime scene.* I may have gotten a little blood on me, but I certainly didn't touch the knife. "What do we know so far? What evidence do we have?" I ask, envisioning boxes of files about my case currently sitting on Amaya's desk.

"Uh, not much, to be honest with you. The prosecutor has some time before they have to give us any evidence. They certainly don't want to give us anything before the grand jury."

"I thought the grand jury was really important. How can they hide evidence? Don't they want the right person caught?" So far the judicial process feels less about a person's freedom and more like the randomness of deciding what takeout to order on Seamless. Despite my lifelong fascination with the law, I find myself frustrated with how far all this feels from justice. I've listened to hundreds of hours of podcasts and watched so many true crime shows. It's all pointless knowledge right now. I don't understand how anything works in real life.

Amaya chuckles without warmth. "They think the right person is you. They're not going to give us anything helpful until they absolutely have to. We have nothing. Not even the name of the victim. Legally they have several weeks to turn over discovery, which is the evidence they have against you."

They won't even give us the name of the victim, the most basic information about this crime. Without that, investigating is impossible. I am literally Amaya's only lead, at least until the media picks up the story and the victim's name is revealed. Despite Amaya's reluctance, I have to find a way to stay as involved as possible in this case beyond today. I never bothered to dig any deeper and question the methods and tools used to get to a conviction as I listened to my true crime podcasts and watched my shows. She's the one with the real-life experience.

The taxi veers down familiar streets. I look out the window at the bodega that has the best bacon, egg, and cheese in Brooklyn. I see the Jewish temples with signs scrawled in Hebrew as people stream in and out. We pass a group of people having a neighborhood barbecue on the sidewalk, farther down a large line forming for oxtail pizza, and finally a Korean restaurant where Alex and I got bao buns after a night of drinking, back when life didn't feel so hard.

A smiling cartoon dog tells me we've arrived at the right place. The investigation is afoot.

CHAPTER 10

I eye the iguana staring at me. The last time someone made such direct eye contact with me was when I was told to piss off after I corrected a passenger's pronunciation of Schermerhorn Street. Dudes hate to be corrected, especially by women. I look away from the iguana and shudder. I look back, and it's still staring at me with its huge eyes. It sort of reminds me of the kid I used to babysit who would stare at me wide-eyed before he burst out crying. Though Ammi and Thathi not so subtly remind me that my body is a ticking time clock, I cannot imagine taking care of a child when I can barely take care of myself. Amaya seems like she could keep a small child alive while balancing a demanding legal career and managing to not look like a total slob. Suddenly, all the little things I couldn't have cared less about—like my split ends and my chewed-up nail beds—come into sharp focus.

We walked into the animal hospital's office a few minutes ago and were told to take a number. "You and your animal will be assisted soon," the receptionist said, not even bothering to look up to see that we didn't have an animal. And by the look of the waiting room, *soon* more likely meant at least an hour. I keenly feel the passage of time like someone stuck in traffic who has downed one too many iced coffees. My anxiety heightens even more. I continue to make a list of all the problems I have: piles of bills, no job, being accused of murder and facing life in prison . . .

I close my eyes and see my brother's face. The image almost always comforts me. Lately, thinking about him makes me worry about my parents. My father seems slower and older. He coughs and his back seems to hurt more than usual. Something is wrong with him, yet no one is telling me what. It's inevitable that eventually both my parents will die; the reason they had two children was to leave my brother and me with each other. Is there a point soon when I will be all alone? I'll feel like an orphan, even though I don't think the term applies to fully grown adults. And sadly, there's no rich uncle to adopt me as his adult daughter.

I open my eyes. "I'm sorry I'm not better at this. At remembering all the details we need to know to investigate properly," I say to Amaya, shifting uncomfortably in my chair, which is stained with God knows what.

"Why are you apologizing?" Amaya asks, not looking up from her phone. "Women apologize too much. Do you notice men apologize a lot less?"

She does have a point. Alex says my tendency to say sorry, even to the furniture I occasionally bump into, is a habit I need to stop. Yet I want to apologize, because I feel disappointment from Amaya, as if somehow I have already failed her and wasted her time.

"I know I seemed annoyed," she says. "I realize I frequently come off as frustrated. This job wears you down a bit. Long hours and few resources." Amaya pauses and straightens her back. She meets my eye. "You shouldn't be here. I've thought about it more.

It's not protocol. After this, you should go home and rest and see your parents. I know they'll be worried about you."

I desperately think of what to say to convince her that I need to stay and be a part of the investigation. This is my life. Yet so far, I've added nothing except a hope that somehow the victim came from this animal hospital's office. My heart starts to beat faster, and my palms become sweaty.

"This is how investigations work. There's a lot of dead ends and false leads," Amaya explains as she continues to scroll through her work email. She's made the animal hospital a de facto office and doesn't seem bothered by the slow service. I can see dozens of emails on her phone. Unlike my inbox, which is mostly spam from a fast fashion website I used one time back in 2013 and Nigerian princes wanting to give me millions of dollars if I only give them all of my personal banking information, Amaya's appears to be filled with important things. I want to ask her what would happen if we fail here, but I don't want to interrupt her furiously replying to emails.

True crime rule number two: Leads are the freshest in the days after the crime and become colder the more time passes. It's why cold cases are so hard to investigate. It's why the delay in getting information complicates things. Witnesses forget or become more reluctant. Video footage is erased. Evidence is lost or destroyed.

I close my eyes and try to imagine the murdered man. He was wearing sweatpants and a sweater. Dressed comfortably and simply. He didn't seem like someone just leaving work. He had a black-and-orange backpack. Then my mind draws a blank. I wish he had something memorable on like the Naked Cowboy who only wears a tight pair of underwear while he roams around

Times Square . . . Well, maybe not *that* memorable. Just something I could remember. I already tried multiple times while at the precinct to replay every single moment of that night again and again, hoping for some clue, some clarity; each time, my mind came up short. I hadn't paid attention. I was listening to my stupid podcast, focused on driving to the airport. I desperately hope the video from the intersection shows something.

I look down at my nails, mangled from years of nervously biting them. My pants suddenly are too tight and my lips are dry. Now my breath feels shallow. *Breathe in and breathe out*, I remind myself. Clear my mind. Instead, thoughts of my parents disappointed in me, of everything Amaya has to do in so few days, and of being prevented from helping the investigation fill my head. I see Ammi crying and Thathi trying to comfort her. Suddenly, all my problems are laid out. Not just this murder charge. I look disheveled (which is putting it politely), eat unhealthy, can't do my job if people are getting murdered in my cab, can't remember critical information, have no friends in the world beyond Alex, and disappoint myself and my parents every single day.

I try to squeeze my eyes shut, as if this will turn off the panicking thoughts. It just helps me visualize them more vividly. My heart is racing, my palms are even more sweaty, and now I start to feel certain I can't breathe. My perfect brother flashes through my mind. He never caused my parents stress. I think about our last fight. He was so angry with me that night. The pain in my chest increases, so searing now I can no longer ignore it. I feel an electric pain shooting down my left arm. I look over at Amaya, hoping I will not have to say anything to get her attention. I don't want to be dramatic. Everything is becoming fuzzy.

"Am-Amaya . . ." I stutter breathlessly.

"Hold on, just one second," Amaya responds, still tapping away.

"Amaya . . ." I say again more loudly and with as much conviction as I can muster, "I'm having a heart attack."

I know symptoms of a heart attack after my uncle had one. I am having all of them. I regret eating all that fried chicken last week, and my lack of exercise.

"What?" She looks up and sets her phone down. I must look really bad, because with wide eyes, she grabs my hand and gets me to my feet. The smell of the animals, the sterile office space, and the bright lights are all beginning to fade to nothingness.

"Come on, let's go outside," Amaya's voice says amid the haze.

I'm not sure if I can walk, but I get onto my feet anyway. I want fresh air and I don't particularly want to die next to the iguana.

"What are you feeling?" Amaya asks as she leads me outside.

"Chest pain, shortness of breath, arm pain." *The hallmarks of a heart attack*, my brain yells at me for the second time.

Once outside, Amaya helps me to the ground and she pulls out her phone and dials 911, giving them our address and location.

"Breathe deeply: one breath in, one breath out. You're going to be okay. Squeeze my hand," Amaya says, her tone very different from the one I am accustomed to. She's still authoritative, only there's now a calmness to it.

I weakly squeeze her hand and she cups it in hers. She takes off her blazer, folds it to make a pillow for me, and cradles my head. I'm glad we are outside, as the fresh air calms me ever so slightly.

"You're okay, you're okay. Deep breaths, deep breaths. I know this is scary. I'm going to do everything I can for you. You're going to survive this and you're going to survive this case."

For a second, Amaya reminds me of my brother in how she comforts me, easing my fears with reassurances and being present when I need it most. Before tests, my brother would bring me Nerds, Takis, and a Monster Energy drink. The trifecta. If I was especially nervous, he would pull an all-nighter with me to help me study. Like Amaya, my brother always tried to find a solution to my problems. He would have done exactly this had he been here. And suddenly, the pain in my chest begins to ease.

"Are you okay?" Amaya asks.

"Yes, just a panic attack." I say, waving goodbye to the EMTs who ran a battery of tests to make sure. They offered to take me to the hospital just in case. I declined. I hate hospitals. They told me to try to find a way to have less stress in my life, a statement met with a cackle so loud I'm sure they wanted to check that I hadn't accidentally hit my head too. I just have to find a murderer so I won't be sent to prison for the rest of my life. Once that's done, life will be a little less stressful. I'm embarrassed I've mistaken a panic attack for a heart attack, and I bet Amaya wonders if I'm the person who thinks they're dying after one glance at WebMD. I wonder if she thinks I'm some sort of hypochondriac. Nope—I just live with them, and can already imagine the stinky and disgusting herbal "remedy" Ammi would be whipping up if she were here. I may be closer to thirty than twenty at this point, but my parents still don't trust me to make the right decisions for myself.

"Have you had panic attacks before?"

"Uh, once, a while ago."

Amaya raises an eyebrow.

"It was the day my brother died. I had one in the hospital. He was undergoing new treatments, and I thought finally we had the answer, and then suddenly . . ."

"Oh my god, that's awful," Amaya says, her face tightening with genuine concern. I appreciate that she doesn't make me tell her the details of how my brother died, and instead lets it hang in the air, now like a weight on both of us.

I hate talking about this, but I can't help myself. "My parents saw my panic attack and they thought I was dying too. I'm so sorry they had to experience that. I'm not a spiritual person, but at the moment I wondered if I would die and get to see my brother again. And that thought made me happy."

I don't recommend telling someone about the worst day of your life within two days of meeting them. I chalk up my uncharacteristic openness to the residual fear of having a heart attack. When you think you're about to die, you're ready to leave it all on the table. I'm alive and well now, and I wish I could take it back. The moment between my brother, my parents, and me isn't meant for others. People always think I'm not strong enough. Not strong enough to be a taxi driver in this city, not strong enough to get my life together, and not strong enough to live on my own. Here I am, telling Amaya just as much through this story.

Amaya squeezes my hand again.

"It's been so long since that last panic attack, I didn't think I was having one again. I'm sorry about all the trouble. The delay. I know we're on a tight time frame for the investigation." I want to shift toward discussing my case again.

"Stop apologizing," Amaya says sternly like it is a direct command, back to her old self. Then, her voice softens again. "The stress you are under, I can't even imagine. Why don't you go home? Rest. I can handle this, I promise."

Just then, the animal hospital receptionist steps outside and calls our number.

CHAPTER 11

The reception desk is chaotic. Only one woman is manning the desk, answering phones and emails, and periodically petting a yipping dog.

"I'm sorry for the delay," she says. "Lucky I saw you step outside, or I'd have skipped you."

Stepped outside? More like thought I was having a heart attack, nearly fainted, had to be carried outside by the woman who happens to be defending me for murder, only to find out I was mostly fine. A scenario probably most apt for an episode of *Jerry Springer*. A mix of panic, embarrassment, and concern returns to me instantly. I take a deep breath. These kinds of frantic thoughts are what gave me the panic attack in the first place.

The pace of service at the front desk is in contrast to the receptionist's fast speech. Despite the EMTs outside, the receptionist managed to miss the noisy sirens and flashing lights. New Yorkers seem to ignore chaos until it urgently requires their attention; no one else in the waiting room seems to have stirred either, instead finding themselves engrossed in years-old *People* magazines.

"We're very understaffed. Four people called out today. I'm doing the job of multiple people," she huffs.

I am sympathetic to her plight. Her predicament reminds me of all the times where people demanded impossible things from me. Like when I've been told to get to Times Square from Battery Park in five minutes in bumper-to-bumper traffic because my passengers have a Broadway show to catch. Traffic doesn't care if you have front-row tickets to Taylor Swift, it'll ruin the best-laid plans. In fact, there seems to be a correlation between how important an activity is and how bad the traffic will be that day. Once-in-a-lifetime opportunity? Bake in an extra two hours minimum.

"That sounds awful. You're doing amazing," I say.

"Yeah, you are," Amaya echoes my sentiments, though she's clearly lying, something I can tell by her impish grin.

"Thank you. You're the first people today to acknowledge that," the receptionist says, instantly softening.

"Actually . . . perhaps you're the one who can help us more than the doctor," Amaya says.

True crime rule number three: Always be polite to get people to talk. All the best true crime podcast hosts know this trick, and Amaya is pretty good at it, even though her outwardly serious and curt demeanor doesn't initially suggest it.

"*Really?*" The receptionist beams.

I smile at Amaya. I try to be immune to cheap flattery, but sometimes a "Girl, your outfit is fire" or more likely for me "Thanks for getting us here so quick" is just nice to hear. In a world where everyone is so self-absorbed, a kind word from a stranger can mean so much. But even that only goes so far. Most businesses aren't willing to give out information to strangers.

"Two nights ago around one a.m. a man was in here—" Amaya begins before she's interrupted by the receptionist.

"Oh god, the man with the snake?" She pronounces every word deliberately, talking at a normal pace for the first time in this conversation.

Amaya's nose crinkles in surprise as she takes it in. Me, I'm wondering why it couldn't have been a puppy, having begged for one as a kid for years.

"Yes, I'm his . . . friend," Amaya responds uncertainly, a rare show of apprehension. The receptionist won't give out information to just anyone asking.

"Oh, thank *god* you're here to pick Frankie up! It's not unusual for someone to come in with a pet so late. Pets are just like humans, after all, and have emergencies. It *is* unusual for someone to forget to pick them up. Was he just planning to leave the snake here?" She rolls her eyes as if her tone wasn't enough to indicate her judgment and displeasure.

"Actually . . . he's dead."

The color drains from the woman's face as if, for the first time today, she's been taken by surprise. "Oh god, I'm so, so sorry. I must have sounded so . . . oh god, this makes sense. He was dropping off the sick snake, said he had to catch a flight, so we were going to treat the snake and then keep it here for two nights, Sunday and Monday, until he got back Tuesday morning. We have a kennel and a pet drop-off. He was supposed to pick up Frankie at 7 a.m. sharp this morning . . ." She trails off.

Mention of the flight confirms to me that we must have the right guy. Besides, how many people drop off a beloved pet and forget to pick it up?

"*Wait* . . . did he die in a plane crash?" the receptionist asks dramatically, already scrolling her phone for the news story.

I hop from one foot to the other, waiting for what Amaya will say. Hopefully, she won't say that the gal to her left may have stabbed him . . .

"No, not exactly . . ." Amaya looks at me.

"He was having heart problems," I blurt out. His heart stopped because someone stabbed it.

"Oh, how terrible. He looked young."

"Yes, well, is there discharge paperwork? I've actually never taken care of a snake, so . . ." Amaya says, impressively changing the subject, a feat I fail at frequently in my own cab. It would mean I'd talk less about people's random medical conditions—like a passenger from last week who detailed her bunion pain.

"It's a python. They're really friendly."

"Uh." Amaya's eyes grow wide with fear. "Is it possible to leave the snake here a little longer?" Amaya agreed to take me as a client, not as a pet babysitter for a dead man.

"Well, he only paid for one night. And so there's back pay owed and money owed for additional nights."

"Which would be . . . ?"

"Well, for exotic pets such as this python, we charge $1,000 a night. He left this python here around midnight on Sunday and now it's Tuesday morning. Meaning there is $2,000 owed but there's a $500 late fee."

I want to protest. He was five hours late because he was dead and now we're saddled with his $2,500 bill that might as well have been a million dollars. It must be the same case for Amaya, because she opens her mouth but doesn't speak. It seems for the first time, I've seen her at a loss for words.

"Well, maybe I'll just leave it here and get back to you?" Amaya suggests. I can see her trying to figure a way out of this.

"Oh, no," the receptionist says stiffly. "I've already got the discharge paperwork ready; we have to give the snake to you." Any sympathy for our situation is already gone. "Don't worry, we just fed it; you won't have to feed it again for another few days." A small consolation. "You can do a payment plan if you need."

The receptionist slides the paperwork toward Amaya and she picks it up, nodding and handing it to me. At the top of the paperwork, there is the owner's name: James Wilkerson-Taylor. We've gotten what we came for, and a little more.

CHAPTER 12

What are you going to do with the snake?" I ask as we walk out of the animal hospital, python in tow. It is larger than I imagined, and heavier, too, so we each take a handle of the cage and carry it together. The python, judging by its hissing, doesn't seem particularly happy with us either.

"I guess I can hold on to it for safekeeping for now." Amaya groans, holding the snake's cage as far away from her as physically possible. "Then hopefully find a good home for him. I certainly don't want him."

I'm surprised she's keeping the snake, despite her real disgust, and half expected her to get animal control to deal with it. Though she tries hard to hide it, Amaya is clearly a compassionate person. After all, she's taken me on as a client, and it's not like I'm even paying her. She presents a steely exterior—a toughness that's probably necessary in the world of lawyering as much as it is in the taxicab-driving business. Yet underneath that hardness is a very good person.

I turn back toward the snake. It doesn't look so bad . . . if scaly, slithering, boneless reptiles are your thing. I shudder. I would have offered to take the snake home to my parents' house, only Ammi is deathly afraid of them. She can't even look at them from a distance. Ammi was once surprised by a snake on television and screamed so loudly the neighbors assumed we were victims of a home invasion and called the police.

At least we found the dead man's name. It is a starting point for a real investigation, even though it isn't the big break I was hoping for. *True crime rule number four: An investigation is sometimes a series of unrelated clues that only come together later.* At the beginning, there's sometimes only breadcrumbs. Eventually we'll find the entire loaf of bread . . . I hope.

"I need to take this snake home," Amaya says glumly.

"Should I come with you?" I know Amaya is looking for any reason for me to not come along. She's made it clear she doesn't need my assistance. Maybe now is the time to make myself helpful, and for real this time, not just dramatically fainting at a twenty-four-hour animal hospital. "I can help you with the snake."

I can see Amaya thinking my offer over. On the one hand, I'm a virtual stranger accused of murder. On the other hand, there's a snake I could help her deal with.

"I do need help with the snake because he's heavy, but you really should go home after that. Your parents are going to be worried."

I nod, grateful I'm still a part of the investigation even for just a little bit longer.

"Should we wave down a taxi?"

Amaya looks at the snake. "Yes, I think bringing this thing on the subway is probably a recipe for disaster." The snake coils in on itself tightly, as if in agreement.

In the taxi, Amaya sets the snake in between us.

"I'll keep the snake around in case I need to throw him at my shitty ex," she says, patting the top of the cage gently.

We both laugh. The tension we've been holding in dissipates, and I'm reminded how good it feels to laugh with someone who seems to really get me. Alex and I joke around, but he'll never understand what it's like to date an emotionally unavailable dude who loves to talk about Bitcoin ad nauseam.

I look at the cabdriver to see how he feels about a reptile in his back seat. He's chatting on the phone and barely notices us.

"So tell me," Amaya says, "about some of your most interesting taxicab passengers."

The taxicab driver is still chatting away, so I feel a little less like an asshole divulging details. It's not like there is a code of ethics preventing us cabdrivers from talking about what happens in our taxis, and frankly, it's not like I have my own crew of drivers to swap stories with. Most people never ask about my job beyond those clichéd questions mostly relating to me being a female cabdriver. *Do you ever feel unsafe?* Rarely, thanks to the bat I keep in my front seat that I've never had to use. *Do guys hit on you?* Also rare, especially these days. *Don't you get bored just driving around all day?* Don't you get bored just sitting at your computer all day?! I know most people mean well, but their questions feel like they're just satisfying some lurid fascination, like my job is somehow beneath them. However, Amaya's question is one I get way less.

"Well, every passenger is different, but they usually fit into broad categories. The best passengers are people who make interesting conversation, or people who are quiet and polite."

"Oh that's boring, who are the worst? Give me something juicy! Have you ever refused service to someone?" Amaya says in a conspiratorial whisper. Obviously, Amaya has a life outside of work, but even so, it's surprising to see this side. People could think we're just friends hanging out.

I talk a big game about threatening to refuse service to people I deem assholes, but the truth is that I can't remember the last time I ever did. I've thought about not picking up the puking drunk or the openly rude business guy, but I realize my cab can be a lifeline for people who want to get home when other modes of transportation are unsafe or unavailable.

"The worst are the actively drunk people. You never know when they're going to be sick . . . and the people trying to get it on . . ."

"Oh god, I hope no one has ever . . ."

It feels strange to be privy to the private lives of others who forget I am driving them or, more often, don't care. I know by now it is more than the plastic barrier that separates me from them.

"Not all the way, but most everything else. Alex calls me the ultimate cockblock, which is a title I'm happy to have in my taxi. It's gross, and you'd think people wouldn't want to, because I'm there, but people just tend to carry on—maybe spurred on by my screen being so murky and probably alcohol and drugs. I've cleaned all sorts of things out of the back of my taxi. I'm still human, though my passengers seem to forget it." The mere thought of what has touched my back seats means I clean them with antibacterial wipes every single day, incident or not. I've finally trained myself not to gag.

In truth, these anecdotes of the worst passengers don't really encapsulate my experience, although they do make for an interesting story. Asking about my passengers is like asking what makes a New Yorker—we're many things. On one ride, a man recommended some stocks, which I would have considered investing in had I had the money. The stocks rose sharply the next few days, and I briefly had visions of me popping open bottles of champagne and taking caviar bumps like those completely unrelatable nepo baby Instagram influencers whom I mostly hate but also secretly envy just a smidge. An obstetrician gave me tips about delivering a baby in a taxicab, should the occasion ever arise. Her vivid descriptions of what happens to a woman's body in the throes of childbirth were the ultimate birth control. A dude detailing his weightlifting and protein goals briefly made me reconsider if I ever wanted to have a taxi conversation again. People want the dramatic story, but my days are usually these simple interactions. Even though some of these conversations are strange and almost all of them take me out of my comfort zone, in some weird way they connect me with this city I love so much. Driving a cab can be such a solitary experience, and sometimes it can just feel nice to be part of the conversation.

As Amaya and I travel along the streets in our own taxi, I try to get comfortable in my seat. I find it impossible given the cage takes up almost half of the car. Amaya's hair isn't frizzy, her suit is neatly pressed, and from afar she looks pretty close to perfect. This would normally be the time I'd compare myself to her, counting the numerous ways I fall short. Yet, up close, I notice a small scar above her lip twisting away from her mouth, almost reaching her nose, like the curling tendril of a plant, faded over the years. I notice her slightly pockmarked skin, likely from angry teenage acne, and her eyelashes that are long and thick. It's a reminder that we're both just imperfect people.

The taxi rolls up cautiously to Amaya's apartment. I can see the confusion on the driver's face, and I know he thinks he's got the wrong address. However, when she confidently gets out after paying, the taxi speeds away. I usually make sure my passengers make it safely to the front door before driving off just in case they have gotten the wrong address. I had—before that terrible night—always gotten my passengers where they were going unharmed. I have blown my perfect record in the most awful way.

I look up at the building. I can discern much more detail in the daylight than I could when I dropped her off in the dark a few days ago. The building is an ivy-covered brownstone, both charming and in clear disrepair. Ivy looks like it has loosened the brick, the paint is chipped, and the gate is rusted—home improvement projects I am all too familiar with. Somehow, though, unlike my home, the weathering of this house makes it look all the more cozy and welcoming, like a refuge on a cold fall day. I assumed that Amaya, a lawyer, would occupy some updated space, some fancy new high-rise that replaced older homes, invaded the neighborhood, and was the death blow to local bodegas.

"It's not much. On a public defender salary, I can't afford a ton of places. But it's home," Amaya says. "Also, for the first time in my adult life I have no roommates."

God, I wish I didn't have roommates. Especially ones that potty trained me.

"It's amazing," I respond. "I live with my parents and I really need to move out one day." I feel embarrassed admitting that I, a fully grown-ass woman, am still living at home with my parents. Of course I want my independence. I don't want Ammi to constantly be demanding I date (and even worse, the son of a family friend) or asking when I'll finally learn how to make chicken curry (for that same son of a family friend).

Mostly, I want to not constantly be accosted by memories of my brother. Despite his death, memories of him are everywhere. His old yellow Livestrong bracelet that was all the rage twenty years ago will show up in the bathroom, an old collar stay embedded in the carpet will stab me when I step on it, and the commemorative cup celebrating his graduation—summa cum laude, of course—stands out on the shelf. Simultaneously, while I struggle with seeing these things, I cannot bear to part with them.

The thought of leaving my parents alone, as they grow older and more dependent on me, breaks my heart. I can't leave them when they are starting to need me most. Thathi is sick with his heart condition, and given his pain and slowness, I suspect he also has some additional illness my mother won't disclose. I help them with their bills, with their doctor's appointments, and with house repairs. They need me, though I wish with all my heart they didn't. I wish I could be a normal, carefree woman in her late twenties, hungover after a night of too many shots and in bed next to a young Ben Affleck. Alex says my crushes are weird, but something about Ben and his unpretentious love of Dunkin' makes me feel like he'd truly get me even though he's from Boston.

Amaya unlocks the town house's gate. As she pulls it open, a few more flecks of paint fall off, glittering in the sunlight like the snow I'm sure we'll get in just a few months. We climb the stairs, and she apologizes for her apartment's place on the top floor of a fourth-floor walk-up. Carrying a snake up four flights of stairs is the most exercise I've done in days, and I try to hide my shallow breathing when we've reached the top. When my brother was alive, we used to go to the gym together. It feels like another life, when I would voluntarily take the gym's Pilates classes, which I'm sure would now feel like cruel and unusual punishment on muscles that only get worked when I'm punching the brakes in my cab. I canceled the membership a few weeks after he died.

Amaya opens the door to a studio apartment. The apartment has what I assume is original crown molding, beautiful hardwood floors, and a tiny kitchen that consists of a two-burner stove and a toaster oven.

"This is so nice," I mutter from the doorway, genuinely taken in by the space, which contrasts Alex's expensive high-rise apartment in every way, one of the only other New York City apartments I've seen and so the only obvious comparison. There are plants and books on nearly every surface, adding to the apartment's cozy atmosphere.

"Thanks. It is nice, isn't it?" Amaya asks.

I stand by the door, aware I haven't exactly been invited in. If this were my house, Ammi would have already shoved a cup of Sri Lankan tea into Amaya's hand (with milk and one teaspoon of sugar) and a plate of short eats, a variety of sweet and savory pastries, which somehow materialized from thin air. It's Sri Lankan tradition, at least for our parents' generation, to always offer your guests, even unexpected ones, food and drink.

I stand on the threshold of the doorway and look at the photographs in frames that line her bookshelves. One photo is with someone I assume is Amaya's mother, another with her father, others with people who appear to be her family members. Everything in the apartment has a slightly worn appearance. Rather than being shabby, it simply looks lived-in and loved. Abstract art in brilliant colors hangs on the wall. I squint my eyes to look closer at the books on her shelves. Some titles I recognize, others I don't—I do see they span a wide variety of genres. I laugh when I see a *Criminal Law for Dummies* book. I wish that's all it took—reading some shoddy book on the subject—or maybe, in my instance, listening to a few podcasts. A few books on the couch have ribbons in them marking the last page read, and I notice she doesn't have a television. She is not just a collector of books, but a reader, which is increasingly impressive in a world where people prefer the internet to anything on paper.

"Okay, I'm going to leave the snake here. If I come back and it's missing, I'm calling you." Amaya laughs a little. "I know none of this situation is funny, but I just can't believe I have a python in my home."

"I think they eat mice; you can buy them frozen," I offer.

"Ugh, that's disgusting. And how do you even know that?"

"It appeared in one of my of my true crime podcasts, actually." Maybe after this, I'll have had my fill of true crime altogether. It can't hit closer to home than this.

"Oh, that's great. I like podcasts too. Sometimes, I wonder if I listen to all of that to keep me from my own thoughts." Amaya laughs again, this time nervously. "Sorry, that was too deep. I sound a little unhinged," Amaya responds, almost to herself.

"No, you don't," I say with a smile, realizing that trying to find a form of escape from present realities is something common to us both. "Luckily, snakes are not big eaters. You'll probably only have to feed Frankie between every five and fourteen days."

"That is . . . helpful," Amaya says, probably surprised by my oddly specific fact. "Anyways, I need some coffee. There's a place around the corner. We should probably try to google this guy."

Searching for someone online is basically requisite research these days. For dates, for colleagues, for some random person you haven't spoken to in years but are now trying to figure out if they've broken off their engagement from a deep-dive Instagram search. I find most surprises about a person these days are bad, like the time I spared myself from a potentially horrible guy when I found out his ideal first date was a strenuous hike and that he preferred girls who were "fit."

"Aren't you tired? You're already home. We can do this tomorrow if you'd like," I offer, always polite even if it's to my detriment. I blame Ammi for my over-accommodating ways. She raised me like this. I can't help but be aware of how much time my case is taking up in Amaya's day—my panic attack likely adding to her stress levels.

"Tomorrow? We don't have time. Grand jury presentation is in five days, Siriwathi." She stops and appraises me. "I'm sorry. I don't mean to add to the stress with the big countdown."

I must seem so much more fragile after my panic attack. "It's okay. Now it's four days and twenty hours. Not that I'm counting or anything."

"Once I get some coffee, I'll be back, good as new," Amaya says as she ushers me out of the doorway and back down the stairs.

The coffee shop is quaint and welcoming despite the gloom outside. Fall in New York City is normally perfect with colorful leaves, the promise of candy in the air, and the Tompkins Square Halloween Dog Parade, where doggos somehow become even cuter by getting into tiny costumes. The air is crisp and comfortable, and I no longer have to worry about shaving my legs consistently, because shorts season is all but over. But lately, every day seems downcast and threatens rain as if we're skipping the precious days of fall and descending directly into a long and cold winter, with its yellow snow piling up on the street corners and me dressed in a jacket that looks more like a sleeping bag than actual clothing. It's the perfect metaphor for my predicament. We find a seat at the front by the window, and Amaya sips on the largest coffee I've ever seen (*Is it a bucket or a mug?* I find myself wondering) while I hold a cup of tea.

"Big tea drinker?" Amaya asks, eyeing the mug. I can't tell if it's an admonishment or an inquiry.

"Oh yeah, actually, yes. My parents drink it a lot."

"Mine too."

I marvel that so much of the world's tea comes from Sri Lanka, just a tiny island nation.

"Have you been back to Sri Lanka since you left?" Amaya asks.

"Once, when my aachchi died. It was sad to be there for that—but even then it was incredible to be back. I didn't realize how much I missed it. It sounds silly, but being born there means part of it is always with me."

I know it sounds like a line from a cheesy yet incredibly poignant Disney movie, but it's true. My first memories are from there. I wish I could visit again, but it is so damn expensive to get there—over $2,000 for the return ticket alone. I miss being surrounded by people who look like me. I love not sticking out for my brown skin or dark hair, and instead sticking out for my awkward sense of humor.

"Aachchi! It's been a long time since I've heard that word. I've always called mine Grandmother," Amaya responds. "It's been a long time since I've been back to Sri Lanka too. I used to go every summer as a kid. Now as an adult it's been hard to find a time . . . or maybe I'm just making excuses. I wasn't born there; I was born here. Somehow, I feel out of place there and out of place here, to be honest. I've never felt quite like I belong anywhere."

I want to tell her that on many days I feel the same. Emigrating from a country for a better life feels like an abandonment of every part of my culture. We make curry here with the exact same ingredients, but it never tastes exactly like it did in Sri Lanka. In NYC, even though immigrants seem to be on every corner, at least in Queens, I still feel different. I want to tell her that she isn't alone, but I am her client, accused of an atrocious murder, and she is my lawyer, so I stay silent.

CHAPTER 13

So let's search for this dude online?"

I'm already dreading the bad TikToks we'll find and all the other weird things that make up someone's online presence. I think I've scrubbed the internet of my angsty online journal entries from 2012 about a foreign exchange student I was convinced I was in love with, but I'm sure if someone tried hard enough, they could be found somehow and would be perfect blackmail material. Sadly, photos of me and my unibrow will live on forever in various Facebook photos. I can't believe a Google search is still our best investigative path forward.

Sometimes I google myself. Only an article about high school honor roll and another about some charity event I ran in college come up. *Unmemorable and unimportant*, the search screams at me. At least that was better than what it will be now. Every time someone googles me now, they'll see my status as a murderer. An accused murderer, but nonetheless, not opening a ton of promising doors for me . . .

I look at Amaya as she sips her coffee and pulls out her phone for the search. Why is she even here? On its surface, this looks like the most obvious case out there. Yet, here Amaya is, taking a chance on me when she could be doing a million other things. I think about an alternate universe where she hadn't gotten into my cab that night and I picked up the guy who waved me down first. I'd probably still be in jail with someone telling me to cop a plea. This isn't how I had thought it would all play out, this murder investigation. Amaya herself, even. I'd expected that an old, grizzled white man with an expensive watch would take over the case. After all, those are usually the people who play attorneys on television. I expected that cops would be swarming and detectives finding clues. Maybe someone who looked like Jack Nicholson would yell, "You can't handle the truth!" That's from a movie of course, but so much of this just feels anticlimactic. As the actual criminal defendant, I'm the most vulnerable person in this so-called justice system. I always thought the good guys and the bad guys were so clear cut. Somehow real life is always more complicated.

"Okay. His name is James Wilkerson-Taylor. It's sort of a common name, though the hyphenated surname may help us narrow this down," Amaya says while typing his name in Google.

I hold my breath, hoping somehow there are only a few search results. Over twelve million results are generated in less than a second. Not a great start.

"Let's try 'James Wilkerson-Taylor NYC,'" Amaya suggests after a short pause.

Less than one million results. We are getting closer; there's still no way we can sort through so many searches.

"Okay, let's do 'James Wilkerson-Taylor NYC python,'" I offer.

"There's no way that is going to—" Amaya begins.

Before she can finish her thought, the screen is filled with more options. I stare at it in wonder. There is a Yelp review for an exotic pet supply store, and given that James owned a pet snake, this could be him. I briefly scan the other search results, and while I don't remember much about James, I'm sure he wasn't a seventy-year-old priest. Amaya clicks on the Yelp review. Though the thumbnail of the photo is small, a shock of recognition runs through my body. I couldn't really describe him earlier, but seeing a picture refreshes my memory immediately. It's the glasses more than anything. When I tried picturing him in my jail cell, I didn't give him glasses. What an obvious detail to forget.

"It's him," I almost shout, forgetting where I am for a moment. One person looks up from her laptop, while no one else notices. It takes a lot more to make a New Yorker look up from their phone or conversation. "I think," I add, just in case I'm incorrect.

"This is great. Okay . . ." Amaya says, leaning in to read the review. "Oh wow, this is a detailed Yelp review about python care." She continues to scan the page quickly. "Damn, he gave the business a two-star rating and ends it with 'would not come again, please consider taking your business for python upkeep items to Amy's Exotic Pets on West Fourth.' Interesting."

"Can we see what else he reviewed? Maybe by clicking on his name?" I ask.

Amaya smiles, giving me undeserved credit for an obvious course of action. I smile back. It's nice to not feel completely useless.

When Amaya clicks on his name, dozens of his other reviews pop up.

"He is quite the prolific reviewer." Amaya clicks through a review. "He's harsh. Although he raves about this cheese shop."

I make a mental note of the name of the cheesemonger, and I'm thinking about cheese plates. A little Manchego with a dollop of fig jam . . . *Focus*, my brain screams at me. I turn back toward the negative reviews. My philosophy is if you can't say anything nice—especially to small businesses, which are most vulnerable—don't say anything at all, which Alex says makes me a pushover, but people have bad days.

"Oh, this one is particularly nasty," Amaya says as she begins to read the review aloud with relish.

"'Lutrino's Pizza is aptly named because the pizza should be found only in a latrine. The pizza, heralded as one of the best in Brooklyn by apparently every other Yelp reviewer on here who is afraid to tell the truth, is limp and soggy. The cheese is greasy. The spices are off. And the pepperoni has probably gone bad. Not to mention the owner, Sal, is a rude man who refuses to provide refunds. Sal thinks because this pizza establishment has been in his family for decades, he has the right to dupe the people of New York into thinking this pizza is good. Well, folks, this just isn't.'"

While it is awful that James died in my vehicle, maybe it will soften my guilt if I find out the guy was a total dick.

"There are responses to the reviews," I say, realizing this is satisfying my Gemini desire to gossip.

"One guy says that 'the pizza is delicious, you dimwit.' Another says, 'Sal is the best and nicest guy around. Yelpers, don't listen to this rogue review.' Oh, boy," Amaya exclaims as she scrolls through all the comments defending Lutrino's Pizza. She doesn't read the ones with curse words aloud, but they are nasty. Just like it's easy to yell at me, an anonymous taxi driver, it's easy to be absolutely horrific to people online.

"Sal responds!" Amaya clicks on the review. "'Mr. Wilkerson-

Taylor, thank you for your comments. I disagree with them completely. Lutrino's Pizza is the best in Brooklyn, possibly all of New York. Some business owners on Yelp say to contact them to make the situation right. I won't be doing that for someone who has trash taste. We have the best pizza and everyone knows it. Period.

It's such a New York City response I can't help but smile.

"Oh my god, James responded and so did the owner," I say, realizing I've been basically holding my breath through the whole ordeal so far.

James Wilkerson-Taylor: Dear Sal. I came again. I thought that maybe you had a bad day and I misjudged you as the other Yelpers seem to think. Your pizza still sucks. It tastes like rat droppings. I'm going to tell everyone I know to avoid this place. You couldn't pay me to eat this putrid shit.

Sal Lutrino: Putrid shit? Come say it to my face, and we'll see what happens. You'll be seeing what Sal Lutrino can do offline.

I look at Amaya. We are thinking the same thing.

"Is that a threat?" I ask to confirm.

"I'd say so. When were the last few messages posted?"

"Just last week," I respond. "Wanna go grab some pizza?"

CHAPTER 14

Amaya reluctantly lets me come along. She says this is really the last leg of the investigation I can join, emphasizing the word *really* for extra effect. I think she's just too tired to argue with me and doesn't want to deny me a slice of delicious pizza. It's probably unprofessional to eat at the same establishment where you're also accusing the owner of murder. I'm almost too hungry to care. Truth be told, I'm exhausted too. My adrenaline is no longer pumping as fast, and the past few days of jail time, stress, and no sleep are starting to hit me hard. I feel my eyes closing anytime there is a lull in our conversation. At least my heart is beating regularly and I have no pains in my left arm. Small wins.

We venture to Gravesend in Brooklyn, a neighborhood that Amaya has never been to. Unable to catch a yellow cab, Amaya calls an Uber, to my dismay. To add insult to injury, the driver has trouble reading the GPS directions to the point where I have to direct him at each turn. This wouldn't happen with a yellow cab. Name a major New York City intersection, and an image of it almost immediately comes to my mind.

I try hard to not feel ill will toward the Uber and Lyft drivers.

It's undeniable that these services have eroded my paycheck so completely that I don't know how long taxicab driving will be sustainable for me. Yet they're just people trying to make ends meet.

"Oh, this is far!" Amaya says. I wonder in relation to what; I figure she means relative to Manhattan, the center of the universe, but there is a lot more to New York City than just Manhattan. So much culture and diversity if people are willing to venture out beyond the safe confines of the Times Square Red Lobster, though I can see why the Cheddar Bay Biscuits are so alluring.

"Turn right," I announce to the driver, who looks as if he is about to turn left.

"You know this area well," Amaya notes.

"Well, I am a taxicab driver." I am pleased that my knowledge of the city's streets, even the less well-trodden neighborhoods, makes me somewhat useful. It's rare I have an opportunity to take pride in my job. "Besides, I used to drop off people at Lutrino's all the time. Not so much anymore." Like Amaya, I guess people found this place too far, and when we turn in to the lot, there are only a few cars parked, far less than I've seen in years past.

My stomach instinctively growls as we approach the restaurant—something it does anytime I'm in the vicinity of good pizza, as if my stomach is its own sentient being. The Lutrino's sign is red, which I heard on *Jeopardy!* is a color that is supposed to trigger hunger. It's working. The exterior of Lutrino's is dated, unlike the new restaurants I've seen popping up all around Manhattan with pink accents and fancy gold light fixtures. The inside of Lutrino's has wood-paneled walls that remind me of my basement, which has not been changed since it was remodeled in the seventies.

As I approach the front doors, the smell of sauce, spiced with oregano, basil, and maybe paprika, creates an intoxicating aroma. I can almost imagine the first bite into the thin crust cooked in a wood-fired oven. I think about the way the cheese pulls as I bite in and the soft pillowy crust that is a hallmark of Neapolitan pizza. I love the little bit of oil in the pepperoni cups, which Ammi always tried to make me dab away with a napkin. On the road, I can enjoy my greasy pizza in peace. Pizza, pretty much nonexistent in Sri Lanka when I grew up, quickly became one of my favorite American foods in NYC. Bread, cheese, and maybe meat. What's not to love? As soon as we reach the hostess stand, my mouth is watering.

"We're hoping to see Sal Lutrino," Amaya asks.

"You've come during prime time; Sal is quite busy right now."

Odd, given how empty the place is now.

"I'm so sorry to bother, but it's urgent," I add.

The hostess smacks her bubble gum and rolls her eyes in teenage defiance.

"Okay fine, I'll see what I can do," she says as she stomps away.

The people waiting in line to be seated behind us audibly groan. I turn around and mouth, "I'm sorry."

A few seconds later, Sal appears. His hair is gray, and the wrinkles around his eyes and mouth have deepened since the photo of him on the pizzeria's website was taken. He looks a little like geriatric Chef Boyardee on the cans of SpaghettiOs that I was only allowed to eat at Alex's house because my mother had deemed it junk. Ammi's words are echoing in my head. *High-fructose corn syrup is not good for you!* She was never so strict with my brother's diet, if I remember correctly.

"How can I help you?" Sal asks in a monotone drawl with a frown.

"Uh, can we speak to you privately?" Amaya asks, reverting to her polite, almost sugary-sweet tone.

"What's this about?" Sal narrows his eyes.

"About James Wilkerson-Taylor."

I notice an immediate perceptible change to Sal's demeanor. He goes from calm and casual to tense and worried. He knows something. The Yelp reviews did look bad, but who kills over a bad review? Amaya reminded me people kill for less on the ride over. So that's the motive. *True crime rule number five: Find the motive.* But the means and opportunity? I look over at Sal and wonder if he could quickly stab someone in a car and run away. I just can't see it. He doesn't look particularly fast. His hands seem designed to make the perfect crust, not the perfect kill.

"Okay, we can talk in my office."

We follow Sal, past an only half-full dining room. He ushers us into a small, cramped back room with a window facing the dining area. The smell of pizza still reaches us here. Amaya shoots me a look as my stomach groans loudly in protest that I haven't offered it pizza yet. We stand awkwardly, and I put my hand on the doorknob. Are we in a room with a potential killer?

I look at Amaya and realize how brave she is, investigating these cases, going to places she's never been, sniffing around stuff that could bring her face-to-face with danger. I solve my podcast murders from the safety of my own taxi. Well . . . it felt safe until a few days ago.

The space is filled mostly by a large wooden desk, covered in papers, which Sal sits behind. I notice that some of the papers have angry red lettering on the top, which, upon closer inspection, tells me they are past-due bills.

"Mr. Lutrino—" Amaya begins.

"Just call me Sal." Sal is perspiring now. The restaurant is hot, but not this hot. "Who are you?"

"Apologies, I should have started with that introduction. My name is Amaya Fernando and I'm an attorney. This is my client Siriwathi Perera."

"Attorney? Are you suing me?" Sal asks, bewildered.

"Why would we be suing you? We just have some questions."

"Do *I* need an attorney?"

"Well, I suppose that depends on whether you killed James Wilkerson-Taylor."

CHAPTER 15

Sal bursts into a fit of laughter that seems to last minutes. With each laugh, his apparent stress and consternation melt away. His rotund belly quakes softly and then more heavily. It's almost hypnotic.

"*Kill* him? Oh, hell no. He's on the payroll. I thought you were here because of that."

"I'm sorry . . . I don't follow," Amaya responds, her nose crinkling in confusion. "Payroll? He worked for you? But he wrote terrible reviews about your pizza place."

"Oh yeah . . . well . . . he did . . ." Sal has a defense up once again.

"And?" Amaya demands.

"Well, I don't want this getting out. Can I trust you?"

Amaya stares at him for a second as if mulling over her answer.

"Can I trust you?" Sal asks again, guarded like a typical New Yorker.

"Yes," I interject before Amaya can respond. "I love your pizza, and we'd never want to ruin your business." I must say it with enough sincerity, because Sal continues.

"He wrote the first Yelp review 'cause he and his girlfriend hated our pizza, but it riled up so many of our customers that they started coming back just to support us. He had the opposite effect; he drove business here."

"So you paid him to write those bad Yelp reviews?" I say. This isn't one of my true crime podcasts, but I can't help trying to play detective. *True crime rule number six: Always keep the suspect or witness talking.*

"Yep. I mean, it got press. The review was featured on some millennial website, BuzzFill or BuzzKill or BuzzMill or something, and even more people were interested, which was wonderful, because as you can tell, business hasn't been great." Sal gestures vaguely to the rest of the restaurant through the window. "People loved our banter back and forth, and they expected me, Sal Lutrino, to have a bit of that Italian mobster break-your-kneecaps effect. I played it up, but I assure you, I'm just a man who makes pizza."

Sal continues, much more relaxed this time. "Eventually, after all the laughs about the Yelp reviews were over, people stopped coming again. It's too far for those Manhattan tourists and everybody else apparently. Some of the neighborhood boys that used to come here all the time, they sold their houses to fancy developers and moved to fucking New Jersey. The *burbs*!" Sal shouts like they committed the ultimate sin.

"So, I got the idea to get that guy to keep writing. For us to get into a real fight on Yelp. Maybe even get some press and get him and his girlfriend to come to the pizza shop—we hadn't actually worked that part out yet." Sal pauses as if just struck with a thought.

"Girlfriend?" I ask.

"Oh yeah, she was some woman. Black hair, slim, in her twenties. They seemed really in love . . . they were necking all over the place. Actually, why are you here? You said that you're here because you thought that I had murdered . . . Wait a second, is James okay?"

Observing Sal's happy demeanor dissipate almost immediately upon the realization that bad news is coming makes me feel sick. Sal would not be one of the close friends and family that police would notify. Most people probably didn't even know they were friends. I don't want the awful news to come from us, virtual strangers.

"I—" Amaya begins.

"I'm so sorry to be the one who has to tell you this," I respond quickly and solemnly. "He's dead." Given that I am the one who met the man, I feel it is my duty to be the one to tell him and not Amaya.

"Damn. That's a shame. A pure shame. Although I thought that guy was an asshole, he really did agree to help us out in the end." Sal's lip quivers, and I wonder if he will break down in tears. I want to put my arm around him and comfort him. "What happened?"

"He was murdered. And we're trying to find the person who did it," I say with trepidation.

I wait with bated breath for the man to point an accusatory finger at me. I am, after all, the accused murderer. Instead, Sal seems absorbed in his own sadness.

"Is there anything I can do to help?" The stoic-seeming Sal Lutrino almost looks childlike as he sits at his desk, shock covering his face. The veneer of the Italian mobster character has disappeared, and I wish I wasn't here for this private moment.

"We weren't good friends, but he was a decent guy. The months he wrote those reviews, and even tweeted some of 'em out for free, were the best revenue months in years. He could have just told me to fuck off when I asked him to keep writing. You know what he said to me? 'If the pizza continues to be shitty, I'm happy to keep writing the truth.'"

The pizza is *not* shitty. It is as delicious as it smells, and I feel sad that a business that has been around for decades with pizza this good is struggling to pay astronomical rent. Some days it feels like the very things that make New York great, like local neighborhood restaurants and small bars, are being forced out, unable to compete in a city that's become prohibitively expensive.

Sal turned over records demonstrating his payments to James at Amaya's request, and with her promise that she'd not show them to anyone without his permission. He then invited us to have some pizza on the house.

"Did you know that Americans eat on average three hundred and fifty slices of pizza per second?" I tell Amaya.

"Let me guess, you got that from a podcast?"

"Nope, a Food Network show I watched with my parents," I say, almost pointing finger guns at her but realizing I've already embarrassed myself enough at this point. I think I'm delirious from exhaustion, or at least I hope that's why I'm acting like this.

Podcasts are the easiest medium for me to consume in my taxicab, where I spend the majority of my time. I also love to read and to watch television. Maybe because school is no longer an option for me, learning on my own has become even more important.

"What podcasts do you listen to the most?" Amaya asks as she bites into a pepperoni slice. I'm already into my second, my first proper food in days.

"Uh . . ." I have half a mind to say something sophisticated and cool, but I can't think of anything, so instead I say the truth. "I love true crime."

"True crime?! The closest you can get to it other than being a murderer is . . ." Amaya pauses "Er . . . sorry, I was just trying to say that criminal defense attorneys have a front-row seat to true crime cases. Ever consider law school? I mean, I know so many of us are assholes," she says with a laugh. I don't think she's joking.

My eyes narrow like she's decided to eat her pizza with a knife and fork. I don't want to talk about this. There are two reasons I didn't go to law school, but I only share one.

"I have a fear of public speaking," I say.

It's a generic but true answer and one that I hope will end the conversation. One-on-one, I can tell people off like the best of them, but give me a crowd, and suddenly I'm paralyzed with fear. It can all be pinpointed to a specific moment in my life. I may have been eight or nine, and I had to recite a poem to my whole class as part of an English-as-a-second-language class graduation. With sweaty palms and clenched fists, I recited the poem perfectly, my confidence growing, until I mispronounced a word, which resulted in rolling laughter from my classmates. I'm pretty sure I'll hold a lifelong grudge against the word *colonel*, and I'm grateful it never comes up in everyday conversation, despite the fact that my English is nearly perfect now. I still worry about my accent, which has faded significantly but still lingers. It's why I'm careful to always speak slowly and pronounce each syllable. I can't speak in front of a judge, in a courtroom, or probably even to an imposing boss with any authority.

"You can get over that! And you don't have to speak in public to be a lawyer, plenty of them just sit behind their desks."

"I didn't want to be one of those types of lawyers; not that there's anything wrong with that work. I just always wanted to be in court." *Like you*, I don't say.

"It's not too late." When I don't reply she says, "Lawyers are always trying to recruit more people to the dark side." She's inviting me to laugh to ease the tension. I can't.

"It doesn't feel important now. I didn't go to law school." I can feel the lump in my throat grow. I know she is well-meaning, one of those "you can do anything you set your mind to" people in this moment. She just doesn't understand my situation.

I'm hoping to eat the rest of my pizza in silence when Amaya comes in hot with another question I don't want to answer. I'm not enjoying the difficult conversation part of this pizza lunch . . . Dinner? Linner?

"How are your parents handling this?" she asks.

"I'd imagine not great." I think of my parents with a pang of regret. I should have gone straight home to them. But I just can't face them right now. Maybe if I go to them with some other leads, they will be less worried that I've screwed up my whole life—which thus far seems to just be one mistake after another. All this stress won't be good for my dad, either, probably accelerating his heart condition—making me responsible for that too.

"I can't imagine. I mean, my parents wouldn't be doing great either."

Amaya must understand better than anyone else what it's like growing up with Sri Lankan immigrant parents with high expectations, who want their children to do well and be good in the world. At the same time, does she *really* understand? My parents are still reeling from the death of my brother, the prized perfect eldest child, and now maybe I'll be locked away forever. I've always been a consolation prize, and now even that is gonna be taken away. On top of it all, we're probably bound to lose the house any day as the bills continue to mount and I've not worked for the past few days. Anger hits me suddenly. I know better than to direct it outward toward Amaya, so I bite down on it and swallow it like a slice of my pizza. She's just trying to help. It isn't her fault that I was arrested and that my life has turned out like this.

"Thanks," I say, avoiding Amaya's eye.

There's an uncomfortable silence before Amaya starts typing away at her phone. I assume it's more emails.

"I found James's LinkedIn. Seems that he worked at a tech company. New Frontier. Have you heard of it?"

I'm grateful that we're back to discussing the investigation. "I haven't," I respond, knowing my brief answers are bordering on rude, but the exhaustion is catching up with me, and today feels like a total bust. I'm waiting for the case to be cracked wide open like on my podcasts. I guess binge listening to podcasts created for maximum dramatic effect makes me want instant gratification. All we've found out is that James wasn't a terrible person, even if he left the occasional gruff review.

"Looks like they have an office in Midtown Manhattan. I may be able to get some leads there."

"That's wonderful. Should I meet you there tomorrow?" I ask cautiously, remembering the onetime-only invitation to the investigation.

"I don't think it's a good idea . . . It's really not protocol."

There's a hesitation in her voice that makes me think she isn't asking me, not because my presence offends her or that I'm shit at investigating, but simply because it's not the way things have been done before. There are probably also some ethically complicated elements. Though if people can represent themselves in court, how bad could it be if I helped in investigating my own case? By her own admission, her office is understaffed.

"I'd really like to be there. This case is literally everything to me. It's my life. I promise to be quiet, to stay out of the way, and simply give you excellent directions. Or maybe a funny story from my taxi driving. I promise brilliant random facts. And maybe, just maybe, I can add something." I stop and realize this is the clearest and most authoritative I've probably ever sounded. I am asking for what I want, for maybe the first time in my life. I won't push her more than this though. She is the attorney, and she knows best.

"Convincing argument, counsel. See you there tomorrow at eight a.m.," she replies with a smile.

CHAPTER 16

At the pizza place, I decide to call my parents. I haven't spoken directly to them since before my arrest, and I know they need to hear my voice. I know I can't avoid their shame and worry forever. I call them on Amaya's phone. I can almost hear the release of fear and stress in their voices when they answer like air escaping an inflatable mattress. I wasn't able to communicate with them during my arrest and subsequent court appearance, despite my best efforts, and I want to apologize for the worry I've caused. The worry neither of my parents should have to endure. There should be a limit for the number of devastating things people have to deal with in their lives.

I try my best to fake my "I'm fine" voice to Ammi, who can usually detect something is wrong just based on a slight change in my tone. I explain to them what Amaya and I have been doing and what is next, and try to calm their frayed nerves just as I saw my brother do so many times before. I tell them I'll come right home after the pizza. Going home means I'll have to hear them cry and wring their hands with fear. They'll wish my brother were here to fix my mistakes once again. This time I have to fix my own problems.

NYC is home to over eight million people. As a kid, I found that walking the streets anonymous and unnoticed gave me a sense of calm. The city streets with their sights, sounds, and smells became my haven, and though I felt out of place, I could still blend in. I take the subway back into Manhattan using the MetroCard Amaya gave me. I walk out of the Twenty-Eighth Street subway stop, and as I do, I see the most beautiful view of the Empire State Building lit up in black and orange, presumably an ode to the upcoming Halloween holiday. Even the rat scampering off with what appears to be an entire slice of pepperoni pizza doesn't take away from the sight.

As I walk across the crowded Manhattan street, I am greeted with the familiar smell of garlic, onion, turmeric, and curry powder. I look up and down at the two New York City blocks studded with numerous Indian restaurants and grocery stores, affectionately termed "Curry Hill," a play on the name of the neighborhood, Murray Hill. The smell alone tells me what kind of cuisine is served, even if I didn't bother to read the signs. I have been to every restaurant on the block multiple times, and each is special to me in its own way. On occasion, when asked my favorite, I'd say it depends on what one wants. Everyone thinks South Asian food is just butter chicken and greasy naan, but it is so much more than that. It is a diverse cuisine with so many different flavor profiles and styles of food. Curry Hill is the warm blanket of familiar comfort I desperately need now. For the first time in days, I smile as I pass the restaurants, many teeming with people. For so long, I thought I had to hide my food and culture, wary of all the kids at school who said I smelled because Ammi cooked curry. Looking at these people now reminds me that times have changed, at least in some places.

I look behind me, and for a second, I feel like I'm being followed. But it's just my exhaustion, which is apparently turning into paranoia. Next thing I know I'll be telling people a group of elites who worship Satan are controlling our media . . .

I walk toward Curry in a Hurry, a fast-casual dining spot, as its name implies. I can't tell if I'm still hungry or just seeking comfort. Curry in a Hurry is both cheap and delicious, a seemingly rare combination in this expensive part of Manhattan, where I am always astounded that a single bagel with cream cheese costs six dollars—a fact I found out the hard way when I once made the mistake of not opting to toast my own at home and wrap it in foil to eat in my car. There was a time when I could get a bagel with cream cheese and a coffee for under two dollars, a thought that makes me feel like the Crypt Keeper even though I don't feel *that* old. Any day now, I'll start to regale the youth with stories about "back in my day." I yawn, as is appropriate for someone of my advanced age, I think. Only one of the *u*'s and *r*'s still works in the neon Curry in a Hurry sign, shining out in the darkening sky. I'd know this place and its blue awning anywhere, sign or not.

"Hello, Siri," the man behind the counter says as soon as I walk in. I hope my haggard appearance and ill-fitting clothes will not elicit any questions I'm not yet prepared to answer. I tell myself I will not think about my case here, not wanting to taint the good memories I have on this block. The man is wearing a white tank top despite the cooling temperature outside. He has a large potbelly—always a good sign for a chef, Ammi says. The man also has a wild mustache that makes up for the lack of hair on his head.

"Hello, Uncle," I say.

The man behind the counter is not a blood relative, or even a particularly close friend, but in my culture, older people with whom you have some sort of relationship usually morph into "Uncle" or "Auntie." Calling someone like that by their first name is a grave offense.

"How are your ammi and thathi?" Uncle asks. I'm touched that he remembers the Sinhalese terms: *ammi* for mother and *thathi* for father, despite the fact he is Indian and I am Sri Lankan.

"They're good." I smile, lying. "They say hello, they're going to come out here again soon." As I say this, I realize how good most of us are at giving the polite answer. How careful we are to hide our problems under shiny veneers. Although, my veneer is pretty gross today. I can't help noticing the growing hole in one of my sleeves.

"Good, you let me know and I'll make them something special to get them to come in. The usual for you?"

"Yes, and two more—one with lamb korma, and the other with just vegetarian biryani and a chicken kabob."

"Good, good," he mutters as he goes back into the kitchen.

I can almost taste the curry and mix of spices as they dance on my tongue. Spicy, savory, and tangy—sometimes all at once. This is my comfort food. This is my happy place. My favorite is the crisp poori, especially excellent here, to soak up all the curries. I tried to learn to make these dishes at home. Other than dirtying up Ammi's pristinely clean kitchen, I didn't make much progress. Even when I follow the recipe exactly, it tastes different from Ammi's cooking. It's as if there is an intangible and unattainable ingredient, like a sprinkle of love, that I can't find in the supermarket.

I take a seat at the counter of the restaurant as I wait for my food. It is nearly empty, save for one man eating in the corner. The man is a reading a newspaper, and the headline catches my eye. **New Frontier Partners with Catalyst Plastics CEO Shirley Lee.** I see a young woman with dark hair and a warm smile. New Frontier is the company James worked at. I try to get a closer look at the paper, when the man turns the page. I make a mental note to look this up at some point.

Restaurants like this have been hit hard by rising rent prices and are barely able to stay in business. So many good places have gone under, unable to continue to pay rent while taking in less money than their more expensive counterparts. Thankfully, and despite the solitary customer here now, this place seems to be doing okay, buoyed by the number of people needing cheap and tasty food quickly. It did seem to scare off fancier people, who took to the restaurants with modern interiors and food triple the price. I look over at a mop in the corner and cracks in the ceiling. Wallpaper is peeling in all four corners of the dining area, and the restaurant signage is certainly original to when it opened years ago. In order for people to come to a place like this, the food has to be good.

I try not to think about the murder. The images of the blood and the dead man I now know as James have replayed constantly in my mind. I've moved on to new worries about money and what will happen if I am sent back to jail. My mother's hours at the local corner store are being cut, it appears, on a monthly basis.

"Your food is ready," Uncle calls from behind the counter. "I put extra samosas and pooris in there."

"Thank you, Uncle," I say, realizing too late that my wallet is with the police. I never leave home without it, but now it's been taken from me. "Uncle, my wallet—"

"Don't worry, you can pay me next time," Uncle says, his eyes giving me a knowing understanding.

I've been the recipient of so many acts of kindness that I know I don't deserve.

"Thank you so much, Uncle. I will be back with the money soon."

CHAPTER 17

I walk back toward the subway to head home. Ahead of me is a taxi stand, filled with yellow cabs, which gives weary and exhausted cabdrivers an opportunity to stop and get a cup of chai. Despite my father's disappointment that I followed in his footsteps to become a cabdriver, I wish more than anything that today were just a regular day and I were here parking my taxi at the stand, ready for a long night of picking up passengers.

My days have changed since I first started what was supposed to be a temporary job. Taxi medallions, limited in number, cost hundreds of thousands of dollars to buy, so instead my father leased one for ten years. It still was a fortune, but there was a promise of a good, reliable salary. When driving a taxi became more difficult due my father's heart disease that he maintained wasn't serious, my brother and I took his shifts over until he could get back on his feet. Thathi never got better, my brother died, and we were trapped in a ten-year lease. It all fell on me. My parents told me I didn't have to take this job, but I knew we'd be financially ruined if I didn't.

Work was busier then, before other car services popped up

and flooded the market. Back then, the world was full of promise and possibility. I would be a lawyer, and my brother a doctor. Together, we'd be two immigrants born from poverty with infinite potential. A cheesy image of me and my brother standing in front of fake fireworks and a faded American flag pops into my mind like a nineties infomercial. How improbable a dream it truly was and how fully I bought into the idea that you can be or do anything in New York City.

I glance around the subway car and wish I had something to read or listen to rather than be left alone with my own thoughts. Sometimes, on crowded train cars, there are subway performers wrapping their bodies around poles, doing feats of strength and gravity-defying tricks. There might be people speaking in languages I can't understand, so I make up stories for what they may be saying. Sometimes, there are elaborate outfits—for humans and dogs. Sometimes people sing (badly), mariachi bands play (generally very well), or someone miraculously manages to make music on an empty bucket (mesmerizing). Like the other subway riders, I wear a frown on my face when these things happen, as if to say, "You're disturbing my very important day." Truthfully, these interruptions delight me. So much talent, or at least fearlessness, is within all of these performers, and all of them seem to have a dream. But tonight, it's just me and two other people trying to get where we need to go.

As the subway makes its first stop in Queens, I am reminded of a sleepover in middle school. My parents invited several of my classmates from my fancy prep school on the Upper East Side, where I had attended on full scholarship given to just a small handful of exceptional low-income students otherwise known as the outcasts. The parents of my classmates all canceled at the last minute: Two were sick, one had a family event that was misscheduled, and two others gave no excuse, just a brief apology that their child couldn't attend.

My mother had taken special pains to find out what American kids eat and, despite her apprehension, bought Twinkies and pizza rolls en masse. *"Did you see the ingredients?"* she whispered to me in the store as if she were about to feed us all poison. The only taker for my sleepover was Alex, a lifelong New Yorker who had never visited Queens before. Ammi thought Alex was a girl—a fair assumption for a gender-neutral name—and Alex's nanny thought I was a boy, never having heard the name Siri. When Alex showed up at our doorstep, Ammi didn't have the heart to turn him away and was probably relieved that at least one parent had let their kid come to this neighborhood. Later that day, I heard Ammi cry in the bathroom.

"Is it my accent that scared them away?" I had asked Alex.

"No. I think some of their parents were expecting they'd be dropping them off at one of those nice buildings in Manhattan. Somewhere in the neighborhood," Alex had explained. I learned "the neighborhood" was the Upper East Side, often directly on Park Ave.

I'd grown up modestly in Sri Lanka, and social division had been a regular part of life even at a young age. I thought things would be different in America.

"Your parents are okay with it?" I asked, surprised that Alex could attend.

"They're not home . . . they're never home. They're always traveling for work. It gets kinda . . ." Alex looked embarrassed.

"Lonely?" I suggested. Years later, I realized that Alex may have had all the outward trappings of a privileged life, but he didn't have what was most important: a loving, present family and, if he was attending my sleepover, friends.

Alex looked at his feet, ignoring me, and instead returned to why no one wanted to come to my sleepover. "Most of those Manhattan kids never leave Manhattan," he had said with a huff, as if he weren't one of those very kids he was talking about. For a while, we both ate pizza rolls, of which Ammi had bought hundreds, and burned the roofs of our mouths in silence.

I exit the subway one stop early. Despite my exhaustion I want to walk. I want fresh air and to feel slightly cold in my ill-fitting jacket, a favorite feeling as fall turns into winter. I see the 7-Eleven where I used to buy chips and where one time I tried to buy cigarettes, only for the owner to dial my parents and rat on me. Most of the places I pass are familiar, though several businesses are shuttered and nothing yet has taken their place. I spot a new grocery store that proclaims to sell expensive green juices and ginger shots. It has seemingly arisen overnight, but it is one of the only signs of gentrification this far into Queens, which is beyond where the tourists lurk for "authentic food."

Each of the front facades in my neighborhood has been imprinted on my mind for twenty years. It was so different moving here from Sri Lanka. On the day we moved in, I stared at each house with awe and wonder. Alex didn't understand why I had been so impressed; they were "just houses" and not like the shining skyscrapers in Manhattan, which were true architectural feats. He'd never understand how for the first time I had my own space and wasn't sleeping in a room shared with cousins. The power didn't randomly shut off, air conditioners came as standard, and cable television was within reach. It was heaven.

Finally, I catch sight of my destination. A modest home with a small driveway. The great affection I once felt for the house diminished as it fell into a state of disrepair. I try to use the rare extra money I earn from driving for house maintenance, but it always goes to some critical problem, never anything cosmetic like new paint or plants. Just a few weeks ago the roof leaked, and then, as if the whole world was against me, the heating broke the very next day, a problem I had to resolve quickly given the increasingly cold fall days. Occasionally, I think that we should sell the house and move somewhere more modern without so many problems. I thought twentysomething me would only have to worry about these things when I had a family and home of my own. My parents bought the house when housing prices in this part of Queens were next to nothing, and they got the place as part of a bankruptcy sale. Despite the healthy profit they could make, my parents, for reasons I understand all too well, refuse to sell.

As I continue to walk, my body aches, likely from sleeping on a wooden bench in a cell last night. I feel my age acutely now. It's like the minute I entered my late twenties, as if on cue, my back started to hurt, and I'm pretty sure I need an orthopedic pillow. Life comes at you fast, I guess. Now I regret my choice to walk. I wish that I were in a cab ushering me right to my door. But I don't have the cash for a cab ride home, both because I'm without my wallet and because the wallet itself contains little cash and a very maxed out credit card. It hits me hard that I can't afford my own services. I couldn't bear to ask Amaya, Uncle, or anyone else for that matter, for any more money. Somehow, they've all already cobbled together $50,000 for my bail. Taking another cent is impossible.

CHAPTER 18

I close the door quietly, hoping my parents are sleeping, nonetheless suspecting they are both up anxiously awaiting my return. It's been hard for them to sleep when I'm not home, something that is probably clingy for the parents of a full-grown adult. Although, they may debate the "full-grown" part. They certainly seem to treat me like a petulant, rule-breaking child by attempting to micromanage every aspect of my life. The double standard between me and my "do no wrong" brother sometimes still annoys me, but it feels weird to be jealous of someone who is dead. And while I dread my parents' reactions to my arrest, after jail there is a comfort in being home. The house smells of cardamom instead of puke, which is a major plus, for starters.

"Putha!" Ammi comes running from the direction of the kitchen. *Putha* means "son" in Sinhalese; those at school always made jokes about how it sounded like *puta*, which is something decidedly less endearing in Spanish. To my parents' credit, they always called both my brother and me putha, the much more endearing and revered term than the one for daughter, trying at least on the surface to make us feel like we were equals.

My mother begins muttering a Buddhist prayer in Sinhalese under her breath. She does this every time I leave the house and every time I come back, believing the words keep me safe. I've also found different trinkets hidden in my taxi, blessed talismans placed there to ward away evil spirits. Given that a man was murdered in my taxi, I'd say they are probably not working.

"Ammi," I say as I stop myself from crying as she squeezes me tightly. I can hear her sniff me a little, a polite reminder that I need a shower. "How are you and Thathi doing?"

"Never mind how we're doing. You're the one we've been worried about."

I look at Ammi. Her eyes are wrinkled with exhaustion. Her mouth is downturned. Her hair, in just a few days, seems more dull and white.

"I didn't do it, Ammi."

"Of course you didn't, chuti." *Chuti* means "little one" or "baby," a name that used to annoy me, but now just feels like a term of endearment I need after this ordeal. I'm fighting so hard for my independence, but now that I'm home, I realize there's no other place I'd rather be.

"Where is Thathi?"

"He's sleeping. He's tired."

I furrow my brow. Thathi would normally be up with Ammi waiting for me—or at least he would if it were my brother in this mess.

"Is he okay? You can be honest," I plead.

"He is fine. You need to get some rest." Her answer is uncharacteristically curt. Normally, Ammi loves to talk.

I remember the bags of food I'm holding, definitely cold by now, and shove them toward my mother.

"You should have come straight home after the investigation," my mother says with a disapproving sniff as she takes the bags from me.

"I needed some fresh air," I reply.

She heads toward the kitchen with the bags with me trailing behind her. I want to demand that she tell me the truth about Thathi's health, only I know that will likely result in her bursting into tears. She's been through enough already.

"I'm going to go back out and investigate tomorrow with Amaya."

"Ah, too bad your lawyer is a Sri Lankan woman and not some handsome Sri Lankan man," my mother says.

"*Ammmmi!*" I screech. I am literally arrested for murder, and my mother is still trying to set me up. I'd imagine this awful situation could be made better with a loving partner—someone supporting me through the roughest time of my life. Or it could be made worse. Ask anyone who has been cheated on. So instead I'll take friendship. Who says that friendship can't be just as good as romantic love? After all, it's thanks to Alex and Amaya that I'm actually out of jail. It's Amaya, not some boyfriend who won't text me back for days, tracking down all these leads with me. She doesn't roll her eyes in annoyance when I share my often crappy investigative leads or theories. I love her heady, loud laugh. How loud she is all the time, actually. My parents want me to blend in, to quiet myself in a country that isn't mine. Amaya makes her presence known.

"Amaya called us and explained everything. What the case involved, next steps. She seems like she really cares. But . . ."

"But what?"

"Your father and I, we can take out a second mortgage on the house if you think we should hire a private lawyer. They are expensive, Siriwathi, but this charge is serious. You could go away for the rest of your—" My mother pauses, with a strange gargle in her throat that makes an appearance when a character on her favorite TV show is killed off or during those ASPCA commercials. She is always so stoic, so seeing this rare display of emotion hurts my heart.

"No. I'll be okay. Amaya is good. Public defenders get a bad reputation. She cares a lot." I feel both annoyed and extremely touched by my mother's suggestion. She wants the best for me, hurt feelings of anyone else be damned. I hate how things and people associated with the poor are always seen as less than, a marker of bad service and poor quality. Am I trying to convince my mother as much as myself that I should stick with Amaya? Are Amaya and I both in over our heads?

CHAPTER 19

I walk up to my childhood bedroom that is now my adult bedroom. Before I know it, the dirty clothes I've worn are on the floor and I'm taking a long, hot shower. Once back in my room, I'm reaching for my familiar pajamas—old shorts and a favorite band tee. My room is filled with lots of books, now mostly ones about the law, the legal system, and legal thrillers. There are a few out-of-date law school textbooks my brother had found at a garage sale and a few we found sitting on neighbors' stoops. My brother could always find treasures in the trash—even turning a truly hideous eighties baby-blue tuxedo complete with requisite frills into the most stylish and unique suit for prom that year. Back then, I thought he had done it to be cool and edgy, and only realized later it was because we didn't have the money for him to buy one at the mall like everyone else.

The posters on my wall are probably over twenty years old, featuring Guns N' Roses and AC/DC—music my parents worried would lead me to a more nefarious life. I have many memories of listening to cassette tapes with Alex. Both of us exchanging a mixtape weekly, and occasionally surprising each other with new songs. Usually, we were just listening to the same classics rearranged in a different order for hours on end. Given the amount of time Alex spent in this bedroom, I could probably consider it his bedroom as well.

Ammi has urged me to update my room so it doesn't look like it belongs to a teenager, but to spend money on changing it would mean continuing to live here longer . . . or maybe forever.

I look up and see a photo of Alex and me from high school sitting on my desk. The other people in the photo are cropped out, friendships that faded as we grew older. He's since grown out of that awkward pimply phase, only I've remained the same with less acne (thank god) but only a marginally better haircut. Somehow, I still don't know my best angles yet. I think I need female friendship more than I realized. Alex takes the worst photos of me, which is why I've had to regrettably include a selfie in my dating profile.

I come down to see my mother setting the table with the food I brought, despite it being well past dinnertime. Ammi tries to force us to have dinner together as much as possible—though sometimes work becomes a suitable excuse. Now that I'm faced with impending jail again, the family dinners I dreaded don't seem so bad anymore. In the past, my mother cooked laborious Sri Lankan meals, each dish requiring multiple ingredients that could only be found at the local Asian grocery store. At one point, back in the day, curry leaves had been so hard to obtain, my parents just grew their own. As I see my mother grow older and more tired, what once were family meals that resulted from a day of cooking are now more simple affairs whipped up in thirty minutes or less. I'm not hungry, but the smell of the curry pulls me in, and I eat at the table in silence. My mother and I fall back into our normal routine of late where she asks me some questions and I provide one-word answers and occasionally a mostly imperceptible roll of the eyes.

I was looking at alternative options for additional income before my arrest. I'd suggested renting out my brother's old room. The mere suggestion had made my mother look at me aghast, as if I'd said that her chicken curry was undersalted or something equally heinous. When I'd pressed her, she had merely said that she didn't want strangers in the house and this wasn't a hotel. I understand that. Our home, as small and now dilapidated as it's becoming, is our private sanctuary. Our place to get away from it all, where people won't comment on the food we eat and the saris my mother wears.

I also know the real reason they don't want to have anyone in his room. They don't want to take down the shrine to my brother that has been there since his death. The photo of him smiling, not knowing that in less than a year he'd be dead, sits in the middle of the shrine. He's forever frozen at the age of thirty-three. His name is written above the photo in calligraphy. The *A* was a little wonky, but even a stranger could make out the name: Ajith.

I avoid going inside his room, or even looking in there. The memories are still tinged with grief, even the good ones. It's hard to remember the laughs without also wanting to cry and maybe punch a wall—emotions I'd hoped would have evaporated by now. People say time heals everything, but I don't feel healed, and my parents still wear the devastation daily on their faces. It's almost as if their physical appearance changed after he died. Yes, the wrinkles were already pronounced and their hair had begun to gray, but the sadness accelerated their aging. Somehow the grief seemed to change the shape of their eyes. They looked sorrowful even when happy.

Yet we moved on as the basic needs of being human prevented us from lying in bed for every minute of the day. We woke up in the mornings and got dressed. My mother works at the corner store, which may let her go at any moment, and my father is a part-time sales associate at a car dealership around the corner—a job taken after his heart condition forced him to pass his taxicab medallion lease onto me. My father has sold six cars—only five if you don't count the one that was returned—six months into working there. It's a commission-paid job, so he can rarely contribute to household expenses, but it's something to do.

Despite an outward appearance of life, we have been ghosts these past two years, shells of the people we once were, going through the days like robots programmed to do certain tasks. There are still joyous moments. My parents smile when someone says something funny on TV. I laugh at amusing things on my podcasts, but late at night when I'm finally alone, I feel terribly sad. Then I get up for work and bury that sadness with a "don't fuck with me" facade.

The death of my brother turned my mother's hair prematurely white, a fact she didn't try to hide. A permanent nod to her mourning. We rarely talk about Ajith anymore. Even thinking about him elicits emotions I hope will continue to remain hidden until they disappear entirely.

After dinner I trudge to my room. Outside Ajith's door I stop and enter for the first time in months. I see fresh flowers and a small plate of kiribath—a traditional offering of a mix of rice and coconut milk—sitting on Ajith's dresser. Other than the shrine, the room is exactly the way it was on the day he died. It is still filled with all the books he loved to read: dozens ranging from nonfiction to fiction, Pulitzer winners to Agatha Christie mysteries. Ajith was so curious about the world. Even the books on his bed, the medical school exam prep guides, remain open at the exact page he had turned to. It is about infectious diseases. I memorized everything on that page. That was during the days I still came back in here often. To keep his room in the exact way it has been is to offer some supernatural, unreal hope that maybe if we wait long enough, he will come back to us.

CHAPTER 20

The next morning, I leave my house just as my parents are starting to watch a rerun of *Jeopardy!* It is one of the many television shows I used to learn English, and it has vastly improved my parents' language skills as well. And unlike in *Friends* or *Seinfeld*, I don't have to navigate the awkward moment where two main characters climb into bed and Ammi starts screaming, "Fast-forward," while Thathi shuffles out of the room, eyes on his feet.

My parents are sitting on the couch, hand in hand. My heart surges with affection for both of them, and for a second I contemplate not joining Amaya and instead spending the day sitting on the couch next to them, eating snacks while Ammi yells at me to not spill crumbs. Next year my parents will be celebrating fifty years together.

My parents had an arranged marriage, and they barely knew each other before their parents promised each of them to the other. The practice is still around but fading rapidly. I can't imagine being forced into a marriage with a virtual stranger. I always expected I would be deeply in love first, though at twenty-eight the pressure to settle down is growing and something my parents will not let me forget. It's only a matter of time before I crumble under the pressure and agree to go on a date with that family friend they have in mind.

My parents tell me they love me as I walk out the door, my mother's prayer following me out. Even before my arrest I understood why they were so fearful watching me go. It was my brother, who on a day just like any other, had gotten sick. My parents had vested all their hopes and dreams on their golden boy. I am the only child left, and the burden to be something more, to get married, to live a good life, feels even more crushing as I get older. Spending the rest of my life in prison is going to dash those dreams.

As I give my parents a hug, I feel how frail they both are. They may be older than me, but I'm reminded of the circle of life and how it's at the beginnings and ends where we need the most love and attention. If my resolve to find the truth of what happened wasn't already at its peak, it is now. I can't leave my parents to wither away without me. I need to do everything in my power to protect them.

CHAPTER 21

Amaya is waiting for me outside of the offices of New Frontier. The company has premium real estate on the twenty-fifth floor of a shiny, tall skyscraper set in the middle of Midtown Manhattan. It makes sense that a technology company is in the center of the city, smashed between the prestigious law firms and bank headquarters likely in need of their services. These places are full of men in suits and women in chic heels, scurrying to get to work under the darkening sky. At any moment, it looks like the clouds will open up.

James doesn't seem to fit the same profile as those on the street, what with his side job of writing reviews for a Brooklyn pizza parlor and his love of his snake, Frankie. I remind myself that people are complex. Full of contradictions and eccentricities. It's another reason why I love this city. One corner may feature a beatboxing priest, another a man dressed in a giant rat suit scurrying around on all fours. New York City is for everyone—conformists and weirdos alike.

As I navigate the sidewalks, I wonder why so many tourists never leave Midtown to experience the sights and delights of the city's other neighborhoods. Yes, there are things to see in the heart of Manhattan, such as Broadway and Times Square, but if you venture a little farther out, you can see a microcosm of so many of the world's cultures right in this city. There are multiple Chinatowns and enclaves of food from around the world. Ukrainian Village features a pierogi that I think of at least monthly, Flushing has some of the best Asian food in the world, and in Jackson Heights, the Mexican food cooked streetside is so otherworldly that eating it makes me have an out-of-body experience. It isn't my business, but when someone asks to get driven to Olive Garden in Times Square, I want to suggest a million other places that will cost a lot less.

As soon as I approach Amaya, I know something is wrong. While she usually looks stressed and overwhelmed, now I can also see worry etched on her face. She furrows her brow, and her forehead wrinkles.

"Is everything okay?" I feel the familiar concern in the pit of my stomach grow. An all too common feeling these past few years.

Amaya hands me a copy of the *New York Post*. "This is going to be hard to see, but I don't want to hide things from you."

I hold the paper in my hands. There is a photo of me taken from court, under the words **Sadistic Taxicab Murderer!** in bloodred lettering. They could have at least given me a more creative moniker. Below are some bare details about my case and more details about James, the dead man. They describe James as a loving environmentalist, survived by his sister and parents. They briefly touch on his work as an activist; there is no mention of New Frontier.

The article is followed by something decidedly less touching: two editorials. The first declares that "women can be killers, too" and details famous female serial killers, which feels equal parts insulting and feminist. The second is an editorial about "how safe are you really in yellow taxicabs," which, based on my quick skim, advocates for greater security checks on a driver's background. I groan. It is hard enough for my fellow drivers to make money at this job, and now they may be plagued with this? It might lead to profiling even more Black and Brown people who drive taxicabs—many of whom had taxi medallions passed down through their families for years. I don't want to belittle anyone's public safety concerns, but usually the people most in danger in the cabs are the drivers themselves. I'd like the writer of the article to deal with passengers who are at least a dozen drinks in.

"I'm sorry. I know it's rough," Amaya says. Her phone rings and she doesn't answer it.

"They couldn't have used a better picture?" I don't want to admit how jarring it is to see my own face staring back at me in the paper just below the word *murderer.*

I read the article again. This time, upon seeing James's name, I feel a pang of guilt for worrying about my own reputation. James was killed on my watch. Even though I didn't kill him, I failed to protect someone in my care. Amaya looks at me expectantly, like I'll tell her how I'm feeling. Of course, I don't want to talk about this now. There's nothing to do except go forth with the investigation.

"How are we going to do this? Just walk in?" I ask.

I try to be polite even though my inner monologue can be biting. At the end of the day, my job depends on being a courteous service worker. To mostly not be seen. Therefore, to simply walk into this building and demand someone's attention makes me feel like asking to use a restaurant's bathroom without buying anything—uncomfortable and invasive. I don't have that luxury of running away. Spurred on by the newspaper, I'm ready to take definitive action.

"I'll walk up to the security desk and say it's urgent," Amaya says. "They'll call up to someone. I'll say we're here about James Wilkerson-Taylor. Maybe they'll think we're police back for a second round of questioning."

I raise an eyebrow at this implausible course of action. Amaya is dressed professionally, but I could have dressed a little better. I thought I had dressed up—when my normal outfit is a ratty band tee and jeans, I guess anything is an upgrade. At least there aren't any holes in this shirt, I think, before looking down and seeing a tiny hole in my shirt that wasn't there this morning.

I admire Amaya's unapologetic boldness—something I desperately wish I could muster more of in my own life. At the end of the day I usually just capitulate to costumers, as I'm too exhausted to keep fighting. Meanwhile, Amaya seems like she would be well suited to a life of espionage if it weren't for her facial expressions. I can usually tell what she's thinking based on those alone. Her tells have become obvious in the short time I've known her.

"What about me?"

"They'll probably think you're an investigator."

"Or they'll recognize me from this!" I say, holding up the paper. My face is clear as day.

"You wanted to come along," Amaya shoots back as if this is all my fault. Her face softens a little. "Worst-case scenario, they'll assume you're co-counsel. I doubt they'll expect their colleague's suspected murderer to be turning up at their door."

The thought of being a lawyer, even just as a fantasy, makes me think of a seminal movie from my childhood, *My Cousin*

Vinny. Sure, it's not one of those hard-hitting legal thrillers, but it's still a favorite. Wisecracking New Yorker goes down south to fight his cousin's murder charge despite overwhelming evidence of guilt and a court system riddled with racism. I'd always related to Vinny and his unpolished yet determined ways. My being any sort of lawyer would make my parents much prouder of me than they are of my life now—but it's more than the external achievements. I want to fight for the voiceless, the people the system uses and abuses—people like me. It's more than my fear of public speaking that prevents me from achieving my dreams.

I can't understand why Amaya allows me to be here, other than to avoid wasting the energy it would take to placate me if I weren't included. I don't question it now though; I'm just grateful to be here.

"And maybe wear this." Amaya produces a worn baseball cap with the Yankees symbol prominently displayed. "I have it for bad hair days."

"I'm a Mets fan," I say, smiling wryly despite myself.

We are granted access to the twenty-fifth floor, home of New Frontier, much more easily than I anticipated. Amaya approaches the sleepy security guard and tells him we are there to see Brett Ryan because we have questions about James Wilkerson-Taylor. The guard simply nods, asks for identification, and phones up before buzzing us through. I wonder if we, as two South Asians, come off as less threatening. Most people stereotype us as nerdy doctors, motel owners, and convenience store workers. Apu from *The Simpsons* was the only South Asian I saw on TV for years. To find out he was voiced by a white dude was infuriating.

I don't tell Amaya, but I spent half the night researching Brett Ryan, CEO of New Frontier. His LinkedIn would move any ambitious finance bro wannabe to envy. Hell, it moved me to envy. He rowed at Yale. His parents are on the board of the Museum of Modern Art. He's interested in improving the environment. I scanned the internet to find something, anything useful. Other than discovering he's handsome, rich, and well pedigreed, I came up with nothing.

But I then remember *true crime rule number seven: Anyone can be a suspect*. Don't discount someone just because Ammi and Thathi would salivate at the thought of having them as a child instead of me. Most anyone can commit murder in cold blood if given the right motivation. And as I've learned in my taxi, being rich, pedigreed, and handsome doesn't prevent you from doing super-shitty stuff.

We pause at the elevator banks. Amaya's phone rings again, which makes me feel unreasonably annoyed. I know she has other responsibilities, but in this important moment, I selfishly want to feel like I'm the only one.

"Are you going to get it?" I snap, regretting my tone as soon as I speak. My nerves are getting to me. I just want to question Brett and get some answers.

"Sorry, it's an unknown caller. I should pick it up. For most people it's just telemarketers, but my clients don't always have the same phone numbers. They may lose their phone, or have a phone shut off." Amaya gives me an explanation I definitely don't deserve and of course makes me feel terrible that I snapped at her. She didn't even flinch. She picks up the phone. "Hello?"

I can't hear what is said on the other side. Amaya's mouth turns into a frown. She hangs up and puts the phone back in her bag.

"What's wrong?" I know it's none of my business. Upon seeing her crumpled expression, I can't help asking.

"They said to stop investigating this case or there would be deadly consequences," Amaya says, looking more annoyed than upset or scared.

"'Deadly consequences'?" I take a moment to let it sink in. "That sounds like a serious threat." I look around as if whoever made the call will pop out and reveal themselves like we're on *Scooby-Doo* and we're the meddling kids. "Should we be worried?"

"It's a big case, it made the front-page of the news today, and this is my work phone. My number is easily found online, and it's been given out to hundreds of people I've represented and their families. This isn't the first time I've been threatened and won't be the last. It could even be the family of the victim, upset about their son. In these types of cases, emotions run high."

"Are you sure?" I ask, wondering if we should call the police, still thinking about my last experience with them—in particular how they had their guns drawn at both our heads. It doesn't seem like they'd be particularly helpful. Maybe the police would even be happy we were getting threats—a morbid but reasonable thought given their treatment of me. Unlike Amaya, I've never been threatened with something so permanent as "deadly consequences," and it freaks me out, even as vague as it sounds. It makes me feel like those scary movies where the lead screams, "The call is coming from INSIDE the house!" I can't shake the feeling that danger is closer than we think.

"Yes, of course, it's just some nutter," Amaya responds casually.

"And I'm sorry," I say, looking down at the ground like a child who's had a moment to reflect on their actions after a much-needed time-out.

"About what?" Amaya's nose crinkles again, and I can't suppress my smile.

"Snapping at you, of course."

"When?"

"Just now, just before the phone call."

"Oh, I didn't even notice. I have so many clients yell at me. If you're not outright screaming, I barely register it."

"God, that must be awful."

"It's hard. It's also hard to be frustrated with the yeller. They are people on the worst days of their lives. They've been manhandled, some of them literally beaten and brutalized. Held in a dirty jail cell like cattle, and told they'll only get out of jail if they're rich enough to do so. Even if all they've done is steal some diapers." Amaya pauses for a breath before continuing. "And most people aren't happy to see me, a public defender, an attorney for the poor and downtrodden. If you're rich, it's a cool idea, but if you're poor and you get me, and you feel like your whole life is in my hands, you start to get nervous."

I remember what my parents offered last night. They could hire a private attorney if they mortgaged their house and sold all their earthly possessions. Even doing that would not likely cover the costs. I looked at the rates online last night—just out of curiosity, I told myself.

"I don't know how you manage it," I reply. It's the truth. If I had half of what Amaya has going on, I think I'd crumble. Some people are meant for important jobs, and others are just meant to drive around a taxi.

"People probably yell at you too. A taxi driver. I honestly can't imagine the type of people you encounter. You mentioned the drunk people in your cab yesterday. I'd freak."

People are rude to me. I just assume that's the life of a taxi driver. In Sri Lanka, the service people who seem to take the brunt of everyone's annoyance are often reduced to "less than" status. It shouldn't be that way. Everyone deserves respect and common decency. Isn't that how I treat people, from the man behind the counter at a bodega to Gary, the sanitation worker who empties our trash every Thursday?

"You ready?" Amaya asks, nodding toward the elevator, interrupting my thoughts.

I don't feel ready, and this sinister phone call only adds to the panic I'm feeling. But time isn't on our side.

The elevator doors open into a beautiful lobby marred only by New Frontier's orange-and-black logo, which appears on nearly every flat surface. There is a receptionist sitting just beyond a pair of glass doors to our left; the blond woman, dressed in a suit, without even asking for our names, waves us through the doors. Her skin looks so perfect, I'm tempted to ask what products she uses. I'm wondering whether it's a Korean twelve-step routine when I remember the consequence of what we're about to do. It's not as if I don't take this seriously—I do—but my anxiety-riddled mind is looking for anything else to think about lest I have another panic attack. But, as my big brother always told me, I have to be brave, especially in those times it feels hardest to do so.

I spot a janitor milling about, but otherwise the entire office is devoid of people. It gives the building an eerie postapocalyptic feel. I assume the absence of people is due to the early hour of the day, not zombies. The reception area is lined floor to ceiling with windows that give a beautiful view of the city. I scan the room and see one man standing by the window with his back turned away from us. This must be Brett Ryan.

"Mr. Ryan?" Amaya asks so sweetly that I'm not sure she's the same person from just a few moments ago. Her different tactics in getting people to speak are impressive. First and foremost, she always comes off as extremely likable, clearly following *true crime rule number three: Always be polite to get people to talk.* It's a surprisingly hard feat given how easy it is for some to label a woman as bitchy or bossy when she's just trying to do her job.

"Yes?" Mr. Ryan turns around. Brett Ryan is conventionally attractive, like a long-lost Kennedy brother. His hair is a little windblown, as if he just stepped off a yacht. For a second, I imagine myself in a Hallmark movie: Woman falsely accused of murder falls in love with a man who helps her find the truth. *No.* This isn't the time to develop a crush. Besides, in the reflection of the glass window, I catch my limp curls, which I spent thirty minutes trying to tame this morning. I'm not melting any hearts today.

"Hi, my name is Amaya—"

"You're the defense attorney, I presume?"

"Yes," Amaya answers. Her eyebrows rise just a little, like she is actively working to keep her face neutral. It doesn't work. I can tell immediately she's surprised, and I wonder if this will throw her off track.

"And next to you is . . . ?" Mr. Ryan asks.

"Uh, my investigator," Amaya says.

My cheeks burn with the lie and the crush I'm trying to suppress. I wish I had worn some makeup—Ammi has tried to force a copious amount on me these past few years—and I know there's some unopened bottle of foundation and probably garish blush somewhere just waiting to be used. I'm grateful he doesn't recognize me; surely he'd kick us out if he did.

"I didn't think you were with the NYPD. They already came here and asked all sorts of details, none of which I assume was of particular help."

"If it's not too much trouble, I'd like to ask you a few questions as well," Amaya says, her voice an octave lower and more like herself now that the ruse is up. To me, the request feels brazen but necessary.

"I suppose it's not the popular choice to answer the questions of the lawyer representing the woman who killed my friend," Mr. Ryan says, and I flinch at his words. "But I was a lawyer once. I learned about the presumption of innocence, and I believe that you should be able to investigate your case and defend yourself. It wouldn't be a fair fight otherwise."

I'm grateful that he isn't turning us away, as he has every right to do. It's actually pretty magnanimous of him—if I were in his place, I'd definitely tell us to piss off. It once again makes me rethink my stance on the criminal justice system and how maybe I've gotten some of it very wrong. Amaya and I are not detectives. We don't have the power of the police force behind us. I am a taxi driver, and Amaya is just a lawyer, not someone with the backing of the state like the assistant district attorney prosecuting my case. We have no power at all. If someone doesn't want to speak to us, then we are out of luck.

"Thank you, we are very grateful," Amaya replies.

"We can take a seat in my office," Brett says as he leads us down a long corridor to a gorgeous corner office with sweeping views of downtown Manhattan.

Amaya and I take a seat across from Brett, who is wearing a well-tailored suit. I can tell it's expensive just from the way the fabric looks. A silk pocket square with a designer logo on it popping out of his breast pocket confirms my suspicions. Brett's suit is probably a whole month's pay for me. I think about my dwindling passengers. Possibly two months' at this point.

"Could you tell us a little more about James?"

"Well, we were friends and colleagues. I have known James for a long time. Since we were young. He is . . . *was* a really good person." Brett's voice catches a little as he corrects himself. I can't help but hurt on his behalf.

I think about how I would feel if someone killed Alex. Visceral anger and hate would course through my body. He's family to me.

Brett continues collecting himself. "We went to college together." Brett gestures toward a "Yale Class of 2018" photo behind him.

I lean in my chair to get a better look. Alex graduated from Yale that year. We both got into Yale, but only one of us could afford to go. Amaya gently kicks me. She must know I'm not paying attention.

". . . started New Frontier together. James was the brains; I was the visionary. I had the ideas and James made them a reality. Without James, there would be no company. I owe everything to him. Everything."

"And what does your company do? Forgive me for such an obvious question. There's not a ton online," Amaya asks politely but assertively.

"Yes, well, when you have a lot of proprietary software, you have a tendency to undershare," Brett says with a laugh, though I don't understand the joke. "We provide sustainable technology solutions to companies. The most important thing about our company, our ethos, is to make the world greener and more environmentally sustainable. If we don't turn back the clocks on CO_2 emissions now, it's going to be too late. We have a roster of clients who are more conscious about the environment thanks to us."

He cares deeply about the environment and is actually making the world a better place. I feel even worse (if possible) about the loss of his dear friend.

"That sounds like incredible and important work."

"Thank you, we're proud of it. I'm not sure how we'll continue without James. I hope we don't get run into the ground without him. My understanding of technology and data was never quite like his."

"Did you happen to know anyone who may have a grudge or vendetta against James?"

Good question, Amaya. Back to *true crime rule number five: Find the motive.*

"Not really . . ." He hesitates for a few seconds before continuing, "He ran in some *interesting* circles. He had a lot of friends in an organization called Green World who didn't love that he was working in tech. They thought he was a sellout. Green World is known for its more aggressive environmental tactics."

"Would you happen to know any of those friends?"

"I'm afraid not." Brett chuckles as if he wouldn't deign to hang out with such a crowd. They probably don't even know how to sail or properly saber a champagne bottle. "They could be pretty hostile to me. Thought I was a bad influence, so I tried my best to avoid them." Brett adjusts his suit, and I spot a gold watch. A Rolex.

"I'm sorry to ask this, but did you and James get along well?" Amaya asks. Even friends hate each other sometimes.

"Yes, we did. I mean we definitely had disagreements occasionally about how the company was run. That was part of the normal course of things. If you ask anyone, this company is not going to run as well without him. His death hurts me personally and professionally."

Brett doesn't seem to have a motive, at least as far as I can tell. And without a motive, he didn't commit the crime.

Amaya continues with her questioning. "Did you see him at all the day of his murder?"

"Well, I did see him at work the day before."

"Everything was normal?" Amaya asks.

"Yes."

"And do you know where he was flying out the night of his death?"

"Yes, I think he was going to Paris. A quick trip."

"Great. You've been of immense help, Mr. Ryan," Amaya says.

Frankie, the snake, was only supposed to be at the animal hospital for two nights, which meant James was going on a very short trip to Paris. He would only be there for hours. Who goes to Paris for such a short trip, even for business? Wouldn't the siren call of the croissants at least merit a longer trip? James's manner in the car was stressed. He was desperate to get to the airport early.

"Do you know why James was heading to Paris?" I ask.

Amaya has asked the questions so far. This may be my only opportunity to speak to Brett. He has no obligation to talk to us further. Amaya shoots me an annoyed look at my speaking up; I can't sit back given such high stakes, and the snake is on my mind.

"I'm not sure. Maybe to meet his girlfriend? Work has been stressful lately, and he said he was ready for a vacation. Actually, I'd better get going. Our workday is about to start and I have a meeting to prepare for," Brett says apologetically, getting up.

Despite the abrupt end to questioning, I'm grateful that we can finally leave and avoid the gazes of James's coworkers. Brett walks us back to the reception area and presses the elevator button for us when his features suddenly transform into a deep scowl as he turns to me. "I have one question for you." He stares directly at me, making eye contact with me for the first time this entire interview. "Why did you do it? Why did you kill my friend?"

CHAPTER 22

I'm rattled the entire elevator ride down and continue to be as we walk into the lobby. It's raining outside, and we pause at the door. Rain is pelting the sidewalks so hard it's like a curtain of water making it impossible to distinguish individual droplets. It's a terrible time to have forgotten our umbrellas. The thought of walking in the rain as I contemplate my life feels dramatic. In real life, I'll just smell like a wet dog and have to suffer a subway ride home in drenched clothes.

"Are you okay?" Amaya asks, a rare tenderness in her voice. She always seems to be directing things and managing crises with the authoritative nature I expect to see in an attorney.

"I can't believe he thinks I did it." I feel stupid saying it aloud. The *New York Post* was impersonal and detached; this accusation came from someone who loved him, and it was directed at my face. It hit so much harder.

"Well, everyone probably thinks you did it," Amaya says matter-of-factly, returning to her normal demeanor.

I grimace at her words. She does have a point, especially after that front-page spectacle. I am the only suspect, and the most obvious one. I remember hearing about Occam's razor in a college philosophy class. The most straightforward answer is also the most likely. I'm the clear culprit. I have the most convenient means and the easiest opportunity. He was stabbed inside my locked taxi. But what's my motive?

"That doesn't mean you did. I'm here, aren't I?" Amaya adds quickly, upon seeing my frown.

"Because you have to be!" I feel like a pouting child throwing a temper tantrum, in need of being soothed like a baby. Is there anyone outside of my own parents who believes me?

"That's true, I am your court-appointed representative, and I'm going to do everything within my power to keep you out of jail." I'm not entirely thrilled with Amaya's refusal to make a sweeping statement about her belief in my innocence or with her formality. I'm not special to her, I'm just like any other client. Any other *guilty* client.

The storm clouds start to look less angry, and the rain begins to slow. I feel guilty even using the lobby of New Frontier as shelter from the elements, as if the mere accusation of murder means that I have no right to seek solace from any place associated with James. I want to get away from this building, and from Amaya, as quickly as possible. I want to be alone. Anonymous. Like I am in my taxi. The past few days, I have been constantly surrounded by people and the center of attention, a position I'm not used to and do not relish. All eyes have been on me at the precinct, in the holding cell, in court, and on this investigation. The rain stops just as suddenly as it began.

"I'm going to go to the office. My colleague dropped the footage off from the intersection where you stopped. I want to watch that to see if there's anything there. Maybe we'll see someone entering or exiting the taxi. It may be too blurry to see a face, but at least we can argue someone other than you had access to the taxi.

"I also have court this afternoon. And I need to find some frozen mice for Frankie." Amaya shudders visibly. "Why don't we part ways for now. If there's anything I think I need your help on, I'll ask you," Amaya says as she walks toward the door.

This feels like a polite way of telling me to get lost. Again, I've been a hindrance. Now it'll be just Amaya fighting for me, and while I believe she is a brilliant and qualified attorney, I can't shake the feeling that it's only a matter of time before we're crushed by the powerful district attorney's office completely.

CHAPTER 23

Amaya calls about fifteen minutes later, when I'm already on the subway back home. The connection is spotty as my train winds its way through tunnels underground.

"We need to talk. Do you want to come to my office?" Amaya asks.

"Uh, sure," I respond. "I can come now." I can't help but feel that this is big news if she wants to discuss it in person. People always want to tell you important news to your face, like a doctor with a cancer diagnosis. Well . . . not always. I guess my ex-boyfriend of two years did break up with me over text. Normal, mature, adult people tell you important news face-to-face. Amaya's tone sounds bad, or maybe it's just professionally neutral. Everything is probably fine and the spotty reception and static are just distorting her voice.

I make it to Amaya's shabby, windowless office. Legal documents and papers are everywhere—though they are in an orderly fashion—and I can tell whatever she is about to say is going to be decidedly bad news. As usual, her face, unlike her tone, is easy to read.

If we were friends, I'd comment on the *Best of Celine Dion* CD, a bag of Cheetos Puffs, which are an excellent snack choice, and her fancy French press. But this is a serious professional relationship, and the news she has for me looks like it may be worse than getting dumped over text because the man in question was cheating on me with my "friend."

"I've got some bad news."

I shift uncomfortably in my chair, wondering how this case could get worse.

"They tested the knife. They found your DNA on it."

My mouth hangs open like I've been slapped. She says it so quickly I'm not sure if I heard correctly.

"That's . . . that's . . . impossible," I stutter like I did when I saw Lindsay Lohan's incredible career comeback and makeover, though this shock and awe are quite different.

She looks at me incredulously. "Are you sure you didn't at any point touch the knife, even accidentally? Maybe you touched it when you were going to check on him? Maybe you tried to pull it out to help him? If so, we can explain that." Her voice is almost pleading. *Tell me something I can work with*, she seems to say.

I go back to that terrible night, replaying the whole horrific scene again and again. No. I didn't touch anything, except the man's wrist to see if he had a pulse. I got a little blood on my hands then, but I didn't touch the knife. I remember thinking, thanks to my true crime podcasts, that I must not contaminate the scene by touching anything. I wanted to be as far away from the blood as possible. Even through my shock, I know I was careful. I'm positive I never touched the knife.

"No. I didn't. It has to be a mistake. They must have made a mistake with the testing." I don't know anything about DNA, but I do know that I'm grasping at straws. I know how I sound.

Amaya shakes her head a little, as if disappointed.

"Mistakes like that *don't* happen, Siri. Tampering happens in cases sometimes, but we need proof of that before we go accusing the state-run laboratory that deals with all of the criminal court samples. We'll sound insane if that's our only defense."

She looks at me, her eyes probably searching for a shred of something redeemable. She must think I've made a fool of her. Maybe she is usually cautious or wary, but with me she let her guard down, hence letting me tag along with her.

"You think I did it, don't you?" I ask. I am angry about the news, but somehow my voice comes out in a meek whisper, as if I should be ashamed by the situation. I would be, if I had killed him. "What about the camera footage from where I stopped?" I know that's where it had to happen. That intersection.

"I got the footage surprisingly quickly. I, too, was convinced it would show someone else stabbing James. It shows you almost hitting someone with your car, but no one going in or out of your taxi except for you." She pauses. "No one ever approaches the taxi."

I am stupefied, and my mouth hangs open for the second time in this conversation, like one of those poor fish that dudes pose with in photos on dating apps.

"I am your lawyer, and I am assigned to represent you and provide you with the best outcome no matter what. However, this relationship is a two-way street. I need to be honest with you, and you also need to be honest with me. I understand that it can be difficult to trust a stranger like me—"

"You're not a stranger! I trust you!" I protest quickly. I know she wants me to come clean, confess all. But I didn't do this. I can't tell her what she seemingly wants to hear.

Amaya ignores me and continues, "I will be honest with you. I will let you know about your options. Siri, they are not great. You're in a locked taxicab. You pick up a man and he is alive, and then drive him to the airport and he's dead. Your DNA is on the weapon." Her voice sounds mechanical, as if now that she's decided I'm guilty, she's flying on autopilot. Get me the best plea deal she can or go to trial. This new information has changed everything. My innocence was already improbable and now it seems impossible.

"I'm innocent. *Please*. I know it sounds crazy. I know it sounds impossible. I promise you, I promise you . . . I didn't do it." I sound like the desperate people on some of my podcasts, with not a shred of evidence on my side. "Didn't they find other DNA in the cab? Fingerprints?"

"No fingerprints other than yours and James's."

"I wipe down my cab because it's dirty!" I had done it right before James got in. Does she not remember when I told her that people try to get freaky in the back of my cab?

Amaya shoots me a look like, *That's what they all say.*

I want to be annoyed with her, but I know I wouldn't feel any differently if the roles were reversed, if she were in my shoes.

I can only assume the investigation is over. This is the end of the road. She can't investigate anymore on a dead-end case when so many other clients demand her time and attention. I wouldn't know where to begin to investigate on my own. I'd probably be charged with another crime if I started interrogating witnesses solo. I can already hear the prosecution screaming, "Witness intimidation."

"In that case, we still have some more leads to pursue, some more investigations we can conduct. I did a background search on James and found a woman named Darla who appears to be his sister. She lives in Staten Island. I'm going to go talk to her today."

I am relieved and surprised that Amaya is going to continue to investigate, but her demeanor has changed. She stands stiffly facing me, the glimpses of a relaxed persona she showed yesterday has totally vanished. The cursory friendship we started to develop has unraveled in an instant. There's irrefutable proof of my guilt. I know, at this moment, she's convinced I killed my midnight passenger.

As if Amaya couldn't be more annoyed, I have the audacity to insist on joining her. I beg, quite literally, and I take advantage of the fact that she is exhausted and fighting with me is something she doesn't have the energy to do. "I fight with prosecutors and judges all day," she tells me when she finally relents. Her face is plastered with a sense of exhaustion that I didn't see yesterday. Maybe she's allowed me to come because she figures there is nothing to lose in this dead-end case. Maybe she wants me to watch as she proves me guilty.

On the ferry ride over, Amaya decides, really and truly, that this time I'm not to say anything. I say "really" and "truly" because I have received similar instructions for nearly everyone else we have spoken to, and I continue to do the exact opposite. I justify my behavior by knowing that my questions usually elicit a helpful answer, but now I vow to stay in line because this time Amaya is probably entirely fed up with me. My DNA on the murder weapon gives her the trump card to definitively kick me out of this investigation at any time.

I'm wearing my glasses and Amaya's baseball cap and look different enough from my *New York Post* photo that I hope my presence will go unnoticed. Staten Island feels like a different world to me. Unlike the bustle of the other four boroughs, Staten Island is only accessible by car, ferry, and chronically late MTA buses. Today, we have opted for the ferry. As the boat moves along, we get a beautiful view of the Statue of Liberty. I relate to the statue inscription's opening line, addressing immigrants both tired and poor. Check and check.

Amaya's hair is blowing wildly in the wind. We decided to stand outside on the ferry deck, as the weather is unseasonably warm, and the sunshine seems to help lift both of our spirits. We do not speak for the first several minutes of the ride, until I break the silence.

"Have you done many murder cases before?" I ask, turning to Amaya. I want to get to know her, regardless of what she thinks of me in this moment. I think about all the times people underestimate us—young Sri Lankan women.

"Uh . . . actually, no." I catch her blushing, as if she is ashamed she didn't tell me before. She looks like she has been hiding some secret, and exhales audibly now that it's off her chest. "This is my first."

In any other circumstance, I would cheer her on, telling her she's an absolute girlboss—actually just a boss—and that she can do anything she sets her mind to. However, it is my life in her hands. I think about my parents' offer to mortgage everything they own just to hire one of those old white men in an expensive suit. For a brief second, I want to call them. Tell them to do it. But Amaya, her stance on my guilt or innocence still unclear, is the person here, by my side, investigating leads. She is going to each place herself. There are few people out there with the fortitude to keep investigating in the face of near-certain guilt. We don't have many clues, but at least we're doing something.

"You may not believe it, but I really am going to do everything I can for you," Amaya says as she looks on toward the Statue of Liberty, again avoiding my eyes. I'm certain she is saying this because of her professional obligations to me. I can't help hoping that it is also because of something more—a kinship she sees with me.

"I know you are," I say, my voice lost in the wind.

CHAPTER 24

I am taken with the house as soon as we walk up. It's a quaint cottage with ivy crawling up the side. For a second, I am transported to an English countryside, like in the quintessential Christmas movie *The Holiday*, starring Cameron Diaz and Kate Winslet. All we need is a handsome Jude Law character who shows his kind and caring side by being an excellent single father to two adorable little rascals.

We disembarked from the ferry, and though I'm not completely familiar with the area, I figured that we were walking distance from the home. To New Yorkers, walking distance could be anything from five hundred feet to a few miles, as I found out when I moved here. This commitment to walking long distances and passing them off as reasonable is only beaten in Sri Lanka, where cars are so expensive that walking ten miles isn't out of the ordinary. Luckily for me, the distance to the cottage was on the shorter side. We both walked in silence, the conversation of the ferry ride lingering in the air like a secret finally come to surface.

Amaya faces the door, addressing it with three assertive knocks. Looking at her, I notice a vulnerability I haven't seen before. I'm not sure if it is because the DNA evidence seems to unequivocally confirm my guilt, or that in revealing this is her first murder case she is showing a side of herself that she hoped would remain hidden. In rooms full of white male attorneys and judges, she is forced to present herself with a certain confidence just to be taken seriously. Revealing her lack of expertise is certainly a chink in what is supposed to be impenetrable armor.

"Hello?" A thirtysomething woman wearing a tie-dyed shirt and paint-flecked shorts answers the door. The woman's outward appearance doesn't seem to match the house. She seems like somebody's kooky aunt who went to Woodstock and had a great time.

"My name is Amaya. I'm a lawyer. I am hoping to ask you a little bit about your brother." I notice she doesn't say whom she represents.

"We're sorry for your loss," I add, while Amaya shoots me a dirty look. *Stay silent*, her face seems to scream at me.

"Thanks for saying that, it's been hard."

I give her a weak smile. I wish I could properly convey to her how sorry I am for her loss.

"Come in," the woman says. I'm always a little surprised at the comfort some people feel with strangers in their own home. Did she not want to see at least some sort of identification? Won't she even ask us to take off our shoes? There are almost three burglaries every minute in the United States and countless numbers of rugs that have fallen victim to dirty shoes.

I look at who I assume is Darla as she leads us into the house. The red-rimmed, puffy eyes, the streaks of mascara below them, and the exhaustion. She looks pale and gaunt. I know how she feels all too well.

As soon as I walk into the house, I smell a sharp herbal scent, one I first smelled on Alex in high school. I look at Amaya, and she at me, both of us registering it. Weed. The woman leads us into the kitchen, where I'm certain the smell will dissipate, but it doesn't. For a second, I worry I'll get a secondhand high somehow, like the time that Alex smoked a joint in his parents' car with the windows rolled up. The one time I smoked, I just coughed until I had to excuse myself. Plus, I still live with my parents, and sneaking in weed as an adult is just as hard as it was when I was a teenager, and even more pathetic.

"You're here about my brother?" She looks like she's holding back tears. The woman hasn't introduced herself. By confirming her relationship to James, I know she must be Darla, the woman listed on the background report as his sister.

"Yes, we're sorry to bother you. I'm the attorney for the person charged with the crime, and this is our investigator," Amaya says, vaguely pointing toward me. So far, I haven't provided any assistance that Google Maps couldn't. Though, technically, I am serving as an investigator of sorts. The fact that I'm also the defendant is just omitted, not a direct lie.

"Oh. So you're trying to help the cabdriver?" Darla says as she lights a blunt. "You don't mind if I smoke, do you?" Before either of us can respond, she lights up and continues. "Maybe the cabbie didn't do it, ya know?"

I raise my eyebrows in surprise.

"What makes you say that?" Amaya asks, exchanging a furtive glance with me.

"I mean, why would a random cabdriver kill him? She didn't try to take anything off my brother. I mean, I have his wallet here.

The police finally returned it to me." She waves the wallet in the air and sets it down on the kitchen table by her side.

"Do you mind if we look at it?" Amaya asks, already reaching for it.

"I don't see why not, just don't take anything," Darla says, eyeing us cautiously for the first time since allowing us into her home. She puffs out a neat circle of smoke, and I have to restrain myself from acknowledging this skill.

Amaya carefully handles the small, worn, brown wallet, taking out the credit and identification cards one by one. After seeing the New Frontier offices and Brett Ryan and his fancy clothing and Rolex watch, I expect an expensive designer wallet, but when the tag inside reads "Kohl's" I immediately feel a sense of camaraderie with James. Something tells me he was a frequent flier at the clearance section of the Gap Factory outlet like me. Inside the wallet, I see he was only one punch card stamp away from a free coffee.

"Also, I realize this is odd, but I have James's snake. I was investigating, and they gave it to me at the animal hospital and wouldn't let me give him back. No other contact information was provided. I got some mice to feed it." I notice Amaya gag slightly.

"Oh, bless you. Yes, I'll take Frankie back. Thank you for taking care of him. I wasn't sure where my brother had dropped him off. I thought he was dead."

She pauses, and then she does the very thing I try so hard not to do in front of others. She cries, just a little. I hand her a tissue from the floral-covered tissue box, and she takes it. "Sorry about that. I just wasn't expecting to have a living connection to him, even if I fucking hate snakes."

Both Amaya and I laugh. If Darla had any suspicion or animosity toward us, it's dissipating. Amaya's care of Frankie has paid off.

Amaya continues to sort through the wallet, and I look attentively over her shoulder. Everything looks fairly normal and explainable. Old receipts, which don't seem to be of value. Credit cards. Business cards. A Werther's, my favorite, which Alex says is an old person's candy. As Amaya continues, we notice a crumpled piece of paper with a number on it: NYCRC #1045. 14-90-18.

I meet Amaya's eyes, and she covertly takes a photo of it when Darla isn't looking.

"Do you happen to know what this is?" Amaya says, waving the little bit of paper at Darla.

"Oh, I don't know. Lottery numbers?" Darla answers as she continues to puff on her blunt, already looking a bit dazed.

"Do you know if your brother had any enemies?" Amaya asks. The question has always struck me. Who hated someone enough to kill them or have them killed? According to three of the true crime podcasts I have listened to, apparently plenty of people. Ninety percent of people are murdered by someone they know. I mean, my aunties and uncles annoy the hell outta me with questions about why I'm unmarried or so dark skinned, two things looked down upon in Sri Lankan culture. I briefly held fantastical thoughts of slapping them, but murder was a step too far even for the auntie who pinched one of my fat rolls. People surrounding victims do have the motive, opportunity, and means. Murder, it seems, is personal.

"Well, my brother was a polarizing person. He cared deeply about the environment. He and I were the same way. We probably pushed ourselves further into the environmental movement than most. Some may have called us radical. We chained ourselves to trees a couple times to protest climate change. We protested often. Even Frankie was a rescue from a rainforest we failed to stop from burning down. We would camp a lot. We took two years off of college and tried to stop fracking in Ohio, attempted to curtail big-game hunting in South Africa, and did a random foray to save an endangered species of snail in Indonesia. People were killing them to make facial products. God, I miss him so much." Darla sniffles, and my hand hovers over the tissue box again, but this time she doesn't cry. Darla's face is animated, but her voice is still low and slow, as if the weed has blunted the strongest of her emotions. She and her brother lived an incredible life, and I can't help being jealous of their passionate dedication to their causes. Dealing with screaming passengers and getting stuck in gridlock isn't my life's passion. Maybe only a few people are lucky enough to do what they love.

"This seems to contrast with the corporate life James led," I say. I don't dare look at Amaya but can instinctively feel her eyes burrowing into the back of my head. It's the same look Ammi gives Thathi when he attempts to shovel rice and curry down with his hands at a restaurant. Eating with your hands as your utensils is traditional among Sri Lankans, despite it being seen as bad behavior most anywhere else.

"You're right. It's probably why so many of the old crew, the Green World guys, were so pissed at him."

"Green World?" I ask. It's the same organization that Brett Ryan had mentioned.

"You probably have heard of Greenpeace. Green World is a bit more . . . radical. Let's just say we don't always take legal measures to further our agenda," Darla says with a conspiratorial laugh.

I think of them ushering polar bears out of a zoo after hours and can't help but smile to myself.

"Do you want to take a seat?" Darla says, gesturing to two couches in the living room that would probably be described as in the style of an "old cat lady" by anyone millennial or younger. They aren't quite what I imagine Darla's aesthetic to be. We walk through and sit.

"And the Green World people, do you have their contact information?" I ask. It's a big ask. Darla would be potentially ratting on people she is friends with, or at the very least, inviting our meddling presence in their lives.

"Um. Yeah. You have to promise they won't know this info came from me. Given our not-exactly-legal nature of things, they're pretty private. I love the Green World people like family, but if there's a possibility that they did this to my brother, I'd probably wanna kill them with my bare hands," Darla says, anger and sadness etched on her face.

I know how she is feeling—probably better than anyone—and had I not been here for an investigation in which I am the accused, I would comfort her. I would tell her that she will feel angry for a long time because death at a young age is just unfair. She will always feel sad. It will come in waves that hit her at unexpected times. In the grocery store, late at night, early in the morning. I would also tell her that one day, she will be able to live her life, maybe not as it was, but that she will find small moments of joy. She'll eat some delicious dosa from the cart in Washington Square Park or laugh at the man feeding the pigeons in Tompkins Square. I'd tell her not to feel guilty about feeling content or even elated when good things come her way. Her brother loved her, and he'd want her to be happy.

Instead, I say, "Of course, we won't tell the Green World people where we got their contact information from."

"They may not even know I'm staying here. It's my parents' house. Certainly wouldn't decorate it like this," she says, rolling her eyes and gesturing to a set of watercolor sunsets and Bible verses that are framed. I think I even spot some Beanie Babies in the corner, still in individual plastic boxes as if they may be worth something very soon. "Staten Island has barely any green points, so it's not okay for us to live here. The bonus is that it makes it a great hiding place."

"Green points?" Amaya inquires.

Hiding place? To me this seems to be the more intriguing question.

"Yeah, it's a system within the organization where we rank everything with points. The more points, the better it is. We support those high-point-ranking places, and we boycott and seek to destroy the others. For example, Amazon has a low point value. They use a ton of plastic, are bad about using recycled materials, their factories pollute. I mean, I could go on and on. They're terrible for the environment. A place like REI has a better point value."

"That's intense," Amaya mutters. I think about how expensive it must be to achieve this level of environmental sustainability. I want to save the environment but am also aware that I probably can't afford any of the places with the most green points.

"You don't even know the half of it. The same points go for restaurants, shopping, grocery stores. It's a little . . . I hate saying this—cultish." I wonder if they all wear purple caftans and chant positive affirmations. "It wasn't always like this though. It was just a dedicated environmental organization at the beginning, with really good people. But, lately, it's gotten extreme. I've, uh, moved a bit away from that thought process myself, and so did my brother. My brother believed instead of boycotting and destroying businesses that were not as environmentally savvy, we could make them better, show them how to make their businesses more sustainable. My brother would have done so much good," Darla says, her fists clenched. Her sadness seems to have turned to anger at the thought of her brother gone too soon.

"Which is why he worked for New Frontier," I say, thinking out loud. Besides, unless James and his sister were independently wealthy, and this house decor suggests they were not, he would have had to work for a living.

"Yes. It's still a corporate business. Based in Midtown, housed in a building with a C energy rating. It is everything Green World has rallied against, even though it's trying to make the world a better place. My brother was trying to do good. In fact, it's my brother who encouraged me to work at Catalyst."

"The plastics company?" I question aloud. Seems like a departure for someone so committed to the environment, but sometimes we take less desirable jobs to make a living. Wasn't New Frontier also working with Catalyst?

"Yeah, that's what I said when my brother first suggested it. Like over my dead body." She pauses, realizing what's she said. "Um . . . I mean, I didn't want to work there, but James was so sure we could try to change these companies from the inside. Once I told the Green World people what I was up to, well, they were pissed. They said there was no changing such toxic places, and anything I would do would be pointless and I'd be complicit."

"Is there a possibility that people from Green World could have murdered him?" Amaya asks. They may be a radical organization, but murder seems to be a step too far. I can't imagine they would want to hurt their own, even if they felt betrayed. These people are meant to be fighting for a better world, not killing those doing something about it via their business—even if it is a corporate one.

"They get angry. And they're not afraid to break the law. I hope they didn't hurt him. Truthfully I don't know. I've distanced myself now." Darla reads a number and address off her phone. "That's Charlie Hall. James's former best friend and head of Green World. He definitely hated James by the end. It's sad. They were so close. I don't think he'll even come to his funeral."

"Did the police ask you about this?" Amaya asks.

"They didn't even come to talk to me. I called the detective, and they said they had the person who did it. They didn't need to waste valuable resources." Darla snorts. It confirms what I've known all along. The police are certain I'm guilty, and if we need other evidence, Amaya and I will have to find it ourselves. Maybe we just did. Another lead, after a seemingly dead end, and this one feels promising.

"Is there any other person that you think would want harm to come to your brother?"

"Well, if I'm going to be honest, maybe me."

Amaya and I exchange another glance and both look to the front door. Women are always looking for an escape route in precarious and dangerous circumstances.

"Look, I would never hurt my brother, but I guess in full transparency, I'm set to inherit about ten million dollars' worth of stock when his company, New Frontier, goes public next year," Darla says as she puts out the blunt.

CHAPTER 25

Darla gets a phone call and gestures for us to leave. I do have some lingering questions, such as: Why is she distancing herself from Green World? Is it because she's working at Catalyst? And why is she hiding? As we walk out of the house, I can't help but feel a little more hope about everything. Even if the police aren't willing to investigate matters of their own accord, our handing them leads will have to make them get their heads out of their asses.

And despite my lingering questions, I don't want to be at Darla's house longer than necessary. I want her to mourn in peace without the prying questions of strangers.

"I don't think she could have done it," I say, thinking of the sadness etched on her face. I remember how hard it was to keep it together in the days after my brother died. Maybe I am trying to draw parallels between myself and Darla that do not exist, but I can't believe she would kill her own brother for his money. Money is a powerful motive, but Darla seems like a genuinely good person who cares deeply about the world around her. As for means and opportunity, I'm brought back to how difficult it would be to murder someone in a locked and moving taxi. Even so, someone did it.

The way Amaya looks at me, with skepticism and slight annoyance, tells me I'm still the most obvious suspect in her book, and with good reason. I don't understand how my DNA could be on the murder weapon.

"If she was guilty, would she tell us she had a motive to kill him? Seems kinda crazy. I think she wants us to find who really did it."

We are walking back to the ferry when Amaya's stomach grumbles loudly. She gives me a sheepish look.

"Do you want to eat something?" I ask.

"We should just go back home," Amaya says, although I don't think she means it. I remember how grumpy not eating makes me.

"You know, we are on Staten Island . . ."

"Yes?" She looks at me like one of those people at the beginning of a Snickers commercial—about to wreak absolute havoc until she's eaten something.

"It's home to multiple Sri Lankan restaurants. *Delicious* Sri Lankan restaurants."

As if on cue, my stomach growls.

"I guess some fuel before we go speak to Charlie Hall wouldn't hurt," she responds, a small smile on her face that she's poorly hiding with a scowl. "But we gotta make it quick."

I'm already thinking of the richly scented curries and fragrant flavors. I know dinner will be awkward since Amaya thinks she's sitting next to a possible murderer, but we don't have to talk; we just have to eat—a social situation I usually prefer anyway.

The restaurant is only a short five-minute walk, all with a view of the beautiful Manhattan skyline from Staten Island.

"And we've arrived!" Amaya says, sounding less sour than just a few minutes earlier.

We enter the restaurant. Beautiful masks line the walls. The raksha masks are vibrantly colored with big googly eyes. Often a tongue snakes out of a sinister smile. The masks, in their sneering and garish vibrance, scared me as a child. My parents insisted on putting them throughout the house, which only served to frighten me half to death when I got up in the middle of the night to use the bathroom. My mother promised me that they were there to ward off evil and that the masks were agents of good that protected us from dark forces. I believed that tale for a long time. Now the masks are sitting in my room, collecting dust in the back of my closet, after being ripped violently off the wall the day my brother died.

"This place is amazing," Amaya says.

Her body relaxes just a little. We rarely see our home country represented anywhere.

I've only been to this place once, having the rare occasion to drop passengers off in Staten Island in years past. I rarely frequent places my driving doesn't usually take me—I can't afford the "wasted" gas.

After we are seated, I open the menu and am greeted with a list of familiar favorites. Most people assume that because Sri Lanka is so close to India, the food must be similar. Looking at the carbohydrate options alone, you'd know this isn't true. In Indian cooking, rice and naan are common. Poori, a fried dough, or roti, a rolled dough cooked in a skillet, are also the norm. In Sri Lankan cooking, there are completely different options. My personal favorites are hoppers, a crispy bowl-shaped crepe; pittu, a rice flour and coconut dish eaten with curries; and a string hopper, a network of rice noodles bound together like a spider's web. At the present moment, my mouth is salivating with the smell from the kitchen. I want it all.

"What do you think the numbers in the wallet mean?" Amaya asks me as we wait for our order.

Her mood seems to have improved at the promise of food, and at the glass of wine she's already made significant headway through.

"I think it must be a locker combination and maybe a locker number? The NYCRC means nothing to me. It's New York City, obviously, but what? Nothing helpful comes up when I google it. Finding a locker in the city will be like finding a needle in a haystack," I reply as the waiter sets down cold coconut water for me, a common beverage native to Sri Lanka. I couldn't believe it when it started to become trendy here and health food stores sold a small bottle of it for eight dollars.

"And the company going public?" Amaya asks. "I'm trying to decide if that's important."

The more questions she asks, the more I wonder if she thinks I may *not* have done it.

"I can't imagine the owner of the company would want any hitches before it went public. I bet James's death actually had a negative effect. Yet another reason that suggests Brett Ryan wasn't involved," I say. Thinking about Brett's sad and handsome face with those chiseled cheekbones, asking me why I had killed his friend, starts to make me lose my appetite.

"It is a motive for the sister. Ten million bucks is a lot of money and could save a lot of trees and animals," Amaya adds.

"Sex and money. The two main motives for murder." That's what my podcasts have taught me. "I just wish I could have asked a few more questions." *Back to true crime rule number six: Always keep the suspect or witness talking.* Darla made that difficult once she began to shoo us out of her house. We couldn't force her to speak more with us. We aren't the police.

Amaya looks up at me, and I brace myself to be chided for once again asking questions out of turn.

"Sounds like you're becoming a real investigator. I'm not sure how the DNA ended up on the knife. Am I an idiot for believing you? For believing you didn't do it?" Amaya crosses her eyes and looks as if she's questioning her own sanity. I see she's surreptitiously ordered another glass of wine and has almost finished that one too.

I don't answer the question. Anyone else wouldn't believe me, let alone agree to eat dinner with me.

"But . . . I believe you," she announces. "Please don't make me regret that."

"Thank you." I say a silent prayer of thanks to this restaurant, and especially the booze, for easing tensions. "I promise you, I'm innocent."

A long pause ensues.

"Anyways, I guess we'll have to see what Charlie has to say for himself," Amaya concludes.

At this moment, the plates of curry arrive at our table. The chicken curry immediately hits me with a wave of familiarity. It smells just like my ammi's. We've over-ordered, an indulgence that I only participate in with Alex, because he almost always pays the astronomical bill. I always offer to pay and on multiple occasions have hidden cash in Alex's house to feel as if I'm not a complete mooch, but Alex's love language is gifts. As money has gotten tighter in our household, the gifts of fancy foods and nice wines that Ammi adores but would never buy herself have become plentiful. When I confronted Alex about it, he just shrugged and said it's long-owed rent for the many nights he spent at my house and all the free food Ammi has fed him over the years. My heart swells at remembering a night from just a few weeks ago when the four of us—Ammi, Thathi, Alex, and I—had played cards while eating and drinking the fanciest wine and cheeses. For a brief moment, on nights like those, my troubles seem far away.

I think about what Alex would do if he were wrongly accused of murder. He'd get the best lawyers and the best investigators to fight his case. Money isn't everything, but it sure is important when you never have enough.

"My friend Alex may know something about New Frontier or even Green World. He's in the tech industry. I should have thought of him sooner. I can call him," I offer.

"The same Alex who helped bail you out?"

"Yes, that's him. My best friend."

Amaya grabs some curry with her fingers. I think of Ammi chastising Thathi for the same behavior, and it makes me feel sad. My parents desperately wanted to fit into their new country, afraid of the consequences if they did not.

I tuck into my food, and the magic of the hopper covered in the coconut sambol distracts me from my worries, if only in this instant. I take the ala kirihothi, roughly translated to "potatoes in turmeric-spiced coconut milk," a comforting classic for me, and pour it over hot rice. The first bite sends a tingle of warmth and comfort throughout my body. We asked for the food medium spicy—which, to quote Alex, is still "butt burning."

We sit in silence as we continue to scarf the food down, not because we don't want to talk, but because we're too busy eating and occasionally smacking our lips in satisfaction. Noisy eating in Sri Lankan culture isn't a mark of rudeness like it is in the United States; it's a sign of a well-cooked meal. I've somehow managed to spill on myself not once, but twice, and I'm pretty sure I've also ruined this white tablecloth. Getting turmeric out of anything is a fool's errand.

Despite everything, for the first time in a long time, I feel okay—at least in this moment. It's a reminder to me how comforting a belly full of good food accompanied by good company can be.

CHAPTER 26

After dinner, we stand outside the restaurant.

"Look, you can see Polaris, almost," I say, pointing toward the sky.

"Polaris?"

"The North Star."

"Where?" Amaya says, looking up in the direction of my finger.

"The two outermost stars in the Big Dipper point toward the North Star."

She pauses, before excitedly exclaiming, "I see it! I never see stars in the city."

It was my brother who taught me about the stars. A reminder, he always said, that we're just tiny specks in the universe. At the time, I found this moment to be ridiculously cheesy and a little cringey—but thinking back on it now, I feel my chest tighten and a flood of sadness overwhelming me. We'd stargaze while attending our neighbors' summer bonfires—roasting marshmallows, mine always catching on fire and burning to a crisp, his always just perfectly toasted. We'd strain our eyes hoping to see something, and then one day, miraculously, we saw the North Star. "It's called that because it's a compass. It'll always guide you," he said before giving me a noogie. He'd always been so wise, so self-assured.

I clear my throat, trying to regain my composure. "It's rare to be able to see anything. There's too much light pollution," I say. Ammi would tell me the chance event of seeing Polaris is a good omen and then mutter some Sinhalese prayer under her breath.

"I should call Alex," I say as Amaya continues to stare at the little bit of light in the sky.

"Alex," I say on speakerphone, knowing I won't have to identify myself, "are you home?"

"Yes, I've been waiting to hear from you!" Alex exclaims.

"We got some tech questions, for the case." I also need to ask him if he knew Brett.

"You got it."

"We'll be there in twenty," I say before hanging up the phone as Amaya hails a cab.

"I know Alex can seem a bit much," I explain to Amaya as I open the door of the cab for her, "but we've known each other since I moved here in third grade and became close friends in middle school. We were both bullied pretty bad. Do kids still give each other wedgies now?" I ask, feeling so out of touch with kids these days, which I suppose is entirely normal since I don't have any of my own.

"I think they've moved on to cyberbullying," Amaya responds. I shudder at the thought and am grateful my most awkward years were kept off the internet. "Or maybe blowing vape smoke in your face." Amaya grimaces as if she's been personally victimized by a bubble gum–flavored vape cartridge like I've seen sold at so many bodegas, clearly marketed toward children and teenagers.

"Alex is basically my brother at this point." Claiming someone as a sibling is the highest praise I can give, knowing what it was like to have had a biological brother that I loved so dearly. "My parents are pretty much his surrogate guardians. They used to even sign permission slips for him since his parents were never home."

"I'm glad you have him," Amaya replies, though her eyebrows are raised in skepticism that suggests otherwise. She must have spoken to him a few times to arrange my bail. His swaggering bravado has either a charming or an annoying effect, and in this case it seems to have been the latter. For most women, it's the former.

We are an odd duo on the surface, but we still both love the same dorky stuff that drove us together in the first place all those years ago. Alex may seem cool now, but deep down he's still the awkward kid who loves watching *Jeopardy!* and cat videos and reading comic books.

"He's been there during some hard times. The hardest, actually." I feel little goose bumps dot my arms, making the hair on them stand straight up. "When my brother died, I was applying to law school. It had been my dream for my entire life." I pause for a moment, unsure if I can continue my story, as even thinking about it induces a panic attack–like feeling. Talking about it feels like having a rat scamper over my sandaled foot while I'm outdoor dining. It's horrible. I can barely begin. Despite this, for once, I can't stop myself.

"Life here hasn't been easy. My dad worked long hours as a taxi driver. My mother worked all sorts of odd jobs. They scrimped and saved and amassed a small, but mighty, savings account. My parents had left Sri Lanka to give us a better life here, and finally it seemed like it was happening. Nothing to make us rich, just enough for school. Then my brother got sick. He got a rare form of cancer, and a lot of his treatments were experimental and they weren't covered by insurance."

Amaya tuts like she knows what I am about to say.

"My parents drained their savings, borrowed money from shady lenders, did anything and everything. At some point, the only money left was what was put aside for my law school." I can't stop speaking now, as if everything I've kept pent up for so long is spewing out like a geyser.

"Siriwathi . . ." Amaya's face is contorted into a grimace, almost as if she can physically feel the pain and sorrow that radiate from my body. She is sitting close to me now, having moved from the opposite end of the back seat to the middle.

"My brother made me promise that I wouldn't use those funds. He said that he was dying and I just had to let him go. How can you let go of the person you love most in the world? He wanted to go knowing that I would be a lawyer; that's all he wanted. He wanted me to go to law school because that was my dream. Not to mention the doors it could open for not just me, but my parents too."

I am crying now, openly, even though Amaya's the one who had two glasses of wine. I haven't discussed this with anyone outside of my parents, not even Alex, and to talk about it makes the grief feel fresh again. I am choking on the words through my tears.

Amaya squeezes my hand. Hugs from friends, an arm around my shoulder, the simple day-to-day things that make us feel connected and human have been missing for so long in my life.

"I would do anything for him, even a treatment that only had a fifteen percent chance of success. Fifteen wasn't the zero percent it would've been if we had done nothing. So I took back the year's tuition money my parents had paid up front, emptied the entire account for law school, and put it toward the experimental treatment. When he found out what I had done, he screamed at me. He told me he would refuse it. He told me to never talk to him again. And for a week of precious time, we didn't talk. I went to see him, but he was so angry he refused to speak to me. The treatment was already paid in full, so he got it. At first, it looked so promising. He was feeling better, but ultimately it didn't help. It bought him one more month, until he was gone, and the last days we had together were still tinged with his disappointment and anger with me. I failed him. I failed my parents. I failed myself."

Amaya hands me a fistful of Kleenex that came from her seemingly bottomless bag, and gives me a hug. I hold on to her tightly as I continue to cry in the back seat of the cab on our way back to Manhattan, the skyline growing larger as we approach.

By the time we pull up in front of Alex's chic condo building twenty minutes later, I am feeling much better. Confessing my feelings released some of the grief and guilt I'd been harboring all these years. Swallowing my emotions and burying them down deep inside has taken more energy from me than I realize. I feel lighter, as if the more I talk about my brother at the end and the more I face my worst moments, the quicker I can accept what happened. When I talk about my brother, I remember the good moments too. I remember when we cut class one time to go have a day at Coney Island complete with those stomach-turning rides, funnel cake, and even a stuffed animal my brother won me at one of those silly games. My parents' anger was lessened when he told them it was *his* idea.

I remember the time my brother took us to one of those fancy French restaurants for Ammi's birthday, and he, insistent on ordering in French, accidentally got us all frog legs, which ended up being pretty tasty. Leave it to my brother for a mistake to become a triumph. I remember when I slugged a kid in the face for calling me numerous racial slurs, but it was my brother who tried to take the blame, and when that failed, he gave a brilliant explanation of why my actions constituted self-defense. I want to remember his face, and his bravery, and I want to live life as he did. With zeal and compassion.

"Has Alex got a good job or rich parents?" Amaya inquires as we approach the building.

"Both," I reply as a congregation of pigeons demolish a hot dog bun.

I confidently stride inside the building, one of the only places I feel comfortable doing so, and lock eyes with the doorman, Ed, who waves me up. The fact that the doormen, in their freshly pressed suits, all seem to remember me is a nice touch. The first few times, they thought I was a girlfriend, but I quickly clarified that no, I'm just a sista from another mista. The front doorman seemed amused and probably relieved that he no longer had to keep the slate of women Alex brings home a secret.

I take a deep breath. The lobby even smells rich, like it's been lightly scented with designer cologne. The closest I can do at my house is to spritz an old bottle of Bath & Body Works Sweet Pea spray, which would probably repel people rather than invite them in. I wonder if fragrances expire, because the one in my room is certainly at least a decade old at this point. It's hard not to be taken with the building's sleek decor—no seventies wood paneling in sight. Yet the fancy exterior and good smells cannot mask the perpetual cloud of loneliness that seems to hang over Alex's apartment. Most of his visitors are the aforementioned cadre of women he dates, and my guilt at my unavailability only heightens when I remember that I am the only consistently present person in his life.

"Hey!" Alex says as he opens the door, arms wide. He eyes Amaya in the same way I've seen him do to women at the club, and I give him a warning look. I finally have another female friend, and he isn't going to ruin that for me by dating her. "Nice to see you again, Amaya," Alex says, sticking his hand out formally. Amaya returns the greeting with a polite shake.

Bella, Alex's dog, runs to me and jumps on me with excitement. I bury my face in her fur. I love Bella. Bella, a German shepherd, seems to understand me better than most humans. Bella doesn't care that I am a taxicab driver. No matter what, she greets me as if I am a celebrity. She just wants scratches and the occasional dog treat—low expectations that I feel particularly suited for.

"Have you found any leads?" Alex asks, handing me a black tea without my even having to ask. He asks Amaya if she wants anything to drink, and she declines.

"Maybe." Now Amaya gives me a warning look. *Don't*

share too much information, she seems to say. Attorney-client privilege.

"James might have had some enemies. We're going to look into it. We did find a set of numbers in his wallet though," I say as I scroll through my phone to find the photo. I understand Amaya wants to keep this investigation under wraps, but thanks to Alex and my community, I'm free. I need everyone's help on this.

"'NYCRC Number 1045. Fourteen-ninety-eighteen,'" Alex reads aloud. "It's a locker combo for New York City Racquet Club."

"How do you know?"

"I have a membership to that place and I have a locker there." For a second, it looks like Alex is flexing the muscles he developed from hitting balls against a wall. "Also, it's written on a piece of racquet club stationery. I can see the embossed racquet, look."

Now that he's mentioned the club by name, I have a vague memory of Alex inviting me to it and me adamantly protesting.

"You invited me once, right?" I ask Alex to confirm.

"Yes! And you refused to go."

If I recall correctly, the price of membership is well beyond my annual pay. It's private and exclusive and apparently ungoogleable. I can already see the employees' eyes narrowing at me if I tried to walk in and chat with them. I'd probably be mistaken for one of the cleaners.

"You know me . . ." Which is to say, I hate inserting myself into uncomfortable situations—like a fancy gym where I'd not only be the least athletic but also the least rich.

"If you remember, you were supposed to go with me in exchange for me going to not one but two film festivals with you!"

Alex retorts. He laughs to show he isn't angry with me. It reminds me that Alex has always been willing to go out of his comfort zone for me, but I've rarely, if ever, done the same for him.

"After this is all over, I promise to join you."

Alex brightens. "This will all be over soon. And you can be my partner for doubles tennis. A certain childhood bully of ours is a member, and I've been dying to take him on . . ."

"Are you okay with us losing, then?" I laugh.

"As long as you're there, I'm happy," Alex responds.

"Aw shucks," I manage to say with a grin.

Even Amaya looks touched from across the room, but soon she's looking impatient. I can sense what she's thinking. *Let's get this show on the road!*

"Another question . . . New Frontier, have you heard of it?" I ask, eager to prove that I can add something to this investigation, even if it is by way of Alex. I detect a hint of recognition in Alex's face at the mention of the company.

"Yeah, it's new. It's still private, so there's not a lot out there on it. Private companies, by their nature, are not beholden to shareholders and have to disclose less. They are going to go public soon."

"Do you know a guy named Brett? Personally or professionally, I mean?"

"Brett who?" Alex responds.

"Brett Ryan, the New Frontier CEO," I clarify.

"Oh . . . no, don't think so. The tech world is small, but not *that* small."

"Are you sure? You were in the same class at Yale. You always go on and on about how you knew everyone in your class . . . at least a little bit."

"I mean, there were over a thousand of us in my class. I didn't know *everyone*. Anyways, I'll head to the racquet club tomorrow. I'll find the locker and call you with what I find," Alex offers, running his hands through his hair. "And keep me updated on your leads. Let me know what's going on. I'm worried about you, Siri."

"Of course, Alex. I will." I'm grateful to have him in my corner.

CHAPTER 27

The Green World guy, whose name I've already forgotten, lives in the Bronx. I usually have an excellent memory for names; less so faces. Noses, eyes, and mouths seem to bleed together, but like the random facts I store in my brain, names seem to stick. The exhaustion of the past few days is beginning to distort my thinking, and even my normal rote memorization is slipping. Even after a good night's sleep, I can't shake the fog that is bathing my brain; it's like a perpetual hangover from too many tiki drinks, aka the world's worst hangover, but this time the symptoms can't be remedied by a McDonald's Big Mac, large fries, and Diet Coke. Sadly, there's no time to waste. It's now just three days before the grand jury meets.

I sit in the car and close my eyes. After parting from Alex's last night, we made a plan to see the Green World guy this morning. I don't put my hands together for fear that Amaya will think I've completely lost it.

If I get through this, if I don't go to prison, I promise I will appreciate what I have. I'll make more of an effort with Alex. I'll try harder to make my parents proud and keep my brother's legacy alive. If I get another chance, I won't be my own worst enemy. I say this to myself and open my eyes, half expecting some sign that the universe has heard my prayers. Maybe a bolt of lightning? A dove? Instead, when I look out the window around me, a woman is hitting a man with what appears to be a baguette, and a rat burrows through trash bags with a full Reese's cup in its mouth, sending what was supposed to be a plea for divine intervention hurtling back toward reality.

Amaya and I ride in a taxi along the West Side Highway, which is lined with a bike path and the Hudson River. The river, while famously polluted, looks lovely today. Jersey City's and then Hoboken's skylines come into view. On my right, I see graffiti that looks like art, that maybe is art, proudly displayed on another building. Farther along the highway, apartments and new condos soar. An ad for a storage company states "For the people trying to make it big whose apartment is a little too small." A reminder that we're all just trying to make it in this big, beautiful, stinky, and expensive city. *Keep going*, I think to myself, *keep going.*

We exit the highway and head into the Bronx, a borough I know well. Few tourists explore the city's northernmost borough. Like almost all New Yorkers, the citizens of the Bronx are kind, but not nice. An important but hard-to-understand distinction for out-of-towners. They'll elbow you out of the way to make the departing subway train, but they'd also pull you off the subway tracks to save your life.

In the years since I became a taxi driver, I've tried every type of food I can think of in the Bronx. Places only insiders would know, suggested to me by the bodega owners I frequently speak to when stopping for coffee. Like Manhattan, the Bronx has its own versions of Little Italy and Chinatown. As we drive, I see a familiar humble deli on the corner, which in my opinion serves one of the best Italian cold-cut sandwiches in the city. The soppressata tastes like it came from the heavens. Far from the expensive restaurants in Manhattan, I know some of the best meatballs and spaghetti are crafted in this borough, by immigrants who came directly from Italy. Who am I to argue with these nonnas and their years-old recipes? And everywhere I look, people from different backgrounds and corners fill the streets. It reminds me of my own neighborhood block.

We pull up to a house with trees and plants overflowing outside. Solar panels sit on every inch of the roof. The lawn is overgrown and probably hasn't been cut in at least a year.

Had it not been for the light on in the house, I would have thought it was abandoned as well. I spot two stray cats and assume there are probably more hidden in the tall grass that surrounds the building.

"Are you sure this is the right place?" I ask. For a second, I imagine Darla giving us the wrong address. Throwing us off the scent to protect her friends.

"I know, I was assuming more of an office building. She said that this was the office address, but it's clearly a house. I guess we go knock and find out?" She's already walking toward the house before I can answer.

Amaya is fearless, or at least outwardly appears that way. I wonder if I'd still be here if I weren't trying to save my own life. It's one thing to listen to an investigator talk to a witness, who also may be the murderer, on a podcast. It's another thing to actually do it. At least we're here together, which has to mean something. Strength in numbers.

I knock on the door assertively as I've seen Amaya do. I feel nervous like I do when I have to take a fare to New Jersey, land of pizza places that *think* they can compete with NYC's slices. Inside, I can hear noises and errant shouts—people talking or arguing. I try to ready myself for whoever will answer the door. I have a bad feeling, which I chalk up to the fact that the Green World guy now seems like the most plausible suspect in the murder of James. Darla and Brett both painted a picture of clear animosity between the two, on both a personal and a professional level. By killing James, New Frontier would certainly suffer, meaning Green World had something to gain, and they weren't above illegal or violent practices. Without warning, the door swings open, startling both of us. We step back instinctively, and I silently chide myself for being more flight than fight.

"What do you want?" the man demands. His hair is messy, and he is wearing what appear to be pajama pants, suggesting that even at noon on a Monday, the man may have just gotten out of bed. Instead of judging him, I find myself a little jealous, as I'm in need of a nap myself.

"We were hoping to speak with Charlie," Amaya says, and I make a mental note to not forget his name.

The man opens his mouth as if he is about to argue, about to demand what we want with Charlie. Instead, he looks us up and down. Forgoing my contacts today, I'm wearing an old pair of thick-rimmed glasses that serve both as a disguise and a necessary tool. I can't seem to throw anything out and have been amassing a collection of glasses since I was eleven years old. Amaya is wearing her suit from court.

"CHARRRLIEEE!" the man screams. We both jump for the second time in just a minute. A second of silence passes.

"WHAAAT?" a voice booms back in response.

"VISITOOORS!" the man responds again.

The loud exchange, with both men refusing to move themselves, reminds me of the times my brother and I would loudly scream at each other from across the house, to the ire of both our parents.

There is silence again and some shuffling. I catch sight of a woman entering through a door in the back of the house. She looks familiar. I squint slightly and I'm sure it's the woman from the intersection. The woman I almost hit. I'm absolutely floored. Why is she here? Despite my bad memory for faces, I remember her because I almost killed her. I want to tell Amaya right now, but suddenly, a man who I presume is Charlie walks down the stairs in a bathrobe. He is large and imposing, and possibly the tallest person I've ever seen, clearing six feet five inches easily. His hair is receding and the bags under his eyes tell me he's probably exhausted. *Join the club*, I think.

"What do you want?" Charlie asks. He has a carton of some drink that I've never heard of in his hand, and he belches loudly. Lovely.

"We want to talk about your friend James."

"James—friend? *Please*," Charlie spits out. "Are you cops?"

"No," Amaya says quickly, and I nod to confirm wordlessly.

"Then who are you?"

"The defense attorney for the woman accused of the crime, and an investigator," Amaya says, pointing at me. Her comfort with delaying our introductions and lying about who I am seems to have grown over the course of our short investigation. *Or I'm becoming a real investigator*, a small voice in my head whispers before I dismiss the thought entirely.

This introduction seems to pique Charlie's interest. He's not expecting this, by the look of surprise and maybe even curiosity on his face. "Okay, follow me."

Charlie leads us to a messy and overcrowded surface that must have been a formal dining table at one point. Now there is not a space to eat or do much of anything else on it; every inch of the table is covered with papers, receipts, and pens. My need to clean goes into overdrive, but I tamp it down. This isn't my taxi—it's someone else's house.

"Our command center," Charlie says proudly, pointing at the mess of papers, as if sharing a celebrated achievement. A stack of White Castle wrappers and what I believe is a used Band-Aid fall to the floor. Ugh.

I like to develop some rapport with the people we speak to, but complimenting the mess just seems too ungenuine.

"I'm Amaya," Amaya says, sticking out her hand. She doesn't introduce me by name for obvious reasons, and I stay silent, instructed as I am again to not ask any questions. "We understand James was once your friend, and we're so sorry for your loss."

"Emphasis on '*once*,'" Charlie says, face contorted into a grimace.

"Any information you give us may help us find the true killer."

The phrase *true killer* is intentional, to get Charlie's curiosity running. For him to angrily burst out that the true killer is caught, or to agree and say there is another suspect, or to maybe confirm that he knows the cabdriver didn't do it, because maybe he, Charlie, did. *You know, just like it happens in soap operas*, I think, realizing Charlie's confession is just as legitimately plausible as a character from Ammi's favorite daytime television show coming back to life for the fourth time.

"Got nothing, don't care," Charlie replies so gruffly and quickly that I wonder why we were even invited in.

"You don't care if your friend is dead?" Amaya is poking the bear intentionally. She isn't getting anywhere with polite questions. *True crime rule number eight: Switch tactics if a witness is reluctant to talk.* Be adaptable. You may come in with a set of questions, but you may not be able to follow them exactly. Charlie clearly doesn't consider James a friend. I gulp and prepare myself.

"No, he is not my friend. And no, I don't care," Charlie responds, now looking bored.

"May I ask why?" I ask. Amaya can get mad at me later for butting in.

"Well, James abandoned us. He *was* my best friend." Charlie's pale skin starts to grow red, as if the sparks of a fire are starting to rage.

I can tell this man is waiting for an opportunity to yell dramatically, to retell his complaints about James to someone who hasn't yet heard them. I think of a fight I had with Alex over something I don't even remember now. I was so angry with him that I said that he was just a finance bro wannabe with bad taste. Did he think he was unique when he said he liked to travel and eat pizza on those dating apps? I was being a total asshole by accusing Alex of being basic, but people always say more than they intend to when angry. Luckily, Alex always forgives me, even if that time I had bribe him with birria tacos that I had to travel to Brooklyn for and help him revamp his Raya profile. The first thing I did was help him get rid of those shirtless photos . . .

"We started Green World together. Decades ago. We knew as PhD students, long before the rest of the world took interest, that we were killing this beautiful planet that feeds us, that houses us, that gives us air to live and breathe. Trillions of pounds of ice are melting every single year, did you know that?" This sounds like the start of a commercial telling me to donate now to save the planet with the backdrop of the 1-800 number being some polar bears stranded on a block of ice.

Climate change gives me palpable fear for the future. As much as I want to dismiss Charlie as extreme, I do understand his panic. Suddenly, viewing him as a murderer becomes harder.

"How were you abandoned?" Amaya asks, her tone less accusatory and more conversational, following my lead.

"Well, I won't lie, James was the brains of the operation. He was really good at planning, and keeping track of our money, and doing certain things so we wouldn't get caught, which I know sounds sort of bad. When we're taking on these Goliath corporations, we have to be savvy. Green World was started because other so-called environmental organizations barely do shit. They don't shake things up. They're fine with the status quo. Drastic results only come by drastic action." Now a vein is bulging in Charlie's head. He looks like he is gonna go full Joe Rogan on us.

In a sudden reversal of my previous position, his anger makes me wonder if he could have done this. Why is it so hard to read people? Charlie pauses and takes a swig of whatever is in his carton. I wish I had coffee—I'd even take the coffee that resembles toxic sludge from that bodega on Houston Street to get through this conversation. All cabdrivers flock there for the legal stimulant that is too much caffeine.

"And he sold out because he moved to New Frontier?" I ask, hoping he'll continue.

"YES! And, look, even before that, he was scaling back. He was saying that we don't have to shut down businesses entirely, because that takes away jobs, blah blah blah. Well, you know what else takes away jobs? Killing the environment and all of us along with it. He was making Green World less radical. He wanted to work with these companies to create environmentally sustainable solutions, and I wanted to gas bomb and protest." Charlie takes a deep breath before continuing. "I realize I may sound crazy to you. I wanted to glue my hands to roads and the fronts of buildings." The thought of how painful it must be to unglue a hand makes me shudder. At least the person doing the ungluing doesn't need to worry about being swatted away . . . "You have to take bold actions if you want people to pay attention. If you're not taking drastic measures, then you might as well give up completely. I never wanted to hurt anyone physically, but if that's an unfortunate consequence, then so be it. Billions will be dead if we don't reverse climate change now." Charlie finishes his carton, which says something about recycled water on the label, in a final loud slurp. He tosses it at the wastepaper basket, missing it and causing the carton to go crashing to the ground by Amaya's feet with a smack. I appreciate the irony of the single-use item.

"What do you mean you never wanted to hurt someone physically?" Amaya asks. Was a confession coming? Could it be this easy?

"Well, the last rally that James and I participated in, I tried to organize. Because I wanted to prove to myself, to James, and to the entire organization that I wasn't some idiot piece of shit.

Unfortunately, it went badly. One of our guys inhaled too much smoke and was trampled on by people trying to flee the building. His family is suing us, and they're still deciding whether to charge us for criminally negligent manslaughter."

I know from my true crime podcast that manslaughter is when someone dies but you didn't necessarily intend for it to happen. Under Charlie's watch, at least one person was killed. He is already involved in someone's death. Is it a stretch to conclude he's involved in another?

I want to ask more questions about that incident. Did Charlie set fire to a building? How exactly did the man die? Before I can ask, Charlie continues to speak, as if in a much-needed therapy session. I'm waiting for a comfortable-looking chaise to materialize.

"If that wasn't bad enough, we're also in the hole money-wise. It's why my office is now headquartered here, where a bunch of us live. We have no money and so many bills to pay." Charlie covers his face with his hands. I don't particularly care for Charlie. His thoughtless planning has resulted in at least one death, but I understand the stress that money problems can bring and the pain of feeling like your life is falling apart.

"I'm really sorry that you're dealing with all of this." Amaya nods sympathetically. She is used to seeing people after they've done horrible things but she still needs to find the basic humanity in them too.

"I'm sorry too," Charlie says. "All our troubles started when James left us. He abandoned us for the very thing we had literally spent our entire lives hell-bent on destroying. I hope neither of you ever have to experience that kind of intense betrayal. And last I saw he was in business with his girlfriend, who runs a PLASTICS COMPANY." He screams the last two words.

"Girlfriend?" I ask.

"Yep. Shirley Lee." I've heard that name before. She was the woman in the newspaper I saw at Curry in a Hurry. She was his girlfriend?

"To be frank with you, I'm not sorry he's dead."

The sentence hangs in the air for a few seconds before Charlie continues. "Actually, I am sorry he's dead, because you can't sue a dead person for damages. Honestly, a part of me thinks he deserved what came to him." Hearing it the second time around, Charlie's ill wishes for his former friend are no less jarring.

"Did you kill him?" Amaya asks, her voice a whisper, so thin and soft it almost doesn't make it to my ears.

Charlie takes a deep breath and wipes his brow. I close my eyes, steeling myself for a confession that I've waited what's felt like an eternity for. Everything we have done has led up to this moment.

"No, but I wish I had," Charlie says. A confession from him would not, it seems, be that easy.

Amaya and I get up to leave, and Amaya drops her pen. I look at Charlie for a second, trying to discern the truth from his appearance alone, but he gives nothing away.

I am glad we are finally out of that crowded and claustrophobic place. As the kids on the internet would say, "The vibe was bad." I learned the phrase from shuttling some teenagers who were filming themselves detailing the top ten things Gen Zers shouldn't do. Number one: Don't wear skinny jeans. Number two: Don't wear ankle socks. Number three: Don't put your hair in a side part . . . So far, I'm three for three in being a loser. The children are our future, but they are also a little annoying. The sun shines brightly and I squint, my eyes still adjusting from the darkness of the house.

"Well, he undoubtedly has a motive," Amaya says. "He seemed very angry."

"It's true." I think of my true crime podcasts. This guy would be suspect number one. I pause, remembering the woman. "This is going to sound crazy. I think I recognized the woman in the house. I can't be sure, but I think it's the woman from the intersection, the one I almost hit." I pause, taking in Amaya's look of bewilderment. I try to look serious for this next part. "Which would mean . . . that Charlie staged the whole thing. The woman runs in front of me so I stop, and then I get out of the car, giving Charlie the opportunity to stab James." The motive, the means, and the opportunity. I know I sound a little unhinged, but this does make sense.

"Okay, Columbo," Amaya says with a smile.

I stare at her quizzically.

"Oh god, are you too young to know Columbo? Peter Falk as an LAPD detective. Normally I'm against copaganda, but my parents watched it so much, and then when I was old enough I always watched reruns." She looks at me expectantly.

"No, I've seen it . . ." It's an unconvincing lie. Amaya and I are probably close to the same age—but having grown up in Sri Lanka, I don't always get the same references as some people, especially ones that predate my arrival to the US.

"Okay, sure," Amaya says, reading me like a book. "I can't

imagine it's the woman from the intersection. It's probably someone who looks like her."

"Maybe . . ." Now I'm starting to doubt my own memory. I had only seen the woman briefly, both on the street and now. It's possible it was a different person and my mind is trying to find connections where there aren't any. But I can't shake that I've seen the woman somewhere before.

"Besides, the footage doesn't show anything happening at that intersection. No one in or out of your taxi."

Check and mate. I'm mistaken then. I switch gears.

"How do we catch him if he's not going to confess?"

Amaya rifles through her bag for just a second before producing a used paper carton. It takes me a moment to register that it is the one that Charlie was drinking out of. It's been carefully placed in a plastic bag, meaning Amaya wasn't just grabbing it to recycle it.

"Is that . . . ?"

"Yes, Charlie's drink carton. Got it when I dropped my pen." Amaya puts *dropped* in air quotes.

"You're going to be able to pull DNA from that, aren't you?" My eyes light up. Amaya is brilliant.

"A lesson learned from the school of true crime podcasts?"

I nod. "Is it legal?" I ask as I stare at the piece of trash.

"Yes, surreptitious collection is legal when the item is discarded. You can take something someone throws away free and clear. We could have looked in his trash, but I really didn't want to do that."

"They probably compost, anyways," I say with a little laugh. Besides, how would we have known which trash was Charlie's? Grabbing something that we saw him use was the right move.

"They say there is DNA on the weapon that matches yours, but maybe he happened to leave DNA behind? And did you notice all the scratches on his arms? Maybe they got into a struggle?"

I hadn't noticed the scratches and am grateful for Amaya's keen eye.

"If there are scratches, then maybe fingernail scrapings from James will provide a DNA profile consistent with Charlie's? They almost always take fingernail scrapings from the victims. It'll be the proof we need," I say, not sure if I'm stating this or asking a question.

"You're absolutely correct," Amaya responds, smiling like a teacher at her best pupil. I've never been a teacher's pet—that was always my brother—so the validation feels especially nice. "Touch DNA could still reveal something."

"Because when you touch stuff, sometimes you leave your DNA behind in skin cells, for example," I say like I've been called on for an answer in a classroom. I am privately thrilled I know what this is, even in the most rudimentary sense. It's gratifying to see what I assumed was useless knowledge come to the forefront of a conversation.

Amaya smiles. "Damn, Siriwathi. Are you sure you didn't go to law school?"

Instead of acknowledging the compliment, I ask, "Do you think his girlfriend, Shirley Lee, is somehow connected to this?"

"Maybe." Amaya shrugs. "She's worth talking to."

Amaya grabs her phone to call a taxi, and she gets a text message a few seconds later. We read the message on the screen.

> Stop investigating or someone gets hurt. Stay away from Green World and all others.

CHAPTER 28

The text rattles us both even though Amaya tries to brush it off. Adding insult to injury, no cabs are willing to pick us up in the Bronx and drive us back into Manhattan. We could take the train from the Bronx back downtown, but according to Amaya's phone, that will take approximately ninety minutes . . .

I think about whom I could call to come pick me up. An acquaintance with a car in the city is pretty rare. Plenty of people I know don't even have driver's licenses. Only one person comes to mind. Alex.

"He's coming to pick us up," I tell Amaya once Alex confirms. He doesn't hesitate to drop everything, and I'm more convinced than ever I need to work on being a better friend.

I turn my attention back to the text message Amaya received. "It has to be someone from Green World, right?" It's not a coincidence that we go to see Charlie and we suddenly get a message telling us to stay away.

"I think that's what makes most logical sense."

"Unless, of course, I'm being followed," I say with a touch of humor in my voice. I don't want to sound paranoid. Truthfully, I feel like I always hear the soft pad of footsteps behind me, but when I turn to look, no one is there. With no proof beyond a hunch, I don't bring it up as an actuality. "Should we file a police report for the threats?" I have no confidence in their ability to help us, but I worry that Amaya is in danger.

"Eh, I don't think filing a police report is going to do anything. Not sure they'll be super helpful to someone charged with murder and her attorney. Besides, we need something more than threats to help your case. The DNA, the evidence against you, still isn't great." Amaya pauses and looks at me. "We'll test the carton, and we should have definitive proof."

I try not to be too hopeful over the tests, considering the many dead ends we've already pursued.

"I wonder how long Alex will take?" Amaya says, a little impatiently.

I hope he comes soon. One time Alex was supposed to pick me up but arrived forty-five minutes late. I only forgave him because the delay was to pick up really good pizza for the both of us. As the minutes fly by, I'm thinking about what may happen if we don't solve this case.

Amaya must pick up on my worry because she says, "We have a real lead, Siriwathi. And I believe you can do anything you want to after this."

"Why are you letting me come on these investigations?" I ask her, quickly switching subjects. "You said it is highly unusual."

She pauses for a second, as if caught eating a dirty-water hot dog at 3 a.m. after a night of drinking. "Well, your instinct is good. Your investigative skills are on point. And I trust your thoughts on the case. If you weren't my client, I'd hire you as an investigator and we could solve crimes and eat all over the city like Thelma and Louise minus us murdering people . . . well, once we clear your name—you know what I mean."

I'm pretty sure Amaya has described my dream scenario. Two kick-ass women taking to the streets (and the food on those streets). I find myself connecting with Amaya in ways that I never did with Alex. Maybe it's because Amaya is also a Sri Lankan woman and understands my unique struggles. I examine her closely.

"How did you get the scar?" I ask, gesturing toward her mouth. It's a more personal question than I should be asking my lawyer, but now that Amaya maybe considers us friends or at least potential colleagues, I hope I'm not overstepping.

"I got into a fight once. Someone said something derogatory to me and my friends outside a bar. I yelled, and the other dude, a big hulking white football-player-type guy, just swung at me. My lip got busted. The police came, and instead of arresting the guy who hit me, I got arrested. I spent the night in jail."

"Oh my god, that's horrible, you didn't even hit him."

"I mean, the case was dropped. A camera had captured the whole incident, but without the footage, no one would believe me over the other guy. Sure, I was the smaller of us two, but it wouldn't be the first time I'm blamed for something I didn't do because of the color of my skin and who I am. That night in jail was terrifying, and they wouldn't take me to the hospital, so it healed pretty badly. I'd never had any contact with the criminal legal system before that. It certainly played a part in me wanting to become a public defender. Of course, what I went through doesn't compare to the shit my clients deal with in and out of court."

I notice she doesn't call it the criminal justice system. There is no justice to be found in her case or mine or the many others she deals with daily.

"I'm so sorry." It's all I can think of to say. In some small way, she knows what I'm going through, something I never thought she could comprehend.

"It's okay. Usually when people ask about the scar, I just brush it away, and tell them they should see the other guy," Amaya says with a quiet laugh as Alex finally pulls up.

CHAPTER 29

"Yo, hop in!" Alex says, and the passenger doors open in unison. It is a rather dramatic car entrance. "I went to the locker. I found something. Wanted to tell you in person just in case your phone was bugged."

"Bugged? You're sounding a little paranoid," I say.

Alex has bought into a few conspiracy theories in the past, though luckily I'm usually able to convince him they are largely without merit.

"Well, maybe not paranoid this time," Alex responds. I pray that what Alex is going to tell us has a little more validity than his briefly held theory on government control through 5G. "Actually, before we get into that, what happened in there?" Alex points warily at the house we just came from.

"We'll fill you in on that in just a second. Tell us, what was so important it couldn't be said over a phone call?" Amaya asks. She taps her hands on her legs, something she does when she's a little annoyed. She's apparently not impressed with the car.

"So I went to the racquet club . . . you know, because I'm a member," Alex begins casually.

I can almost feel Amaya's annoyance and impatience roll off her, her tapping even louder now. We have clearly established that he is a member of the racquet club. I want to shrug my shoulders and say, "Men, am I right?" But Alex has done so much for me, I can't be an asshole now.

"I go to his locker. I enter the locker combination . . ." Alex pauses, as if for dramatic effect. "Inside, there was a USB."

"What was on the USB?" Amaya demands.

Alex looks back at her and laughs a little as if she's asked a stupid question.

"It's password-protected. To hack in, I need a truly powerful computer like the type that I have at work. There is some software out there that could probably do it on my personal laptop, but it's sort of illegal and I really can't risk it."

Alex has done plenty of illegal things in the past. I wonder what's changed now.

"Discovering any material illegally could preclude us from using it in court anyways," Amaya replies, seemingly agreeing with him.

"We have to decrypt it though," I protest.

Amaya pauses. "We can try our best . . . we're already on shaky ground getting this out of the locker . . ."

My life is on the line here, but before my annoyance can build, I remind myself how much Amaya and Alex have already done for me. It's ridiculous, not to mention selfish, to ask someone to risk so much for me.

Somehow we need to find out what's on that USB without getting anyone in trouble.

On the way to Alex's office, Amaya and I tell him about Charlie and Green World, and about the threatening text situation. He takes it in in silence, which is surprising because Alex usually provides a nonstop commentary about everything.

Once we arrive at Alex's office building, somewhere I've never visited him before, I find it is even more impressive than his home. Everything is sleek and smart. Temperatures adjust to the people in the room; doors open only after an eye scan. I can't imagine how much this all costs, and it looks like it belongs in a James Bond movie, not an office. I'm waiting for Daniel Craig to pop out of a closet.

"Okay, take a seat here." Alex directs us to two chairs. My chair is possibly the most comfortable thing I have ever sat on and probably the most expensive, too, if you didn't count the seats in Alex's Porsche.

I take in my surroundings as Alex taps on his computer aggressively. I didn't realize that Alex now occupies a corner office. Did he get a raise? A promotion? Why didn't he tell me? Did he keep good news from me so as not to rub it in or hurt my feelings?

I spot a toy car on Alex's desk. The first thing I ever gave him back when we were kids. It was my favorite car, one of the few toys I owned, which I bestowed on Alex. I am touched it is in such a coveted position in his office and that he hasn't lost it over the years, especially as I can recall the much more expensive toys, like G.I. Joes, that Alex's parents hurled his way to make up for never being around. His parents didn't know the things he really liked to play with. They never really seemed to know him at all.

Alex looks up from his work and catches me staring at the car. "You remember when you gave that to me, right?"

"I do." I smile.

"It was after someone made fun of my 'Jewish nose,' an insult you didn't understand at the time."

I didn't know exactly what a Jewish nose meant, but I got the idea. Besides, a preteen boy singling someone out for their personal appearance was usually a bad thing.

"I have a big nose too," I had replied.

"Not as big as mine," Alex had replied, tears in his eyes. "Mine is bad because of who I am."

"Mine is brown, and people don't like my skin color," I had said. I had been made fun of so many times in my nearly completely white school that I had lost count. It didn't make the additional insults any easier to hear.

"People suck sometimes, don't they?" Alex had said, looking up.

"Not all of them," I responded, holding out a hand to Alex. "Wanna go to the bodega and grab some snacks?"

To this day, Alex and I use food to turn around a bad day. Back then, it was Fruit Roll-Ups and Snickers bars. Now it's sushi (if Alex is buying . . . that stuff costs a fortune), or bodega bacon, egg, and cheeses and pizza if I pick up the tab.

Deep down inside, no matter the money or flashy things, Alex will always just be the kid on the playground that day.

"Um, hello . . . let's get back to work?" Amaya chides.

"Any chance you can guess the password?" Alex asks, seemingly half-joking, half-serious.

"It could be literally anything . . . Uh—" I pause to think.

"Well, I can't get in without the password . . ."

"My password is my name and one-two-three-four-five," Amaya offers.

Alex types while rolling his eyes. "It's not his name and one-two-three-four-five. And I'd suggest you change all your passwords now. That's a predictable password. Have you heard of two-factor authentication?"

"Alex. We have to focus. Um, maybe try . . . 'Frankie'?" I offer.

An angry-sounding beep tells me I'm wrong.

"I feel like you're on the right track," Amaya says as she rummages into her bag.

"It's not going to be that simple. He's a tech guy. So it'll be a combination of letters and characters," Alex mutters under his breath.

Amaya pulls out the documents from the animal hospital from her bag. "Maybe it's Frankie's birthday?" The sheepish look on her face makes me think that Amaya uses her own birthday as her phone password. Nearly 60 percent of people do this and I make a mental note to tell Amaya to change hers.

"Try 'Frankie' followed by his birthday," I state.

Alex is trying to say that won't work, when I push past him and try it. There's a chirp and . . . we're in.

"You cracked it," Amaya says with a rare smile.

I look at Alex, vindicated. He simply shrugs.

I stand up to get a better look at the computer. Amaya does

too. I expected this code breaking to take hours or even days. I guess James didn't think anyone would ever find the USB and therefore it wouldn't require the complex passwords we all need to use online.

"Oh shit, this looks big," Amaya says, mouth open, scanning a screen filled with thousands of numbers. "What does this mean?"

I take a few minutes to scan it, making sure I am understanding correctly.

"I think these are balance sheets," I say before scanning for another few seconds. "But the numbers don't appear to be adding up."

I grab my phone and start to add some numbers on the calculator app to confirm. "That's odd . . . there's something missing. Money missing." Math was by far my worst subject, so I look to Alex to see if he's seeing what I'm seeing, and he is reviewing the screen just as intently as I am.

"What does that mean?" Amaya asks.

"I think it means that someone is stealing money from New Frontier. The money that is supposed to go toward the so-called environmental solutions is, in part, going into someone's pocket. This is proof the environmental fixes New Frontier promises are not being delivered."

"I mean . . . what if these aren't complete balance sheets? Maybe these have been tinkered with," Alex says.

"Why would James create fake balance sheets and put them in an encrypted USB?" Amaya asks.

"Seems like hundreds of thousands have come from oil and gas, plastics producers. New Frontier says they are working toward getting better energy ratings for these polluting companies, but at least according to news coverage, they've done some stuff but not much," I say.

"Environmental change takes time," Alex responds as if he is a New Frontier spokesman. "Who knows what's happening behind the scenes."

"Here it states 'Money moved to JT account' . . . " Amaya says.

"James Wilkerson-Taylor? He was stealing the money?" Alex asks, frowning.

"It looks like it . . . Catalyst is one of the companies buying 'services' from New Frontier," Amaya says, looking as if she is deep in thought. "I think I've heard of them . . ."

"Yes, you've heard of them because they're accused of deforesting millions of acres in the Amazon," I offer. "You've also heard of Catalyst because James's sister works there. And his girlfriend just so happens to run the place." *True crime rule number nine: Coincidences in criminal investigations should raise suspicion.* Investigate them.

"If this got out before the company went public, everything would go south," I declare.

"Why would James keep a USB with proof of his wrongdoing on it?" Amaya questions. "More likely someone other than James was stealing money and James was trying to show that he was being framed."

"Or . . . Charlie knew what James was doing and was trying to use the USB as leverage. Maybe gave him a copy—could be anything," Alex says. "Charlie was clearly the angriest. He felt James had ruined his life. He betrayed their friendship and literally was a part of something that went against everything they had ever believed. If it's the way you guys described it, the guy had motive for murder. For everyone else, it's just money."

When you're poor, you'd certainly kill for money, but Alex can't appreciate that.

"What's next?' Alex asks.

Everyone instinctively looks at Amaya's purse, thinking of the carton within. So much riding on a piece of trash.

CHAPTER 30

Amaya explains to us that DNA testing can take months, which is not what *CSI* would have you believe.

Things always seem to work faster on television. The accused can be left waiting in jail for evidence to be tested and for attorneys to investigate. I again realize how lucky I am to be on the outside. At least for now.

"Maybe I could—" Alex interrupts Amaya's explanation of the process. Alex, unlike the rest of the world, doesn't often have to wait. He is, I know, used to getting things quickly.

"No." Amaya cuts him off. "All labs have a backlog right now. The ones we can use for this case are few and far between." I can feel the tension between Amaya and Alex grow, and it's not the sultry kind, like in a perfectly plotted rom-com. It's more like the tension in *Rocky* where you know someone will be punching the other by the end.

"Why don't we try to speak to someone at Catalyst? All those companies that paid New Frontier may have some information. James was dating Catalyst's CEO, Shirley Lee. And James's sister was working there. Shirley must know something. Let's talk to her and see what information we can learn. It's something to do as we wait for the results on the carton." I'm uncharacteristically assertive in order to convince myself everything is going to be all right.

Alex insists on coming along. Amaya tries to protest by claiming that a group of us coming to speak to someone at Catalyst is not effective and will only cause them to clam up.

I tell Amaya that while three is a crowd, I know Alex is tech savvy enough to have a proper conversation with Shirley. Alex gives me a thumbs-up like he's an old politician or someone who tells too many dad jokes. *Rule number infinity . . . no, ten of true crime podcasts: Don't overwhelm the witness.* I can't help but wonder if I'm making a mistake.

I envision it clearly. Go talk to Shirley, wait until she gives us critical case information, and secretly record it and use it. So far, nothing in the past few days has gone as planned.

We roll up to the Catalyst office like the Three Stooges. Alex appears to have no clue what is going on, I look like I was dressed in Goodwill discards, and Amaya is just fully waking up from the nap she took in the car. We enter by following someone in through the front door. Unlike New Frontier, which is housed in a fancy office building, Catalyst's building is much smaller with apparently no security. I marvel at how easily we can get in. Isn't this a multimillion-dollar company? They've probably spent their money on things I don't understand like NFTs and cryptocurrency. I wait for some bro to pop out like a jump scare and explain it all to me.

A woman greets us as soon as we arrive off the elevator. This must be Shirley Lee. I recognize her from the newspaper.

"Hello, Ms. Perera, Ms. Fernando, and Mr. Feldman."

While I know who she is, how does she know who we are?

She must register the shock because she says, "We have state-of-the-art facial recognition technology in our lobby. We know who you are." So they do have security . . . you just can't see it. "How can I help you?"

I'm momentarily creeped out by this technology before focusing on the task at hand.

"I'm sorry for your loss," I say to Shirley. Her face crumples for just a second before forming itself back into a neutral expression, like her sadness was a figment of my imagination.

"Well, yes. It's very sad. Thank you." Shirley wraps her arms around herself. "Let's talk in my office."

We follow her to a modern, sparse room. In comparison to Shirley's personal style, my room looks like it could be featured on the show *Hoarders*. There's barely anything in here besides a sleek table, chairs, and a MacBook Pro.

As soon as we sit down, Amaya gets right into it. "Catalyst is working with New Frontier?" No more pleasantries.

"Yes, that's well-known news," Shirley responds.

"I suppose what is less well-known is that Catalyst paid for services from New Frontier to improve its energy efficiency, and it's still waiting on most of those services," Amaya says. We don't know for sure this is the case, but asserting it as fact and waiting for a denial seems like a good strategy.

Shirley's lips turn into a sour frown.

"It's not our fault that New Frontier is slow on delivering product."

"You didn't know your boyfriend's company was taking money from you and not giving you anything in return?" Amaya says. She's on fire.

"James hasn't been my boyfriend for a little while," Shirley responds more meekly than I anticipate.

"He hasn't?" I can't keep the surprise off my face. People break up all the time, but they've been described as being very in love.

"Not that it's any of your business, but we broke up a few weeks ago." The post-breakup "I'm trying not to cry at work or in public" face is evident on Shirley. Sending her strength, because haven't we all been there? Sounds like James did the dumping.

"And he never told you that someone was stealing money from New Frontier?"

"Stealing money?" Shirley looks momentarily surprised. I imagine someone like her isn't easily taken off guard. "I had no clue what was going on. Why would I pay New Frontier to steal money from me and the company I worked so hard to build? I paid New Frontier with the understanding that we'd get services in exchange. We did get some initial documents . . . and minor services. I was waiting. Things did feel off. I asked James repeatedly why things were so slow, but he was evasive and weird. Then he broke up with me out of the blue."

"And?" There's more to this story.

Shirley doesn't say anything.

"We can always send a hot tip about your company not improving its environmental standards to *The Wall Street Journal* . . ." Alex threatens. I don't think Alex has ever read *The Wall Street Journal*, let alone met anyone there. Come to think of it, when was the last the time I even saw Alex read?

I see a flash of anger in Shirley's eyes, similar to how I look when I'm really hungry, before she composes herself once again. "I don't like being threatened. If you do it again, I will find a way to ruin you." Her tone is harsh, scary even. "Ultimately, my company isn't guilty of any wrongdoing, but I don't need this type of publicity right now. If you promise not to break this story, I will tell you what I know."

I nod my head, surprised she thinks we three hooligans are capable of breaking any story.

"I wanted to know why James was acting weird. Brett wanted to know too. We had a lot of long discussions about James. We cared for him. We were worried about him. I started to suspect James was hiding something, and I think he broke up with me so I wouldn't get implicated in his wrongdoing. Brett and I . . . well . . . we began to date at that point . . ."

Messy. Dating her ex-boyfriend's business partner . . . Trust me, I get the appeal. Brett is fine and I admire her chutzpah, but what a move!

"Do you think James was the one stealing from his own company?" I ask.

Shirley shuts her eyes tightly and tenses. "James had something to tell me just a few days before he died—maybe he was coming clean about this?"

"Brett must have at least known!" I interject.

"I don't think so. He does the publicity—the flashy marketing—he's not the brains side of the business. He doesn't deal with the money. He's not . . . very smart."

"He went to Yale," I retort.

"Legacy admissions and money will get you far," Shirley counters. Ouch. Clearly Shirley isn't with Brett for his keen intellect. I think about his dazzling good looks and his apparent charm. If he were single and asked me out, it would be hard to say no . . . I guess until we had a conversation of substance. Try as I might, I'm a sucker for a man with brains.

"Maybe James was just over it? He used to hate companies like New Frontier. He was a member of that radical group, Green World. And he started to go back to some of those meetings in the weeks before he died—"

I interrupt Shirley. "Wait, James was involved in Green World again?" This feels contradictory to what his sister, Darla, had told me. So who is lying?

"Insane environmental actions were what he loved for so long. Maybe he decided to tank his own company by stealing all the money from it and giving it to Green World. Your guess is as good as mine," Shirley offers.

I'm about to tell her that this explanation doesn't feel right, when Alex speaks up.

"Makes sense to me," Alex says while nodding his head. "James stealing money to give back to his favorite organization."

Everything about this case feels like my head is swirling in a dense fog, one that won't clear anytime soon.

"James stole the money." Alex won't drop it, but maybe he is right. I'm always assuming the victims are completely blameless individuals. On TV, podcasts, and everywhere else, there is a clear-cut black-and-white duality between victim and perpetrator. Why was James acting strangely before his death? Why did he break up with Shirley so suddenly?

"I guess it makes sense. James even had his sister working for

Catalyst. Maybe they were in on it together. Abandoning the environmental stuff and going for the money," Amaya says. "James's sister was his woman on the inside. Maybe that's why she was hiding out on Staten Island."

"It doesn't seem like James," I say. "He turned from die-hard environmentalist to a guy that was taking money from the very companies he hated and then not actually making them more sustainable? Just stealing from them? It doesn't really make sense."

"You didn't even know him," Alex replies.

"Maybe James and his sister needed the money for something. Desperate people do desperate things," Amaya offers, as if she's seen it all too often. I think of what I would have done to save my brother. I'd have entered into an arranged marriage with a rich, icky old dude if I thought it could have changed his circumstances. "And what better people to take money from than the companies that are destroying the environment?"

"Then who killed him?" Alex asks.

This is the million-dollar question.

I am exhausted. My feet hurt, and my body feels physically heavy, as if trying to walk around and keep it upright will take all the effort I can possibly muster. I wish something, anything about this case was straightforward.

We exit Catalyst into a large crowd of people. It seems there are always large crowds in this part of Manhattan. This particular group is dressed in costumes and reminds me Halloween is tomorrow. Some of them are tourists; I can tell from the way the Marvel characters walk slowly and every few seconds stop to look up at the skyscrapers, seemingly oblivious to the downpour we are all about to be caught in.

I spot a man wearing a Boston Red Sox hat and sunglasses meandering away from the group of tourists. Odd attire, given the darkening sky and how terrible a hat it is to wear in a city with two perfectly good baseball teams. The Red Sox man is no longer aimlessly walking about and has instead picked up his pace. He is heading toward us, and that's when I see something shining and sharp in his hand.

CHAPTER 31

"Amaya, watch out!" I scream. Alex turns his head, and we stare at the man for a split second in stunned silence.

He has a set of keys in his hands that he's swinging and catching. It's nothing more than my imagination running wild.

"What's that about?" Amaya asks me.

"I'm sorry, I'm just on edge," I reply as I relax my shoulders, which I didn't even realize were tense. The threats Amaya has received have shredded my nerves even though they are as cheesy and generic as a bad made-for-TV movie, which, yes, I do watch on the rare occasion I'm home alone.

The crowd is basically at a standstill as we wait for a green pedestrian light. I know this crowd consists of tourists because of their refusal to jaywalk. After Amaya, Alex, and I cross the street, we'll part ways.

The crowd is filled with all sorts of different costumes, most of them from recent TV shows or movies. Some of them are political. Some are old-school costumes, like the Mickey Mouse that is right behind us. On further inspection, it's "Magnus Mouse," probably because the company didn't have the licensing from

Disney to be the real thing. Only recently has Mickey Mouse entered the public domain. It's a full costume, with a head and body, like the characters that dress up in Times Square and stop to take pictures with people.

I look around, and again I think I see the woman from the intersection who is also the woman from Charlie's house . . . Is she following me? I try to strain my neck for a better look, but I'm interrupted by a very impatient Magnus Mouse, who tries to push past me. His watch catches a little bit of light from a restaurant, and it temporarily blinds me. I look over at Amaya.

"Oh my god!" she gasps. With her flair for the dramatic, I think she is about to yell at Magnus Mouse for pushing past her so roughly. It's our God-given right as New Yorkers to shake our fists in the air about these sorts of things and, for some, to accompany such fist-shaking with expletives.

Then I see dark red blood trickling down her shoulder. A Halloween trick? It takes another second to process what's happened.

"Alex, Amaya's been stabbed!" I scream as I catch Amaya in my arms when she stumbles.

"What?" Alex says, confirming that he's heard correctly over the din of the crowd.

"Magnus Mouse stabbed her!" It's a phrase that I never thought I'd say. I point to the quickly vanishing black-and-red-costumed figure.

"*What?*" Alex says, confused.

"The mouse!"

As soon as it hits him, Alex runs after Magnus Mouse, and I turn my attention to Amaya. This isn't the first time Alex has willingly walked toward danger for me.

Her eyes are wide in shock.

"Give us room!" I say authoritatively as the crowd pushes back. "Call 911."

One or two people already have their phones out, which I desperately hope means they are calling 911 and not just taking photos of the scene out of some lurid fascination to later post on TikTok. This isn't a tourist attraction; this is a real-life emergency. *True crime rule number eleven: Stay calm in high-stress situations.* This seems like an obvious rule, but it's much easier in theory, because at the present moment, I just want to scream my head off and wait for an actual adult to come. Yet, here, I am the adult.

"You're going to be okay," I say instinctively, unsure entirely if she will be. I rip a segment off my jacket, which is easy given the cheap fabric, and stanch the bleeding from her shoulder. "I'm here with you."

I try to think of everything my brother learned in those premed classes. He talked about them all the time; it almost felt like I had sat through the lectures myself. I lean Amaya against me to make sure the wound is elevated above the heart to slow the bleeding. I apply more pressure, and Amaya gasps. I'm taken back to my panic attack outside the animal hospital and my feeble attempt at returning the kindness she showed me.

"Well, this isn't how I hoped to spend my day!" Amaya growls more than verbalizes, her animation making her sound a bit like herself. She is lucid enough to joke around; this is a good sign. In the distance, sirens are blaring, and I know EMTs will soon arrive and place her on a stretcher. She just needs to hold on until then.

"How are you?" I'm unsure what else to say to someone recently stabbed by a stranger. I imagine that a shoulder isn't a bad place to be stabbed, all things considered. If she had been stabbed in the heart, like James in the back of my taxi, she'd bleed out in just a minute. This probably isn't the comfort she is looking for, so I stay silent.

"It fucking hurts," Amaya says, a small grimace plastered on her face despite what must be excruciating pain. I can't believe she isn't crying, though she looks as if she might at any second. If I didn't know her, I would have thought her a stoic person, but I can see through the tough veneer she puts up at her most vulnerable moments. A practice she probably developed through her years as a public defender fighting judges, ADAs, and everyone else who thought the worst of her clients. Inside, though, she is as sensitive as me. Or almost as sensitive. I adjust her body to minimize the blood loss, while keeping a steady pressure on the wound and praying an ambulance will come soon.

"I want you to know . . ." I say, pausing, "that I promise to bring you both chicken curry and pizza from Lutrino's so you don't have to eat the hospital food every day."

Amaya laughs a little, a tear escapes her eye. "It's going to be soggy . . . you know that pizza doesn't travel well," she manages.

"Don't leave me, all right?" Amaya asks as another reluctant tear slowly rolls down her cheek.

"I'm not going anywhere," I respond.

CHAPTER 32

I've managed to avoid hospitals in the two years since my brother died in one. I am grateful for my decent health, and that my parents and Alex have remained relatively healthy, though I do worry about my dad. No distant relatives have croaked. Now that I'm back, I feel my skin prickle with anxiety. The bright hospital lights seem to present everything in a slightly sinister manner, making everyone's skin glow unnaturally. It smells like cleaning fluid and bad cafeteria food. That's why I could never have followed my brother into medicine to become a doctor. In Sri Lankan culture, the most prestigious job is a doctor. Is there anything more important than saving a life?

I take out Amaya's phone, which she shoved at me, telling me the passcode, which was, as I suspected, her birthday.

I call Amaya's parents, who, in typical Sri Lankan parent fashion, scream dramatically and don't stop until my third or fourth repeated promise that Amaya is really all right. It is something I know my own parents would do: grow hysterical over the bad news until they could see how bad it is for themselves. They will be here as soon as possible, they say. They live in Delaware, I remember Amaya telling me.

"Can we speak to her?" they ask.

"No," I reply gently, "she's with the doctor and no visitors are allowed right now. But soon. She's okay," I promise them once again.

Finally, through breathy sobs on the phone, Amaya's mother asks, "Who are you?" I tell them that I am a friend. That I promise I won't leave her until they get here, and hearing that, they finally seem to calm just a little bit.

I remember how my parents were when my brother got sick. They barely slept for months, the image of their son withering away in a hospital bed keeping them up at night. My mother spent the first months at my brother's bedside, until finally and firmly my brother said that our mother should sleep at home. It was pointless that both of them should lose sleep. The insomnia for both our parents and me continued at home. For the months my brother was in the hospital, my mind felt foggy, as if I was going through the motions of life but not really doing anything. I still live in the fog—just doing the bare minimum to stay alive.

Once I finish filling out the ER intake forms—thanks to Amaya's driver's license, I learn she is three years older than me, a fact I had been trying to figure out since I met her—I think of Alex. Alex, shit. I scramble to call him, sweating profusely at the thought of Alex also lying somewhere stabbed. Why had he chased Magnus Mouse? Probably because I told him to, I scold myself.

Pick up, pick up, pick up, I pray as Alex's phone rings and rings before going to voicemail. I end the call and stuff my phone back into my pocket.

Suddenly, my phone rings, startling me. Alex. I breathe in sharply, realizing I had been holding my breath while I struggled to reach him.

"Hello? Are you okay?"

"I'm fine. I lost the guy," Alex says, his ego sounding more wounded than anything else. Losing a chase to a man in an off-brand mouse suit is something that Alex would require me to take to my grave. "How is Amaya?"

"She'll be fine."

"Thank goodness." The relief in Alex's voice is palpable. "Do you think it was a random attack?"

Of course it wasn't. "It seems a pretty big coincidence to be random. Whoever is behind this made good on all those threats," I say.

"Crazier things have happened than an evil Magnus Mouse stabbing people in NYC," Alex says unhelpfully.

"Did you get any promising information? A description? Anything we could tell the police?" I am still nervous about police involvement after my interactions with them, but who else could we turn to?

"Around six foot, black fur, red pants, two large circular ears . . ." Alex says.

"Alex!"

"Well, I couldn't see his face, but he did drop a menu for a pizza place, somewhere right before I lost him."

"Okay?" I say, wondering why that matters. "What pizza place?"

"A place called Lutrino's in Brooklyn."

I think of Sal Lutrino smiling at us in his back office. It is, I know, too much of a coincidence.

CHAPTER 33

Amaya's parents arrive, bleary-eyed and exhausted. For a few shockingly real seconds I picture them as my parents arriving at my brother's bedside. I blink this vision away. That scene ended differently, and for that I am grateful. Amaya will be okay.

Both Amaya's parents cry when they see her there, as she begins to wake up from the grogginess of surgical drugs. The reunion makes me emotional, and I slip away unnoticed before prying questions can be hurtled my way. Had I been someone to Amaya, a proper friend, I would have stayed. But that is not our relationship. We are not friends. Our relationship is a professional one, brought together by a terrible tragedy and nothing more. I found myself in the position of bringing her to the hospital by happenstance, convenience, and urgency. I've done my duty, ensured that she would be okay.

I walk out of the hospital alone, eager to leave the place that has so many sad memories. I am relieved to be away from the lights and the smells. The doctors delivering bad news and the families practically living at the bedside of someone sick.

I see something in the shadows outside the hospital.

"Hey!" I shriek. This may be the first time in my life I've willingly walked toward danger.

It's the woman from Green World and the intersection again, I'm sure of it. I start to run. She is involved. I just had no name, no information, no way of tracking her down until now. I run, and she starts to run. I'm not in shape by any means, but adrenaline courses through me, allowing me to run faster than I ever have. She's quicker.

"Stop!" I yell uselessly.

She runs into traffic, is almost hit by a car, and at the last minute darts away into a crowd. I've lost her. I'm out of breath and mad at myself.

I look up at the night sky. "Why is she following me?" I demand of no one. A few people walking by move away from me before crossing the street.

There are no stars that I can see. They are there, I remind myself, just hidden from view by the clouds and light pollution. I think of Ammi, who once said that just because you can't see something doesn't mean it isn't there. Have faith in the unseen. I always wonder if she was talking about my brother. Does Ammi think my brother's spirit or soul is here, without a body? This seems to go against all science and reason, but I can't help wondering—no, hoping—that some part of him will always be with me, even as my memories of him begin to fade.

In the distance, an ambulance siren blares. I think about the time my brother collapsed. How I rushed him to the hospital, how certain he had been that it was just low blood sugar and stress, until it wasn't. Until I held my parents as the doctor told us all that my brother, my best friend, my guide in this world, had terminal brain cancer and just weeks to live.

If he is out here, guiding me, unseen, why do I feel so lost? Why do all the promising leads seem suspicious with no single clear suspect? If he is really looking out for me, why didn't he make sure that James Wilkerson-Taylor never got into my cab that night? Why didn't he give me some clue as to why there is a woman following me? No, my mother is wrong. My brother is dead and gone. Amaya is injured and out of commission. I am going back to jail.

I walk down the streets of Midtown, which are much quieter now that it is late at night. The suits have gone home only to rest ahead of coming back and doing it again tomorrow morning. Midtown isn't really a place to live, more a place to work. I pass by a bar and stare at it, contemplating going in.

It takes six minutes for the brain to react to alcohol. Six minutes to begin to forget. Maybe I will order vodka, the most popular alcohol in the world, with five billion liters consumed every year. I walk inside the bar. It's wood paneled and cozy, and I see a few dates snuggled up in the booths in the back. A big mirror behind the bar makes the space seem a little bigger than it really is. I scooch onto an empty leather stool at the bar; it's the farthest away I can get from the other people. My brother wouldn't be happy that I'm numbing my feelings with alcohol. He always encouraged me to feel things, whatever that meant, but he isn't here to stop me.

I contemplate ordering a glass of red wine in a sad attempt to be more sophisticated, but eventually capitulate to my adult baby ways and order a mango margarita. I still need drinks to be sweet enough to cover the taste of alcohol, like a high schooler at their first party. One glance at the bartender tells me this isn't a mango margarita sort of place, and making it is going to involve a lot of effort he doesn't want to expend. I should call my parents so they won't worry. I should do a lot of things.

But I am tired. And sad. And so I will drink away my sorrows, and ready myself for the day I have to return to jail.

I take a sip of what is most definitely a regular marg, and I gag slightly. A man sits next to me, and I notice his expensive watch. I'm about to feel sorry for myself again, when I remember something. Something important.

CHAPTER 34

I grab my cell phone.

"Alex?"

"Sup?"

"I think I have something." I want to blurt it out to Alex now, but his paranoia about surveillance and surreptitious recording has gotten to me. It doesn't help that I now know for sure someone is following me.

"Come right over," Alex says immediately.

"Thank you." I look at the still nearly full marg, and instead of feeling a rush of shame, I'm a little proud of my investigative skills. Hours and hours of those podcasts are finally paying off.

"I remembered something," I say as soon as I walk in.

"The pizza menu?"

I've thought about that long and hard. It's not a coincidence. Lutrino's is far away from where the menu was dropped—a good hour's train ride given the poorly functioning state of the subways lately. To have the very menu turn up with the man who stabbed Amaya means something. I have half a mind to go over there and confront Sal Lutrino. Maybe he killed for money? I remember all the past-due bills on his desk. But how would he earn money from James's death? We need something more than accusations without proper proof.

"Oh, no. It's more than that," I respond. "So, you were running after . . . Magnus Mouse. He's weaving in and out of people . . ."

"He was fast even in that bulky suit. I wonder what kind of workout he does—"

"Alex!"

"Oh yeah, sorry."

"So as he's running away, I remember a glint of something. At first, I thought it was the knife. But it was on his wrist . . ." I say, waiting for it to hit Alex. *True crime rule number twelve: There are no clues too small in a criminal investigation.* You don't know what will break the case wide open.

"A watch? I didn't see anything, I mean, he's ducking in and out and around and dashing in front of cars and then, well . . ." Alex trails off sheepishly. Alex is getting into CrossFit, and being fit enough to run and catch someone in a bulky mouse suit seems like the basic requirement of entry.

"Well, he couldn't wear his white mouse gloves to stab Amaya, so his hands and wrist were visible. I saw a watch that looked . . . unique. I think it had a blue band. It had gold and diamonds in an intricate pattern on the face."

"Are you sure?" Alex asks, looking unconvinced.

"Yes, I'm sure."

"Well, a ton of watches probably have that design." I'm a little surprised at Alex for saying this. He is a connoisseur of watches.

"Actually, only one brand makes those watches. Rolex." I beam. Thank you, Google Image Search.

"Okay, so where does that leave us on identity? Perhaps the pizza place hired him?" Alex asks.

"Maybe."

"The coincidence just seems to be too much. Did Sal seem, like, I dunno, suspicious? Capable of hiring a hit man?" Alex asks.

"He seemed sad that his friend was dead. I couldn't really discern much more than that." *I'm not a human lie detector*, I want to add.

Alex rolls his eyes like I've missed some critical clue because I was too busy feeling sorry for the guy.

"Well, let's see what we can do." It's not the ringing battle cry Watson would have for Sherlock, but I'll take any help I can get.

"So how do we find this guy?" Alex asks. "We don't even know what he looks like. Even if I could remember some defining characteristic of the guy, we can't find him on description alone." New York City is home to over eight million people, and we don't even know if he lives here.

"I guess we could start at the Rolex store. Alex, you know people at the store." I know this for a fact because Alex has more than his fair share of those watches.

"Oh yes, you're right," Alex says, as if he's forgotten he has a small fortune of wristwatches in his walk-in closet upstairs.

"Yeah, I mean, I've given the sales associate on the floor so much commission. Maybe he'll help me out if I offer to buy another watch."

"Alex, you don't have to do that for me."

"I'm prepared to make such a sacrifice for you," he says with a wink that I find both charming and incredibly irritating. Dropping thousands of dollars on something so frivolous annoys me. I'm not sure if I'll be able to afford heat next week. "So should we go?"

"It's past ten p.m."

Alex just shrugs and I'm reminded that, if you have enough money, any door will open for you.

CHAPTER 35

Even after regular business hours and upon invitation, I feel sure someone is going to kick me out of the Rolex store. As soon as I enter through a side door, which feels more comfortable than walking through the front door, I can tell everything in this place has a high-end finish. I don't fit in here. Had I come here during regular hours through the front door, I have no doubt I would be closely watched, unlike Alex. Death, taxes, and racially profiling Black and Brown people in expensive shops: the three certainties of life.

The first time I knew I should be jealous of Alex was when his parents' apartment elevator dropped us off right into their home. His nanny, a plump woman with a strong German accent, usually greeted us with Alex's favorite snack of Cheetos and Starbucks, and for me, the ever-elusive Twinkie. I look at Alex and feel a pang of gratitude for my family—blood and chosen.

The Rolex store, after hours, feels a bit eerie. The retail space that is normally well illuminated is now dark except for the glow from the lights shining outside the front door. The only other lights come from a back room filled with boxes and a few computers. Here it smells a little like leather, as if they lit one of those candles marketed toward men with scents like tobacco and charcoal because apparently real dudes can only enjoy rugged scents. Rolex uses the most expensive steel in the world, 904L, which was a question on *Jeopardy!* once.

I look at the man who led us inside. He had unlocked it almost as soon as Alex had knocked, lying in wait for us. The man who opened the door is slight, but wearing a formal suit, likely what he wore today on the sales floor.

"Okay, so you sent me the picture from your Google search and you're right. It is the Master II, Special Edition," the Rolex employee whispers. I want to ask for the man's name; however, I realize he is breaking some sort of rule for me. Maybe I feel a mutual understanding because we're both service workers at the whim of often demanding customers. I can't imagine some of the assholes who probably frequent this place.

"And there are only twelve, right?" Alex asks.

"Yes. And you have to buy them from the flagship store, which happens to be this one. Out of the twelve made, only four have been sold so far. Here's the list. I can't print or send it to you, because that would come back to me. And no photos!"

I make my way toward the shining light of the screen and wait as the man taps quickly on the keypad. One of these four names is Amaya's attacker. I assume we won't recognize the name, but we've narrowed it down to four people in the world. Just four! We can go back to Alex's and investigate each one. I feel like we're narrowing in and reaching the end. After taking as many steps back as forward the past few days, it now feels like we're making progress. The warm glow of a newly loaded page lights up my face, and I realize no investigation will be necessary.

I recognize a name immediately.

CHAPTER 36

If my podcasts have taught me anything, it's that anyone can be a murderer and not just the bro who's a dead ringer for Patrick Bateman from *American Psycho*. They can be any race or religion. Rich or poor. It's just like in my cab. It's impossible to discern the good passengers from the bad ones on appearances alone, unless, of course, they're already super drunk.

I stare at the screen and rub my eyes. The name on the screen is Charlie Hall. The head of Green World. I scan the rest of the names just to be sure. It's no mistake. The sales associate steps out to take a call, and I start snapping photos like an unhinged paparazzo of sales receipts and whatever other paperwork is associated with these sales. I hate doing exactly what I was told not to do, but this is just too important.

"Do you think it's another Charlie Hall?" I say, mouth agape, as soon as we're hurried out of the Rolex store by the helpful, nameless employee. It's a dumb question. The night is chilly, and I hug my jacket around myself tightly. "Charlie Hall tried to kill Amaya on the street in broad daylight?"

"Wait . . ." I'm slowly trying to piece things together in my head. "I'm not sure that could have been Charlie in the Magnus Mouse costume—that guy didn't seem as tall as Charlie is."

"He's hired someone else, a professional hit man maybe. Someone we don't know," Alex counters.

"Maybe one of the other names on the list is the hit man and they both coincidentally own the same watch," I posit, though even I know that I'm grasping at straws. *Back to true crime rule number nine: There are rarely coincidences in criminal cases.*

"The most plausible scenario is that Charlie is paying off the hit man with the Rolex watch. It does cost a lot of money . . . It's smart paying him off like that. Paying him off with any sort of cash payment would immediately look suspicious. Any sort of withdrawal would be problematic," Alex says.

I'm impressed with Alex's keen investigative eye.

"You're pretty good at coming up with these theories."

"You know why that is?"

I'm about to say it's because he's a genius. I don't get it out before Alex speaks again.

"It's because I'm used to seeing the worst in people. I also usually expect the worst too." There's a rare seriousness in Alex's face. "I think you see the good in everyone, so it makes you blind to their true possibilities."

I'm not sure what to say. I sense Alex is about to tell me something important. He has a pinched look on his face.

Instead, he goes back to the investigation. "Charlie is behind this."

"But Charlie is bankrupt. I saw it for myself. How could he afford such an expensive watch? What about the pizza menu? There are hundreds of pizza joints in the city—I can't believe our killer would have a menu from that particular place by accident."

"Maybe Charlie embezzled funds from Green World? Does it really matter what the motive is? And maybe the pizza guy is just a red herring?" Alex remarks.

"A red herring?" False, convenient clues don't just pop up. Motive is critical.

Alex doesn't address the comment. While the best true crime podcasts are filled with twists and turns, I now realize that's probably careful editing and storytelling to maximize drama. In real life, red herrings don't seem plausible. I wish my own life situation were a little more straightforward. For a second, I wonder who would play me in the TV version of all this, and my mind draws a blank. Mindy Kaling is far too beautiful, but since it's a movie, a little embellishment can't hurt . . .

Alex interrupts my admittedly poorly timed daydreaming. "Charlie must be the one behind the threatening texts and the stabbing of Amaya. Who else knew you went to Green World the day you got the text to stay away from there?" Only me, Amaya, Charlie, and the few people in Charlie's house.

This is, I must admit, a good point. Even Alex didn't know we were going there until after I told him. Charlie does fit in with my true crime rules. He has a motive. He wished the victim dead. He almost surely sent us the threatening texts. Could it be any more obvious?

"Maybe there's more to the story . . . something doesn't add up. Something I can't put my finger on."

"Always seeing the best in everyone," Alex says with a shake of his head.

"Is that such a bad thing?" I respond loudly, irritation coating my words. He's used this line as an insult before.

Alex stops walking and looks directly at me. "It's not a bad thing. In fact, it's the best thing about you," he says.

We wait until we get back to the safety of Alex's apartment before looking at the photos of the other documents. I'm still feeling spooked after the attack, worried that the man who stabbed Amaya will spring out of any dark corner like my life is part of the *Scream* movie franchise.

"Anything in there helpful?" Alex asks from the kitchen as he makes himself a sandwich.

I scroll through the photos on Alex's phone, and suddenly it buzzes. Someone is calling. The caller ID flashes *B-Dawg*. I can't help but roll my eyes at the cringey nickname.

"Alex, someone's calling!" I call out, waving the phone in the air.

"Who is it?"

"Someone named B-Dawg?" I say, poorly stifling a laugh.

"You can let it go to voicemail, I'll call them back," Alex responds, face a little pink as he walks toward me.

I return to the phone, which has now stopped ringing. I continue to scroll through the photos hoping that something will stick out at me. I need to find something. My life depends on it.

CHAPTER 37

"Let me just send those to you," Alex says, plucking the phone out of my hands, like I'm his parent about to search through his internet browser history.

Alex sends the images to my email, which I pull up on one of the three Mac laptops sitting about. I will be able to examine the documents properly on a larger screen. Alex eats his sandwich in silence as I do so.

"I think I've found something. A note, probably by the sales associate. In pencil. Charlie paid for the watch and left it at the store to be picked up by a man named Harvey Pembroke. There's an address and a number too."

Alex gets out his phone. It looks like he's texting someone back and forth, the phone buzzing with each new message.

"Everything okay?" I ask as Alex looks at his phone with furrowed brows.

"Yep, just googling Harvey Pembroke. Yale grad. Lots of degrees. Lives in New York City."

"Another Yale grad! Did you know him?"

Alex has a pensive look on his face, then shakes his head. “Again, I don’t know everyone who went to Yale, Siri.”

“Well, fast find regardless!”

“Just good online sleuthing. It’s all on his Instagram, which isn’t private,” Alex responds, shrugging and holding up Harvey’s account to prove his point.

“So Harvey is Magnus Mouse?” I ask.

“Maybe. There’s one way to find out, or at least get more information.”

“And that is?”

“Let’s go stake out his address.”

“Harvey’s? That’s a terrible idea. He literally stabbed Amaya in front of dozens of people. He’s unhinged. Besides, Amaya already said I can’t get in trouble. It will make my bail situation worse.”

“Let’s just go check it out. What could happen?” Getting stabbed or murdered?

“We won’t even get out of the car. We’ll just follow him. He won’t even know we’re there. Siri, how many times have I gotten you in trouble?”

“Many,” I say with an uncertain laugh.

“How many times have I gotten you in trouble where the consequences are life in prison?”

He does have a point there. I look over at Bella, Alex’s German shepherd, who is staring at us with mournful eyes as if she knows she is about to be left alone.

“Should we take Bella for extra protection?” I ask, knowing full well that Bella is the gentlest dog anyone could meet. “Or in case we’re seen, we can say we’re taking our dog for a walk.”

Upon hearing her name, Bella stands at attention. Ever the good dog, she’s ready for her first investigation.

CHAPTER 38

As we exit onto Roosevelt Island, I feel like I'm in a Hallmark Christmas movie. Big-city working gal goes back to her small hometown and finds out the true meaning of Christmas. Roosevelt Island does feel like a place where I could fall in love with a man trying to save his Christmas tree farm. Roosevelt Island is not easily accessible by car, and no passengers ever request to come here; most people take the tram and subway. It is considered part of Manhattan, even as an island in the East River. The strip of land is narrow and only about forty blocks long. The skyscrapers filling the horizon bring me back to reality, reminding me we're still in the city—no handsome lumberjack in sight.

"Odd place for the Mouse to live," Alex remarks as he zips through the barely present traffic.

"Odd that a guy who has degrees from Yale is a hit man too," I say. I wonder what happened in his life that made him veer off the path of the typical Ivy League graduate. No tech bro startup wannabe here.

We don't know for sure that Magnus Mouse is Harvey, but the Mouse nickname is hard to abandon. It's a little harder to be scared of a grown man who voluntarily wore a costume that is mostly a black jumpsuit and red shorts. The more I appreciate my situation and the looming jail time, the more I realize I need to channel my inner . . . Who's a modern-day detective? Benoit Blanc from *Knives Out*? I could never pull him off, but he's a little more chic than Hercule Poirot or Sherlock Holmes.

As we drive past average-looking apartment buildings and houses, I wonder what a normal place would be for a hit man to live. In the new Brooklyn high-rise that everyone compares to the evil tower in *The Lord of the Rings*? I guess a house on Roosevelt Island seems just as likely a place as any other for a hit man to live in. I just wish we were in a less conspicuous car. We stand out like those Tesla trucks that seem better suited for warfare than driving to the store for some milk.

"I'm getting family-friendly vibes here, not 'let me stab you in a crowd of people' vibes," I say.

"I doubt he'd wanna call attention to his off-the-books job," Alex says. "He's not fitting any professional hit man stereotypes, which is probably his goal."

If there's anything my true crime podcasts taught me, it's that evil can hide in plain sight.

Soon we pull up to a quaint house, with a literal white picket fence. Toys are scattered in the yard. The house seems to be pulled out of a Norman Rockwell painting. All that's missing is an adorable pup running around.

"So now what do we do?" I ask uncertainly.

"We wait. Good ol' fashioned stakeout," Alex says as he pulls a bag of Flamin' Hot Cheetos, a top-tier snack choice, from the back seat.

"We can eat in your car now?" I ask. Alex is fastidious about keeping his car and his home spotless. He has a strict no-eating rule in the car, which makes me a little sad, as I'm frequently tempted by roadside bodegas. I can't resist a good snack. I wish I had some Takis right now.

"Special occasion, this one time. Plus, I'm starving," Alex says, his mouth already half-full of Cheetos.

"Cheetos . . . they're not your normal fare of protein shakes and egg white omelets." Alex normally only eats junk food when he's feeling very stressed. My arrest has taken a bigger toll on him than I realized. I should feel bad about this. Instead, I happily crunch on the delicious treat and feel grateful that Alex isn't forcing a chalky protein bar on me.

Alex and I have made it about halfway through the bag when I see something.

"It's him! He's wearing the same watch." I gasp, impressed with my ability to recognize something so small from a dozen or so feet away. Looking at my outfits of late, you wouldn't be faulted for saying that I have no eye for details. The dawn is just breaking. My one and only foray into understanding luxury goods is working.

"Oh shit. Okay. So we know it's him," Alex whispers. "The Mouse is Harvey."

"He's coming to the sidewalk. Does he recognize us?"

Alex carefully cleans his orange fingers on a wet wipe before placing his hand on the ignition, ready to speed away at a moment's notice. I stop licking the orange dust on my fingers and use a wet wipe like a civilized person too.

Magnus Mouse has a black bag in his hand, which he dumps in the trash can on the curb. Seeing him in the daylight, taking out his trash like the rest of us, demystifies him ever so slightly.

He's muscular, but not overly so, and balding. Not quite the secret assassin I was expecting.

"Seemingly normal," Alex comments as Magnus Mouse shuffles back into his house. I bet Alex is wondering how he got outrun by this guy.

Suddenly, Bella jumps out the open window of the car.

"Oh no," I say, immediately running out after her, images of her alone on the street and getting hit by a car flashing through my brain. I couldn't care less if Magnus Mouse sees me. Instead of running far, Bella makes a mad dash to the trash, grabbing the bag.

This is pretty typical behavior for Bella, who was very defiant of all her doggy training classes. I'm able to separate Bella from the bag on the street, but I realize that maybe there could be something useful in the trash beyond some food scraps that Bella was probably trying to eat. I guide Bella and the trash bag into the back seat and trunk of the car respectively before scrambling into the passenger seat, out of breath. I look back to the house, fully expecting Magnus Mouse to be charging after us, but we've miraculously managed to escape detection.

"Why did Bella do that?" I wonder aloud, envisioning a dead body in the bag, which actually happened in one of my true crime podcasts.

"Maybe she smelled chicken?" Alex offers. Or a dead body . . .

Like me, Bella does love to eat.

We both turn around and stare in the direction of the trash expectantly as if waiting for something to jump out. It does smell. Not as bad as a random body part might, so I try to reassure myself it's just normal, innocuous trash with some potentially valuable clues.

"There might be something in there . . ." I trail off.

"It's probably going to stink up my car soon," Alex says with a wince. He unbuckles his seat belt as if to get out and throw out the bag.

"Just keep it for now. I think tha—" I'm interrupted by Alex.

"Wait, the Mouse is out again." I'm glad the tint on these windows is dark. "He's getting onto a motorcycle," Alex whispers.

Where have I seen that motorcycle before? I rack my brain.

"Let's follow him," I say. Something in my gut, an overwhelming pull, is telling me I need to follow the man. I know that Alex won't take much convincing to go on a probably reckless car chase.

"Sure," Alex says, "but I think the better driver of the two of us should do it."

"Me? You want me to drive your car?" I say, incredulous. Never in the four years that Alex has had this car has he ever offered it up for a drive.

"Yes, hurry up and switch with me! You're the better driver and you know the streets better than me; you drive a taxi for a living. And with a motorcycle like that, he is gonna be weaving in and out of traffic."

Yes, I'm a good city driver, but not in cars like this. Magnus Mouse is already on his bike. Before I can think, I jump out and Alex does the same. Once in the driver's seat, I buckle in and adjust it. The wheel feels soft and sleek under my hands. As soon as I start the car, the engine purrs just slightly. Bella barks as if cheering me on. I love my taxi, I remind myself, but this car is a thing of beauty. I grip the wheel tightly, keenly aware of how much this car costs and how much horsepower I command under my foot. While I think dudes' obsession with their cars is a little weird, driving this car, I sorta get it.

"I wonder where he's going," Alex wonders aloud.

"Clearly back into Manhattan or to the Bronx. Maybe to see Charlie?"

"That would be helpful. We might catch them together. I could take photos," Alex says, hand on his phone, ready to use it at any moment.

I continue to follow two cars behind, inching closer if it looks like Magnus Mouse may shoot ahead at a red light. We pass the exit to go to the Bronx.

"I guess he's not seeing Charlie, at least not at his house or business or whatever that place is . . . Maybe he's just running an errand?" I offer, thinking about the kids the Mouse may or may not have living in his house, which looks like it's made for a big family.

We continue to drive, unclear of where we're going. We pass some of the spots Alex and I frequent together. Were I not so focused on driving, I'd take a minute to revel in the nostalgia. I'd remind Alex that we should go back to our favorite Japanese restaurant and finally finish that sushi boat we've always wanted to conquer.

As we continue on, weaving in and out of traffic, I realize that I've been in this neighborhood recently. In fact, I was in this neighborhood two days ago.

"It sort of looks like we're headed to the hospital," Alex offers, his voice a little shaky. It is something I know too, but I'm hoping at the last minute the car will veer off in a different direction. Turn onto another street. The car continues to make its way toward the hospital situated on the west side of Manhattan. There isn't too much else out here so close to the water. Finally, after some careful maneuvering, our car is alongside his bike. Harvey looks over, and a shot of recognition seems to run through his body as he looks at our car, because suddenly, just a few blocks away from the hospital, he speeds away, accelerating on the yellow light so quickly even I can't follow.

The implication is clear.

"Call Amaya NOW!" I demand, revving the engine.

CHAPTER 39

By the time we get to the hospital, the sun is starting to rise. I hold my breath as I run inside with Alex, leaving the car illegally parked and its doors wide open. I'm ashamed to say Bella didn't even cross my mind. Right now my only concern is Amaya, and I run as fast as I can toward the reception desk.

I remember where Amaya's room is and run toward it. And that's when I see him outside her room. A deranged mouse holding a gun, about to open the door.

True crime rule . . . I don't think, because if I did, I would have considered another course of action. I dive at the Mouse from behind, giving me an advantage that prevents him from shooting at me immediately. I land on him with a sickening crunch, Magnus Mouse breaking my fall. I jump to my feet quickly to look for the gun. It has skidded across the hospital floor. Alex grabs it, but he doesn't need to. The Mouse is curled up in the fetal position on the floor.

"Fuck," he yells. "You broke something!"

I start to apologize, when I realize he's here to shoot my friend. I look at him and the gun and appreciate that he's now much scarier than any off-brand Disney character.

"Police, police!" Alex yells, his faith in them not shaken as it has been for me.

A few seconds later, hospital security streams in and I instinctively put my arms up, but they go directly for Harvey. They've gotten the right guy for once, and relief washes over me like a wave.

"Nice work," a nurse says, and it takes a second before realizing she was talking to me. "You're pretty damn brave."

I'd thought the stabbing was just a warning. Never did I anticipate the man would come back to finish the job. The seriousness of the situation hits me all over again.

I ponder the implications of this arrest. I know all too well that after an arrest, you're brought in for questioning. Will Harvey spill the beans, or, like me, will his attorney caution silence? Is what he may say enough to clear my name? Charlie hires Harvey and pays him with a Rolex? Harvey takes the Rolex and stabs James and Amaya? And then my DNA somehow ends up on the knife? The connection is tenuous and confusing.

A few minutes pass before I'm allowed to see Amaya. She looks exhausted but better, and is able to move her arm now, something I can only assume is an excellent sign.

"Thank god you're okay," I say, approaching her bed. "I'm so sorry I've put you in this position."

She opens her eyes and gives me a weak smile. "It's my job, you know."

"Not to get stabbed! Or shot!"

"I guess I'm bad at my job, if that's happening." Amaya laughs.

"Ow, don't make me laugh. It hurts. And . . . thanks for taking down a shooter for me. You've raised the bar for friends in my life."

Still, I'm the luckier one in this friendship. I found someone who will quite literally defend me from murder.

"Why do you think this happened?" I say, changing the subject.

"You're going to have to be more specific," Amaya responds, sharp as ever. Stab me in the shoulder and my brain is going on vacation for a good month—no critical thinking skills to see here.

"Him, coming after you. Why not me?"

"Well, usually you don't wanna kill the woman you're trying to frame for murder. Better to kill the meddling attorney, I guess?"

Just then Amaya's parents walk in, carrying coffee and looking exhausted. They seem to not know about the situation that has just transpired, likely missing it in its entirety while in the cafeteria. The police still haven't come to Amaya's door, probably calling for backup. Remembering their previous hysteria, I'm grateful for their ignorance. No use worrying them when Amaya is okay.

"Oh hello!" they say, looking from Amaya to me, me to Amaya.

I can tell that they are trying to discern exactly who I am. Amaya must have left it ambiguous when they asked earlier about me, the woman waiting by her bedside until they arrived. I'm grateful that she hasn't introduced me as a maybe murderer. I can see how that conversation would play out. *Mom and Dad, everyone thinks she murdered someone in her cab, and she's really the only viable suspect, but I believe she may be innocent.* Even the least discriminating parents would find me problematic company, and it's likely her parents are picky. Besides, I'm already a disappointment enough without the murder accusations. In our culture, the prestige jobs are limited to doctors, lawyers, and engineers.

"She's a friend," Amaya says quickly, as if she hopes her parents won't ask any prying questions. "She's Sri Lankan too." They seem comforted by the fact I'm Sri Lankan, as if the shared heritage makes me more trustworthy.

"Thank you for watching out for her," Amaya's mother says as I turn to go. "She's lucky to have such a good friend."

"No problem," I mutter under my breath, afraid to meet Amaya's parents' eyes. "I better be going. Take care, Amaya," I say as I show myself out of the room.

Thankfully, when Alex and I get back to his car, Bella, ever the good girl, is sitting patiently inside, guarding the parking ticket we've received.

CHAPTER 40

"I can't believe you're back here so soon," I exclaim as I help Amaya get out of her taxi. I know she is back here for me. Between her and Alex, I'm not sure how I got so lucky. Amaya discharged herself out of the hospital this morning. Later this afternoon is the big grand jury presentation we've been counting down to.

"Oof, that guy didn't drive so great. We need you back out there, Siriwathi," she says with a smile. "Besides, I wasn't going to miss this very important meeting with the district attorney's office about your case today. Usually my cases are only worth a phone call. I guess when you're representing the alleged murderer on the front of the *New York Post*, you get a little better treatment."

"Thank you for at least saying 'alleged.'"

"I certainly wasn't going to let another attorney take credit for the outcome of this case. I paid my dues," Amaya says, pointing to her shoulder.

I brighten at this. "Do you think this meeting will be positive?" I've learned not to assume I know what will happen next.

This isn't a carefully edited podcast directed to maximize anticipation. Today, the grand jury could vote to indict me. I may be heading back to jail. We know Harvey tried to murder Amaya, but did he also kill James?

"It better be," Amaya says as she drags herself up the front steps of the courthouse with effort, grunting a little but refusing any help. "Just don't say anything. *I'll* do the talking." This time we both look at each other and laugh.

"Honestly, at this point you can say whatever you want to these idiots," she jokes.

This time, I'll leave the talking to Amaya, glad that I won't have to fumble with my words in front of the assistant district attorneys. Amaya cautions me about how my words can be used against me, a spiel I've heard dozens of times on the cop procedurals my parents still religiously watch but that now make me uncomfortable. If you're not guilty, I'd once naively thought, it doesn't matter if you say something to the cops. It's hard to believe I was so uninformed only five days ago.

Harvey, who I can't help but think of as Magnus Mouse still, has been arrested for the attack on Amaya. "*Mickey Mouse?*" Amaya asks quizzically, before I can explain that Magnus is Mickey's cheaper and unauthorized brother. Thanks to Alex's sleuthing, we turned over the Rolex documents that prove a definitive connection between Harvey and Charlie. The watch was paid for through an offshore Cayman Islands account, apparently standard practice for rich people. But we can't yet prove that Charlie hired Harvey to kill James or even Amaya. I pray that this meeting is happening because that final piece of the puzzle is in place. Maybe the police have decided to dig deeper, though I don't feel entirely confident in that.

The other urgent question is how my DNA ended up on the murder weapon. I can't be cleared until that is solved. My hand is sweaty, and I fidget nervously. Every bad scenario, which I went over many times during my sleepless night courses through my head.

The district attorney's office isn't what I expected. Perhaps I thought that I'd be going through some gilded chamber of justice that resembles the ornate and beautiful US Senate building I once saw on a tour of the Capitol. Instead, it's just an ordinary office building for ordinary prosecutors who don't always get it right. I see a roach scuttle on the stairs out front.

The security guard lets Amaya in without going through the metal detectors as soon as she flashes her public defender badge, but I'm forced to place all my items in a plastic bin. I set off the metal detector, and the officers pat me down. I can't help but think back to my pat-down at the police precinct. Try as I might, I cannot excise it from my memory. I know that no matter what happens in this meeting, even if the case is dismissed, the trauma and fear of what happened will stay with me forever. I think about all those women in the cell with me who may still be incarcerated.

After I get through security, beltless and shoeless, Amaya guides me toward the elevator. I scramble to get my belt and shoes back on. Everyone is wearing suits, and almost all the people are white. They either look at me with disdain, maybe having recognized me from the newspaper coverage, or they ignore me, which I much prefer. I'm wearing a nice blouse and slacks, hoping to convey that I am taking this meeting seriously. I can't help but feel uncomfortable in them. The shirt is Ammi's and feels foreign on my body. I firmly refused Alex's Gucci belt, one he claims an ex left at his house, which I'm sure the ADA on the case would assume I stole. Besides, I can't pull off Gucci. My skin only seems to feel at home in itchy, cheap fabric. I realize I am sweating, and not just my hands anymore. My heart is pounding. I am glad, if not a bit embarrassed, that Ammi encouraged me to wear a little extra deodorant today. Even still, I'm going to have to dry-clean this shirt for her.

My nerves must be showing. "It's going to be okay," Amaya whispers to me. She feels like the only safe person here, the only person I can trust. "If at any time you need to talk, just let me know. We can step out and have a conversation privately."

My mouth is dry. I nod. I am going to meet with the very people who want to see me in prison.

Amaya opens the door to a large conference room. Three men, all white, stand up. No one bothers to introduce themselves, and I figure they are important enough at the district attorney's office that they have never thought to do so. I recognize the man sitting in the middle from the DA's website—he's second-in-command to the DA himself. He's short but seems to have the confidence of a much taller man with that smirk that's plastered across his face.

During my sleepless night, I was curious about what the people who were prosecuting me looked like. I tried to search their online photos for any hint of kindness; instead they all looked like they belonged in one of those fraternity class composite photos. I wonder which of them can do the longest keg stand.

"Thank you for meeting with us today," the man in the middle says, extending his arm for a handshake. Amaya shakes it, but based on her poorly covered grimace, she does it against her better judgment. The man does not extend a hand to me, something I'm perfectly fine with. I didn't want to shake his hand either.

"Obviously, this case has garnered a lot of attention," the man closest to the door says.

"Yes, obviously," Amaya says, the irritation oozing out of her voice. I appreciate how Amaya is past pleasantries.

"As you know, we arrested the man, Harvey Pembroke, who tried to attack you in the hospital," the man at the end of the table says. He nods to Amaya's arm, as if she possibly could have forgotten. The man speaking looks like he's the youngest, the least senior. He's wearing pants that are so fitted they don't leave much to the imagination. Ew. I don't recognize his profile from the website. Probably the line assistant district attorney actually in charge of trying the case, unlike the other, older men at the table managing the office.

"Harvey refuses to talk, but we feel as if we have enough information to charge him in Ms. Fernando's attack. We captured him on his motorcycle on a variety of surveillance cameras leaving the scene of the stabbing. He was easy to find in that . . . mouse suit." He chuckles as he says this, but stops when he sees our scowls.

"What was his connection to James's murder?" Amaya asks. She seems to care less about what happens to her knife- and gun-wielding attacker and more about what's going to happen to me.

"Even though Harvey is lawyered up and won't speak, we believe we'll have enough to charge both him and Charlie for the murder of James Wilkerson-Taylor. We believe the Rolex was payment for everything."

Amaya blinks. My mouth—like the world before me—falls

open. This is what we wanted. I never expected it, but I'm delighted . . . though I still feel unsettled. Could it be this easy? I almost laugh to myself at this question. I've been asking for an easy and simple solution this entire time, and when it presents itself, I can't help questioning it. It's too surreal.

"How did you get Harvey on the murder?" I ask.

"His DNA was on the knife."

"You said my DNA was on the knife!" I'm confused.

"That was a happy accident," he says this time, as if we're talking about Bob Ross painting on PBS and not about a murder investigation. "Well, for Harvey at least. Have you heard of touch DNA?"

The ADA continues, a little too smugly for my taste, "Our DNA is everywhere. We have it in our hair roots, in our skin cells . . ." This is beginning to sound like an obnoxious science lecture. "So when you touch something, you sometimes leave behind traces of your DNA from the skin cells you shed. In years past, it was just too little DNA to do anything about. With today's DNA technology, a swab can give you a profile. So, yes, your DNA was on the knife."

My mouth drops. "I didn't touch the knife."

"We believe you. Your DNA was probably all over your cab. So when James touched the cab, the door handle, the seats, whatever, he picked up your DNA on his hands. And then when he was stabbed, he touched the handle of the knife. Either to pull it out, or in surprise." I think back to all the things I touch in my cab every single day. Even though I wipe down the seats regularly, my DNA is still all over my taxi.

I look at Amaya, dumbstruck. My DNA was on the weapon after all. Completely innocently.

"So there were three people's DNA on the knife?"

"Yes." The ADA smiles, probably happy to show off again in front of his bosses. "Your DNA, James's DNA, and Harvey's DNA were all on the knife. We didn't know about Harvey because we compared the DNA on the knife to James, the victim, of course, and also to you, our suspect. We didn't have Harvey's DNA until we arrested him two days ago."

"And Charlie? You believe the Rolex was payment for the murders? As in you don't know for sure?" I ask.

"Harvey has no money in his bank accounts. The Rolex was worth thousands. We are working to connect the Cayman bank account to Charlie as we speak."

"You have proof from the store?" Amaya interjects.

"Yes. We strongly believe Charlie bought the watch, but we haven't been able to question him directly since he lawyered up too," the line assistant district attorney says with an eye roll as if Charlie asserting his basic constitutional rights is so inconvenient. I want to tell them that the police probably tried to continue to question him anyway.

I wonder why Harvey didn't ask for cash. Maybe he thought a watch would be harder to trace.

I'm elated that I'm off the hook, but it still feels a little unsatisfying somehow.

Charlie seemed disgruntled, and his history of unpeaceful protests and a pending manslaughter case did not play in his favor, but could he really hire someone to kill his best friend even after the falling-out? The evidence seems to suggest as much.

"We're willing to admit a mistake when we've made one, and here it seems we've arrested the wrong guy." The man says this so easily, as if it's just a wrong order at a restaurant and not something that has fundamentally changed my life forever. I half expect him to shrug and say, "Whoopsie daisy."

"We are hoping in exchange for dropping the charges you will consider avoiding a civil lawsuit."

I am willing to do or say anything for this ordeal to be over. I look over at Amaya, though, and am wondering if she will transform into the Incredible Hulk. I can see her seething with anger and appreciate the big breath she takes in so she won't start screaming.

"You're not doing us a favor here," Amaya says. "She's innocent, we're not waiving anything. You're dropping the charges because you've made a grave error with lasting repercussions."

I nod along dramatically as if I totally understand what's happening. I'd have agreed to anything to get the charges dropped. It's why I'm glad Amaya is here. Before this arrest, I may have even thought Charlie lawyering up was incriminating. Now I know that is a ridiculous thought. People need lawyers to protect them at every stage. Being innocent doesn't matter if the police think you're guilty.

"Understood," the middle man says gruffly, probably unused to being told what to do, unused to being challenged.

"So the charges will be dropped? You'll be making a statement to the press?" Amaya demands.

The men shift uncomfortably but don't say anything.

"You've put this woman through hell. Her face has been splashed on the front page, she dealt with the trauma of being arrested. You better right your wrongs now." I nod again. I'll need a full public retraction to ever get a date in this town again.

"Yes, we will put out a statement that your client is no longer a suspect. We're officially dropping all charges."

I exhale sharply. Relief washes over me like a wave. For a second, I feel dizzy.

"We are sorry for this . . . inconvenience."

"It's much more than an inconvenience," Amaya retorts, clearly restraining herself from saying anything worse.

CHAPTER 41

As soon as we get out of the district attorney's office, we hug on the street.

"Thank you so much," I say finally when I can get the words out. I need a minute to process everything that is happening. Amaya and I have formed an unusual bond these past few days. We've accelerated our friendship, tested it, and somehow it has survived.

"Thank *you* so much," Amaya says in response.

"What for?" I ask, confused. Asking Amaya to take a time-consuming job with no extra pay at the expense of her other cases feels more like a curse than a gift.

"For taking a chance on me. This was my first murder case. You could have left." Amaya looks down, not meeting my eyes.

"I guess we both just believed in each other." I realize how cheesy I sound. This feels like a direct-to-video movie from the aughts, which, while tacky, was incredibly heartwarming.

"You were a great investigator. A keen eye," Amaya acknowledges. "There were some good questions back there. You've got a good instinct," she says.

My instincts are telling me something still isn't right.

"Do you think it's a bit odd that Charlie, in near financial ruin, had the money to buy the Rolex?" I ask, hoping that my continuing need to pry into the case doesn't appear as if I am not grateful for her help. I desperately want to move on with the rest of my life; I just can't help feeling that this isn't the end.

"Yes, a bit," Amaya says. "But I don't see any other explanation. The goal here was to get you out of jail and get the case dismissed. We've done that job. You're going to let this go, right?" Amaya's eyes narrow suspiciously.

"Right," I say uncertainly. I understand the pain of being falsely accused.

Alex arrives outside the DA's office a few minutes later. He's fidgeting a little and running his hands repeatedly through his hair.

"How did it go?" he asks.

"Charges are getting dropped!" I practically scream.

Alex pumps his fist in the air. I haven't seen him this happy in a long time. He also seems relieved, the stress of the last few days melting off his face. I didn't appreciate how hard this has been for him. I know our friendship has had its problems lately, but I'm determined to work on it. This is a friendship that means everything to me.

"Congratulations. How does it feel?" Alex is beaming.

"I feel great. Truly." I must have a slight frown on my face, because Alex looks at me with raised eyebrows.

"What are you not telling me?" Alex asks. He knows when I'm holding back.

"I just can't help but feel like there's more to the story."

"*Siriwathi*." He only uses my full name when he's truly annoyed with me—so pretty often. Alex has picked up more than a few annoying habits from my parents after years of crashing at our house. "You need to drop this. You're free. This was the goal. We have other things to conquer now, like a giant sushi boat."

"That's what I've been telling her! Well, not the sushi boat part, but . . ." Amaya says. Both of them are on the same page—a rarity.

"Even though the paperwork said Charlie bought the watch, is there any way to trace the wire transfer?" I ask.

"Tracing a wire transfer is police work. And it's definitely Charlie," Alex says with an exasperated sigh.

I can't help thinking of *true crime rule thirteen: Even if someone is the obvious suspect*—which I guess was me for much of this case—*continue to investigate if the evidence doesn't line up.*

"Maybe, but if he's so broke, how could he have bought the watch?"

"You need to drop this," Alex says through gritted teeth. Once I have my mind set on something, I can be quite persistent.

As we all begin to go our separate ways, I hear a rustle behind me, like someone tripping. I turn around expecting that some passerby has fallen, when I see her again. The woman following me. This time I'm really ready. Without saying a word, I sprint and finally catch up to her. I don't want to tackle her so instead, I grip her arm, hopefully not too firmly.

"Why are you following me?" I am yelling by the time Amaya and Alex reach me. Once I catch my breath, I realize the woman is just as scared as me. "I'm sorry. I don't mean to scare you, I just want to know why."

"I don't know," she responds.

"What's happening?" Alex questions.

"This woman has been following me! This is the same woman from the intersection and Charlie's house that I mentioned to Amaya . . ."

"Oh god, someone *has* been following you! I should have listened to you," Amaya says.

"Why have you been following me? Were you at the intersection the other night? Where I almost hit you?" I release my grip on her wrist.

The woman looks at me blankly, no recognition of what I'm saying on her face. I may have been mistaken about the intersection, but I'm sure I saw her at Charlie's.

"Please tell me who you are," I say again, as politely as I can. I've backed away from her, hoping to show that I don't want to hurt her.

She relents. "Look, I was hired from a job board for a few days for some private investigator work. I was only told to follow you and record your movements. No one said why. And I have no clue what you're talking about . . . almost hitting me with your car?" She backs away a little farther.

"What's your name?" I ask, softening my tone.

"Melissa."

"Melissa, do you work for Charlie? You were in his house?"

"Uh . . ." She hesitates. "Am I going to get in trouble?"

"No," I reply as Amaya glares at me. "I just want to know why you've been following me and what you were doing at Charlie's house."

"There's a ton of people in that Green World house going in and out. I snuck in to hear your convo. No one seemed to care who I was."

"Charlie didn't hire you?" I ask now, genuinely puzzled.

"No. A woman named Shirley Lee did. She only communicated with me via email and paid me through a direct deposit from a bank account. I normally wouldn't take such a shady job, but I really needed the money."

Amaya, Alex, and I look at each other. Shirley Lee. James's ex-girlfriend.

"So Shirley Lee is behind this?" Amaya asks.

"Why would she kill James? Why would she have her ex-boyfriend's accused murderer followed? I know I'm cleared and my involvement in this is done . . ."

"But you need to find the truth. No more innocent people in jail. No more having more questions than answers." Amaya looks at me with a true sense of understanding. "We need more evidence to prove Shirley hired Harvey to commit the murder. Maybe she just wanted to keep tabs on you because you were accused of murdering her ex-boyfriend? We could have tried to get something more from Melissa, the amateur PI."

Amaya eyes me with an annoyed look I know all too well.

"She was scared. And she clearly was just doing someone else's bidding. Besides, we got her info if we ever need the police to talk to her. We can find something more on our own. Having someone followed and hiring a hit man are two very different things," I retort. One is technically legal. The other, very illegal.

"I think we've got this resolved. I don't know if this has anything to do with anything," Alex says. I'm shocked that he doesn't find this suspicious. "Siri, looking into this . . . someone's already been caught. It could be dangerous."

"No. This clearly isn't the end. We should look through the trash."

"What?" Amaya asks, probably bewildered at the thought that this is some sort of weird ritual between Alex and me.

"You kept it, right?" I ask Alex, before explaining to Amaya that we, or rather Bella, took the bag from Harvey's house. I now doubt the plan to look through it, realizing it'll probably show nothing and be equally disgusting. But I'm not going to give up a potential lead no matter how minor it might be.

"Well, actually, I took it to our trash room . . . it was starting to smell," Alex says with a grimace.

"Let's go try to see if they've taken it down to the dumpster yet." While Alex lives in a fancy building, the trash collectors aren't necessarily the most efficient. "Can you call your maintenance guy? Ask him to look? To confirm the trash hasn't been put in the dumpster?"

CHAPTER 42

We make a quick detour to pick my taxi up from the police impound. The car looks the same as it always did from the outside, though perhaps a little dustier and dirtier. Usually, I take her for a wash weekly. I find that people don't want to get into a dirty cab, and I don't want to drive one. I'm mostly worried about the inside. Surely the police would have taken out all the blood for evidence purposes? Even so, will I ever feel comfortable driving it again? Will the tinny smell of blood linger so that at unsuspecting moments I'll be brought back to one of the worst days of my life, second only to my brother dying? I look over at Amaya, who is eyeing me sympathetically.

I open the car door tentatively. The keys feel odd in my hands. I take a deep breath. It smells of cleaner. There is powder everywhere, which I assume is from taking fingerprints. I brace myself as I open the back door of the car. They've cut out a small chunk of the seat. The taxi has undergone surgery and not been stitched back together. I assume it's been cut out because of a few droplets of blood that fell there.

"We can get the state to pay for that," Amaya says matter-of-factly as she regards the situation over my shoulder.

"Thank you. I'm glad it's all out. Not just scrubbed out but *out* out," I respond, looking at the partially maimed seat. "Cleaning blood out of the seat doesn't make it all go away." I think about how blood shines under infrared light despite being scrubbed out with bleach. Thanks, *Forensic Files*.

"Unfortunately, I don't think anything can make this all go away. You're still stuck with memories. And I'm sorry for that."

"You have nothing to be sorry for," I say.

I've missed my taxi more than I thought I would. Society at large always asks us to aspire to something better, bigger, and bolder. It looks down on the people who are essential to making our daily lives function, who are relegated to the background. I've missed seeing the city; discovering yet another bacon, egg, and cheese in a hidden bodega; and hearing about the drama of the Upper West Side dog park from a passenger. I am important to New York City, maybe even an iconic part of it.

Alex climbs in the back, on the half of the seat that can still be sat on, and Amaya sits in the front. Passengers aren't usually allowed in the front of a taxi, but this is a social ride. Unlike the last time I picked Amaya up in my cab, she isn't a stranger heading home from work. That day feels like a year ago.

The trash, luckily, hasn't been taken out, and I'm surprised it can prove so interesting. We'd have turned it over to the DA's office if we thought it was genuinely something other than just trash. Now we know Harvey has a cat with a specialized diet, Harvey goes through a lot of Xanax, and somebody in that house is having sex, hence the empty bottle of lube. We all gag a little upon touching that last item, even with a gloved hand. However, the most interesting thing is the cheap phone sitting at the bottom of the trash covered in food scraps. It is not a smartphone, and clearly cannot even access the internet. It is for the sole purpose of making phone calls, like the phones marketed to old people with a large font or my first cell phone, hard-won after finally convincing my parents I would be safer with one on me. I can easily convince my parents of almost anything if it improves my personal safety or academic prospects.

"It's a burner phone," Amaya says confidently.

People, from drug dealers to garden-variety cheaters, buy temporary phones and trash them so nothing can be traced back to them. Of course, my ex was stupid enough to use his own cell phone to cheat.

"Let's see if we can turn it on," Alex says after he wipes off the phone multiple times with a Clorox wipe to hopefully rid it of any trash particles it has been buried with. Alex still holds it at arm's length as if it is radioactive.

I wait for the telltale glow of the phone screen.

"Nope. It's dead," Alex says anticlimactically.

"You wouldn't be a tech guy if you didn't have a charger for every device, right?" I say, already rummaging around Alex's drawer of different chargers without permission.

"Reminds me of my parents' clutter boxes," Amaya says as she appraises the drawer.

"Oh, do your parents keep a bunch of odds and ends in old cookie tins?" I ask.

"Yes!" Amaya says with a laugh.

The butter cookie tin that hasn't actually held any cookies in years seems to be a staple of many Sri Lankan households. It is usually filled with buttons or cords and other bits and bobs.

"And, if you look into my parents' fridge, you'd also see—"

"A billion yogurt containers?" Amaya says, finishing my sentence.

Food containers that could be reused, from plastic yogurt tubs to glass condiment jars, filled with random leftovers, dot my fridge, often leading Alex to open a container expecting one thing only to be greeted with a completely different food.

Alex is looking at the phone intensely, waiting for it to turn on.

I get up and go to Alex's kitchen.

"You wanna order takeout?" Alex asks. I'm not surprised that even at a time like this Alex is thinking of food. There's a reason we're friends.

"Just grabbing some rice to see if the phone is waterlogged and needs to be dried out," I respond, rooting through his kitchen cabinets. I place the phone in a bowl of rice, and a minute later, the phone turns on with a ping. Rice usually takes hours to work, so the phone must have just needed some juice. We stare at it like it is some sacred relic.

Amaya rubs her hands together as I grab the phone, the glow lighting my face.

"Let's see what's on here," I say like I am about to crack a safe in a heist movie.

I can't help but be nervous, even though my charges have been dropped. Even Alex is leaning forward in anticipation, despite his previous protests that I need to move on. The phone is not password protected. I doubt a phone like this even has that feature.

"We have a list of past phone calls. Multiple. To the same

number." I write the number down on a piece of paper. "Look up the number on the internet."

"Nothing is coming up. Probably a private or protected number," Alex offers.

"Well, I guess there's only one more thing to do," I say, picking up the phone and dialing the number.

We collectively hold our breath as the phone rings and then goes to voicemail.

"It's Shirley Lee. Leave a message."

CHAPTER 43

I wouldn't have pegged Shirley for a murderer," Alex remarks.

"She did hire someone to follow Siriwathi, so she's clearly involved somehow," Amaya says, probably offended by Alex's insinuation that a young woman couldn't hire a contract killer.

"Maybe she was in on stealing money with James, and the whole 'breakup' was a ruse," Alex offers. This explanation feels flimsy, but the proof seems to be in the pudding, or in this case, the cell phone.

"Then what about Charlie?" I ask. "Maybe he didn't send those threatening texts after all. I was being followed by Melissa, the amateur PI, so she knew exactly where I was. Maybe she was reporting back to Shirley, who then sent Amaya the messages."

Charlie has been the most obvious suspect this entire time. Brash, rude, openly wanting James dead, and having a motive to kill him. Statistically, men are behind most murders. A woman-run world would likely be a utopia. But Charlie certainly didn't have the kind of money to hire anyone. And wanting someone dead in a fit of anger doesn't necessarily mean you'd kill them yourself or come up with a calculated plan to have them killed. There would probably be a lot of dead people if that were the case.

"If there's another innocent man in jail," I say, "we have to right this immediately." I wouldn't wish my experience on anyone. My protestations that I hadn't done anything were ignored. I won't let that happen to Charlie if, in fact, he is innocent.

"There's one way to find out for sure," Amaya says. "We could see Charlie in jail."

While I wouldn't normally choose to go to Rikers Island for a day out, as I sit on the city bus, I observe all the people who don't have the luxury of that choice. The bus is filled with mostly women, many of them accompanied by young children, likely visiting loved ones. Alex offered to drive us to Rikers Island, but visitors can't do that. We all have to take the bus, which is an inconvenience, almost a punishment for wanting to visit an incarcerated person. Even taxis aren't allowed on the island, ensuring that the journey is made as arduous as possible.

When we finally arrive, we are immediately told to line up against the wall as drug-sniffing dogs greet all the new visitors. We throw our belongings, including our cell phones, into a small, dirty locker. From there we are escorted to a large white school bus that drives us to one of the several housing units on Rikers. After a short five-minute drive, we are at our intended destination, and once inside, Amaya is given paperwork by the sour-faced guard, all to be completed by hand.

"Damn, this place needs to be digitized," Alex announces once we all sit down, as if that is the biggest problem here.

About an hour later, we are escorted to a small booth, where we are separated by a plastic barrier, and Charlie is brought in by a guard.

"It's you!" Charlie hisses as he sits down. He sounds angry, which I can't fault. We are part of the reason he was arrested.

"Hi, Charlie," Amaya says, her voice softening in that familiar way. "We just have a few questions—"

"I didn't do this," Charlie says, fists rattling the table in front of him. He's so tall he makes the table in front of him small by comparison. I can see how his presence and personality could mislead someone to think him dangerous. I think about how I let it affect my own perceptions.

"Do you know why you would be connected to this?"

"I have no clue," Charlie responds, sounding genuinely confused. I believe him, realizing that this is probably how I sounded at the beginning. No clue what happened, and only able to assert my innocence. I hear all the people in my head who tell me I shouldn't believe Charlie. *Of course he'll deny it. They always do.*

"I was angry at James, but I would never kill him. He was my best friend," Charlie says as he buries his face in his hands and sobs, his big body heaving violently and the tough-guy facade finally fading. Rikers Island jail can break even the toughest people.

"Do you know anything about the Rolex watch?" I ask. It is the only so-called connection we have between Harvey and Charlie.

Charlie looks at me quizzically.

"I do," he replies. His voice has a lilt to it that makes it sound almost like he is asking a question.

So I am wrong. He is involved.

"And what is that?" I ask.

"Rolex is not a very environmentally friendly company! They use about eighteen metric tons of—"

"Sorry to interrupt, but we're not talking generally, we're talking about one specific watch," Amaya responds.

Charlie's face is clouded with confusion. "I have no clue what you're talking about. I don't know how to prove my innocence, but I didn't do it."

Finally off Rikers Island, I still can only think of Charlie. Another possibly innocent person behind bars. My thoughts are cut off by a news alert blaring on our phones. It's a Google alert—we all set alerts for people involved in this case.

Shirley Lee, CEO of Plastics Company, Dead at 37

I click on the article, heart pounding.

> Lee was found dead in her residence of an apparent suicide.

"Suicide?" I scan my memories of Shirley's face to see if there was some indication of her distress. She seemed to have a zest for life, but I realize that appearances can be deceiving. I'm all too familiar with people burying their feelings.

"Maybe she was involved and the guilt drove her to end her own life," Alex remarks, head down.

"We should talk to Brett. He was her boyfriend. Maybe he'll have some answers." I don't want to intrude on him again, in another moment after he has lost someone, but Shirley's death has to be connected to this. No coincidences. I have to find the truth.

We arrive at New Frontier's reception desk around 7 p.m. I'm surprised Brett is still around and even more surprised when he agrees to speak with us, and I'm ready to go in guns blazing. Upon seeing his face, I have second thoughts. He seems to have shrunk in just the few days since we saw him last. A dead best friend and now a dead girlfriend. It's horrible. His shoulders are slouched, and his once perfectly tailored suit now seems to dwarf him like he's a coat hanger. There are dark circles under his eyes, and his face seems plastered in a permanent grimace. He looks as if he hasn't slept in days, and I can't help but feel ashamed that my presence will add to his unhappiness. I'm surprised that Brett is at work and didn't go home after hearing the news about Shirley. After my brother died, I let my taxi engine grow cold until we needed a paycheck to put food on the table.

"Is there something else I can help you with?" Brett says stiffly, eyeing me with unease.

"We're sorry to bother you again; we'd like to talk to you about something." Amaya glances over at one of the women who passes us. "Perhaps we could meet somewhere privately?"

"I'm having a hard day. Now is not a good time," Brett responds.

"We're so sorry for your loss . . . about Shirley." I realize I need to clarify, and my guilt for all this man has suffered comes back again.

Brett's eyes narrow. "How do you know about her?"

"She told us that you two were dating."

"We were. I'm devastated . . . I didn't see it coming," Brett says, now crying.

"Did you know about James, what he had been doing? Stealing money from the company?" Amaya asks gently.

Brett's face turns pale, something I've only seen on the *Maury* show when the dude was, in fact, the father. I watch as the blood drains from his face and his eyes bulge out of his head as if he were slapped. People may try to hide their emotions, but his physical reaction shows his hand.

"Let's speak in my office." Brett ushers us into his corner office with a beautiful view of the Brooklyn Bridge and skyscrapers shining in the setting sun. He gestures for us to take a seat, and Amaya and I find ourselves in two chairs across from his desk, relegating Alex to the couch by the door. I move an orange-and-black backpack emblazoned with a New Frontier logo off the chair, eager to finally have some answers.

"How did you know about James?" Brett asks. His question confirms what the USB said all along. James was stealing money. Before we can answer, Brett continues. "I didn't know about it until the suicide letter."

"Suicide letter?"

"Shirley and James were embezzling money. Taking it from companies with no plans to provide full services to our paying customers. I suppose I should have known what was happening in my own company, but I was busy with taking us public. With marketing. With all the flashy things when I should have been making sure everything was going to plan internally."

I swallow. It's hard to believe he couldn't have known. Maybe he was myopically focused on the other things. He is a flashy person, compared to the down-to-earth and environment-loving James. I wonder why Shirley was taking money? Why would she risk her company?

Brett continues unprompted. "We don't know how she killed herself or James in that locked taxi. She didn't elaborate in the letter. But my girlfriend killed my best friend. I'm feeling pretty messed up right now." Brett begins to cry again as Amaya fishes in her purse for what I imagine will be tissues.

Shirley did what? I think back to how sad she looked with James gone—there was love clearly still there. She couldn't have killed him even if they were no longer together. "I'm sorry, but that doesn't sound right." I'm not an investigator, but I know when an explanation does not seem plausible. In true crime, a conclusion must be supported by evidence, or you end up with an innocent person behind bars.

"Unwell people do terrible things," Brett responds, eyes downcast.

"With all due respect . . ." I begin. I know people say that when they are about to convey the opposite sentiment. "Why would Shirley date you if she and James were the ones embezzling money?"

"Probably to throw me off the scent or something. Shirley could be a distraction."

I'm slightly offended by Shirley being a mere distraction. She was smart enough to be the brains of the operation. I'm unsatisfied with this answer, but I don't think probing further on this line of questioning will get me anywhere.

"Why would James be stealing money? Do you think it was his plan all along?"

"How would I know?" Brett responds, his face turning into a

scowl. I'm surprised this man has so little insight into his supposed best friend.

"I still feel like something is off, possibly . . ."

"You won't let this go, will you? You're free." Brett's demeanor changes suddenly, and he seems angry. His fists clench, and the vein in his forehead bulges.

"Brett, don't . . ." Alex says.

"Well, I guess this won't end as nicely as I hoped."

"What do you mean by that?" Amaya asks as we both eye the door.

Then I look at the backpack, the initials JWT staring back at me. James Wilkerson-Taylor. This is James's backpack. The backpack that was in my taxi the night of James's murder. The backpack that was taken by the murderer.

I glance at Amaya, and we make a run for the door.

CHAPTER 44

The door is, of course, locked.

"Alex, can you please restrain your overly curious friend."

Alex looks at me, pain etched on his face.

"Alex . . . you know him? You—you're involved in this?" It takes me a second for my brain to catch up with what's happening. My heart feels like it is ripping in two, and I have to grip the top of the chair to stop from crying. I am seized by a visceral pain, much like the panic attack at the animal hospital.

"Should I explain or should you, Alex? Our friend has endless questions. She could have just accepted she was off the hook, but she had to keep digging."

"I . . . I swear I didn't know anything about the murder," Alex stutters. He moves toward me as if to take my hand. I flinch.

"Well, if I go down, you do too," Brett says, perhaps a bit too calmly for my liking. He's now sitting with his feet propped on top of his desk. He's enjoying this.

"What does he mean, Alex?" I demand. I move toward Amaya and try to catch her eye. We need a plan to get out of here. Alex moves in front of the door, thwarting any attempt at escape.

"I . . . I lied. I know Brett. We went to college together, like you said. He had this idea for this incredible company, New Frontier, and he needed my advice, so I gave it to him. And suddenly he needed my money—and I gave it as an investment. I gave him a lot of money, including a lot of money I didn't have to give. Once the company went public, I would make all my money back. It was a sure thing—until I looked at the numbers. The company wasn't going to be even close to profitable, and probably wouldn't be for years. If we just got those investors . . . if we just slightly modified numbers just a little bit . . . we could take into account future value so it wasn't illegal per se. Once we made the money back, we'd be okay. I didn't realize—" Alex gulps as if he is running out of air. "Brett was stealing from the company, so adjusting the numbers a little was actually a crime. It was no longer just a gray area. I *unknowingly* helped him commit a crime. Of course, no one would believe I didn't know. Only an idiot would be so careless as to not thoroughly vet the numbers beforehand."

My stomach is doing flips, and I feel bile rush to my throat. Somehow, Amaya looks calm and collected. I know it's a facade. She is bouncing her leg up and down—her obvious tell.

"Alex, you can get out of this. Even if you're in a little bit of trouble, it's not as bad as being complicit in murder. You can still make this right," Amaya says. I'm not so quick to forgive, but we need Alex on our side to get us out of here. I'm so mad at him, I never want to speak to him again. I can hardly look at him, I feel so sick.

"Oh, you wish that's all he did." Brett laughs. He's sitting upright in his chair now. The same things that made him seem sympathetic when we first arrived, like his gaunt face and sunken-in eyes, both of which I assumed were from crying, now make him look sinister.

Alex has moved away from the door and is now pacing while running his hands through his hair. He looks at me pleadingly, but I turn away.

"Initially, before I looked at the numbers myself, Brett told me James was stealing money from the company, so I told him to deal with him. I swear that I didn't think dealing with him meant killing him. I just thought it meant a stern talking-to . . . or something . . . I could never imagine . . ."

"Sure, the idea to kill Shirley and James was mine alone, but you were certainly the inspiration, Alex. Take some credit. Like you always said, '*Success at any cost.*'"

"This is not what I meant," Alex responds through gritted teeth. He genuinely looks pained at what he's done.

Brett gets up and stands between Alex and me before advancing toward me. Brett's face is now inches away from my own. "Don't be so sad. Alex finally did some due diligence after the murder and realized that I had stolen the funds, not James, and he threatened to out me. This, of course, would have implicated him, but he didn't care as long as you got off the hook. He is a loyal friend. He said we had to find the true murderer. So I said James's friend Charlie had the most motive to kill him. And Alex believed it. Or maybe just wanted to believe it." Brett looks gleeful.

I can't believe what I'm hearing. Alex has known Brett this whole time and has taken him at his word. I'm surprised that Alex, as a lifelong New Yorker, has managed to be so naive. He was going to make sure I didn't go down for this crime. It didn't absolve him of his secrets and betrayal, but he certainly wasn't in the same league as Brett.

"Siri. I swear I didn't know you were going to be involved in this. I didn't even know James would get into your taxi. When I found out what really happened, I was trying to make it right immediately . . . I'm so sorry. I should have been honest from the beginning. I didn't want you to hate me, and I thought I could get the guy who did it and everything would resolve itself. I only realized Brett was stealing funds after you got charged, and I didn't think Brett was capable of murdering his close friend and business partner. I should have asked more questions . . ." Alex turns to Brett. "I mean, how did you even know James was going to get into Siri's taxi, Brett?"

"Harvey was following Siri. I thought that if Alex had some second thoughts about outing my criminal activities, I'd let him know I was keeping tabs on his most favorite person in the world. Then I thought I'd have even more leverage over Alex with Siri behind bars."

I still couldn't figure it out. "How did you ensure James would get into my cab?"

"I work at a tech company. Some geek hacked the Curb app to make sure you'd be right by where James would hail a cab. Don't ask me how he did it. James and I shared a Google Calendar for work, and he had 'snake drop off 1:15 a.m.,' so I knew where he would be."

The night of the murder, I remember being hailed on the Curb app and then the cancellation. Then seconds later, James was at my door.

"How did you do the rest of it?" Normally, I'd relish this satisfying explanation at the end of it all, like a British murder mystery that neatly wraps up despite a few gaping plot holes. Instead, actually living it feels terrifying.

"I hired my friend Harvey to kill James. James found out I was embezzling money from my own company. I covered my tracks for a while, and James's hippie-dippie ass didn't even notice. Eventually, Shirley mentioned something about her deliverables still not being sent to her, and James realized I had taken the money her company paid us to get her that stuff. We probably could have worked something out, but James was insistent on outing me. He was going to fly to Paris to reveal all to our investors. I tried to talk sense into him, but he kept saying I had committed a crime. He really gave me no choice."

"But . . . how did you kill James in my moving taxi?"

"You can thank Harvey for that," Brett says, nodding to the photograph of the two of them on his desk. "He's pretty awful at everything, and I guess that extends to killing people. Don't send out a Yale grad to do your dirty work, but my options were limited. Harvey was so desperate for money for his little drug addiction that he'd do anything for me. He followed your taxi on his motorcycle. He was going to wait until you stopped, force you out of the car, stab James, and flee. Or follow you to the airport and stab him at some point. He didn't have it fully fleshed out, yet knew he needed to do it before James got through security and got on that flight. Then you stopped at a red light, and the passenger window was open. He stabbed James and literally rode away into the sunset."

It was nighttime, but I get the metaphor. Brett gestures over to the gorgeous view of the sun setting behind him. It would be a breathtaking moment to behold if I weren't worried about leaving here alive. I think back to the night of the murder, to the moment the motorcycle rode up next to me. There was a commotion up front, and I remember sticking my head out the window to find out what was causing all that incessant horn beeping. With a sinking feeling in my gut that makes me want to vomit, I realize that's the exact moment James was murdered in my car.

And finally, we have it: means, motive, and opportunity.

"He got very lucky. Until he totally spun out and tried to kill Amaya at the hospital. I didn't think he was stupid enough to attempt that. I told him just to scare her. He was really strung out. Harvey followed you to throw you off the trail with that pizza menu and those anonymous threatening texts. Turns out you were hard to scare off." It's a compliment from a literal psychopath, but in a twisted way it still makes me feel a little better about my investigative skills. "When Harvey couldn't follow you because he was trying to keep tabs on Amaya and Charlie," he says while looking at her, "I hired some girl to follow you. Of course, I created a dummy email account to make it look like Shirley was hiring her. Obviously, I have to cover my tracks." It wasn't Shirley Lee who hired her after all. But the voicemail on the burner phone . . .

"And Shirley?" I ask. Brett's on a roll, and I need to keep him talking. Always keep the suspect talking.

"Shirley had been demanding the environmental work we promised for months. At first I thought I could hold her off because she was interested in me." Brett retreats behind his desk and starts rummaging through his drawer for something.

"And did she stop demanding the deliverables when things got . . . intimate?"

"Not really. That bitch was suspicious from the start. I think she only came on to me to find the truth. I'd only even gotten together with her to shut her up. When James died, her suspicions grew, and she thought she was hiding it from me. I knew she was too smart for her own good. She would have figured it all out in the end."

"So you staged her suicide?"

"I tried to get her to stop without taking such . . . drastic measures. Harvey called her and left threatening messages. That only seemed to fuel her curiosity." That's how her number ended up on Harvey's phone. He was threatening her. They weren't working together.

"How did you kill her?"

"I don't need to tell you all my secrets, do I?" Brett grabs a letter opener out of his desk drawer. "I wasn't anticipating having to kill anyone myself, but I guess this little thing will have to do. It's dull, so this will most certainly hurt," Brett says with a manic smile.

"Please spare Amaya," I plead. "You have me."

Brett is standing up again and advancing toward Amaya and me.

"Sorry, y'all got to go." For a second Brett sounds like a Southern belle. I remind myself this situation is anything but funny. "And, Alex, you have to help me. You may not have committed murder, but financial fraud is certainly a crime punishable by prison time. And so easy to prove too. I have receipts. You don't *have* to go to jail for your friend, Alex."

"Brett. Just calm down. We can work this out," Alex says, voice frantic.

"Time is past for that. I think we can kill both of them, take them out the service corridor, and then dump them in the river . . . also open to other creative solutions."

"You won't get away with it," I manage to eke out. "There are cameras and DNA evidence and . . ."

"I'll help you," Alex interjects.

My stomach flips again. Alex is tossing aside years of friendship to save himself. I'm about to die. This is how it ends. Nosy investigator who can't stop asking questions finds herself as a true crime headline. Why couldn't I just keep quiet and be happy the charges against me were being dropped? Why do I always have to figure out how it ends? I wonder if Amaya and I can bum-rush both Alex and Brett, but we are at a disadvantage. Amaya still has the injured arm, and I'm a string bean compared to Alex and Brett.

I'm thinking about our exit strategy when Alex approaches me gingerly. He grabs me.

"Alex, I can't believe you're doing this." I dig my fingernails into my palm, but I can't stop a few tears from stubbornly making their way out. I'm momentarily frustrated at my inability to hold my emotions back when I need to be tough—or at least pretend to be.

Alex looks at me so sadly, for a second I feel bad before remembering that this is all his fault. "Siri . . . I—"

I interrupt him. "There's nothing you can say to make this better. There's nothing you can do to fix this."

"Do you remember the Great Noogie Incident of 2011?"

Brett, Amaya, and I all stare at Alex like he's hit his head. What the heck is he talking about, he—*oh*. I nod almost imperceptibly.

In what feels like half a second, Alex pivots and pins Brett to the chair as I swiftly punch him. It happens so fast I feel like I've hallucinated it except for the pain radiating from my fist. The Great Noogie Incident was payback to a certain middle school bully. Back then, the noogie, not a punch, was the torture of choice.

The letter opener falls to the ground with a clatter.

The punch was enough to knock Brett out temporarily, just until the police and medics arrived. The *New York Post* headline the next day spared no mercy, just as they hadn't for me a few days earlier:

LOVE TRIANGLE: Man Hires Hit Man to Stab Best Friend and Poisons Girlfriend!

The article has a quote from Brett Ryan's expensive lawyer stating that they vow to take his case to trial. According to sources Amaya has in the DA's office, the Cayman Islands account that was used to buy the Rolex and hire an expensive attorney for Harvey so he wouldn't talk was arduously traced back to Brett, resulting in Charlie's name being officially cleared. In light of the overwhelming evidence against Brett and his own plea deal, Harvey confessed to the murder for hire. In the story, my name is cleared, but only toward the end in small print. Brett's trial is quickly becoming the murder case of the year, and I'm sure I'll be called to testify—a thought that would normally bring me crippling anxiety. This time, though, I'm ready.

CHAPTER 45

Two months later, I call Alex.

"Wanna come over for dinner?" I ask.

"You still want to see me?" he replies.

We haven't talked since Brett was arrested. It feels both long and short at the same time. Too short to be speaking to someone who betrayed me so deeply, but far too long to go without speaking to my best friend. I saw in the news that Alex was also arrested on felony fraud charges. I imagine he could use a friend right now. I want to hate Alex, but he never set out to hurt me. He kept a major secret from me, but he would never, ever try to harm me intentionally. When I got arrested, he did everything he could to help me. He thought he was doing right by me. Yet I'm also still angry. He betrayed my trust. I don't forgive him. But I also can't help but miss him. It's complicated, but if we ever want to repair our friendship, I have to make the first move.

"I'm still angry at you. I need to know if I can ever forgive you. In order to do that, I need to see you. Come over."

"Is Ammi cooking?" Alex asks almost shyly. Over the years, Alex has taken to calling my mom Ammi too.

"Yes."

"I'll be there."

After I hang up, I call Amaya.

"Any interest in dinner at my parents' house?"

"We're celebrating?" she asks.

I just wrapped up the grueling process of testifying in the grand jury against Brett Ryan. It's the first step in his prosecution; his actual trial won't happen for months. Unlike my grand jury process, which was set to happen just days after my arrest, Brett's lawyer did something I'm not sure I legally understand to get it delayed.

"I mean, I know you have a lot to do and are still rehabbing that arm, but you still need to eat."

"You don't have to convince me. I have been dying for some good home-cooked Sri Lankan food since my parents left. And I do need to eat."

Most people would not be able to have a whole meal ready to go in the one-hour notice I gave, but most people are not Ammi, who has been cooking for large crowds of people her whole life. She is especially adept at making sure people who have never had Sri Lankan food try it. People who say they don't like spicy food, and especially people who say they don't like curry, are simply challenges for my mother. She prides herself on converting even the most skeptical, believing that some food—her food—is universally delicious. Nearly everyone on our street in Queens has had Ammi's chicken curry at least once.

As I look at my home and notice the siding falling off, I worry what Amaya will think. I love my home, despite the constant complaints I've had about it over the years. I'm proud my family worked hard to buy it, with no generational wealth and no help. The home isn't perfect, but I belong here. Anyone who needs a hot meal and a mother to love them is welcome.

I see Ammi is busy in the kitchen stirring multiple pots simultaneously. The work that goes into the Sri Lankan feast she is preparing is enormous—she was likely cooking even before I called her. A mother's intuition. The smell of the food hits my nostrils immediately. I can recognize each scent individually: garlic, turmeric, coriander, mustard seeds, curry powder, onion, curry leaf. They all meld together into a beautiful harmony.

"Oh, this calls for a celebration," she says as I walk into the kitchen. She hugs me tightly, the stress of the past few days melting off her face, making her look younger. This time, I wasn't the one in trouble, but my having to go back to court still made Ammi anxious. One good thing about the process? I also saw Alex exiting the grand jury room one day. My heart tightened at seeing him. I knew I had to reach out.

"Siriwathi. I am so proud of you," she says, smiling.

"Why? I didn't do anything," I say in genuine surprise.

"You did. You got yourself out of this on your own. I know you think we've been harder on you than your brother. It's just that I know how hard it is to be a Brown woman in this world." Ammi's face softens. "We just wanted to protect you. And I doubled down after your brother got sick. We couldn't save him, but I'd be damned if we lost you too." Ammi is crying, a rare occurrence for a woman who has carried the weight of this family on her for decades without flinching.

"Ammi . . . I didn't realize. I thought you just loved him more. He was a boy and going to be a doctor and . . ."

"I love you both with every ounce of my heart. And we don't thank you enough for everything you've done for this family. You've kept us going these past few years, and I think Thathi and I are ashamed at how reliant we've become on you. You're our child. You shouldn't support us—we should support you, and we will. Ajith isn't coming back, but we must find a way to enjoy life."

I feel a strange gurgle in my throat again and dig my nails into my palm.

"Thanks, Ammi—"

We're interrupted by the doorbell ringing. Alex has arrived.

I greet him at the door. He looks gaunt, like the one time he was hospitalized for food poisoning and couldn't eat solid food for weeks. I fight back an urge to shove a sandwich into his hand.

"I'm so sorry, Siri. I—" Alex begins before I interrupt him. He's already starting to tear up.

"Let's not do this here." Upon seeing his anguished face, my stupid bleeding heart melts a little. "We'll talk more later. But for today, can you please just try to act normal?"

Alex wipes his eyes and takes a deep breath. "Yes, I can. Of course."

We stand in silence for a second, looking at each other. In this moment, I know we'll be okay . . . eventually.

"Come on in," I say as I wave him in.

Alex's crumpled expression is replaced with his million-dollar smile as he strides toward the kitchen.

"It smells delicious here. Did you happen to make your famous chicken curry?" Alex asks my mom with a wink as he makes his way inside, bags of fancy wine in tow. Alex never comes to my house empty-handed.

"I always make your favorite," Ammi says with a smile as she leans in to pinch him on the cheek as if he were a child. He smiles in delight.

"You're the best, Ammi. Thank you for everything." Alex smiles, and I know this isn't just about food. I groan outwardly. Inwardly I think it's cute how charming my mother finds Alex and how much he loves her. I spared Ammi the details of Alex's involvement in my case, not wanting to taint her beloved memories of him. It would kill Alex to know that a woman he views as his surrogate mother was disappointed in him. Somehow, I feel like I owe him that.

"When is your friend coming?" my mother asks.

I walk into our small kitchen and dining room and notice the paint peeling from the walls and the cracks in the ceiling. There are family photos and plates of food filling up the tables. I look at my college graduation photo on the fridge, growing yellow with age. Just then, Thathi steals a kiss from Ammi. A half-completed thousand-piece puzzle sits on the coffee table.

The doorbell rings again. It must be Amaya. I open the door to see her smiling, a paper gift bag in her hand.

"Ko ma tha?" Amaya says. *How are you?* in Sinhalese. The simple phrase makes both of my parents smile in delight.

"Welcome to our home." Ammi beams as if welcoming in an honored dignitary. I think for a second. She is more than that. She saved my life.

"This is for you," Amaya says, handing the bag to my mother.

"Oh, thank you, you didn't have to bring anything," my mother demurs. I know Ammi well enough to know the complete opposite is true. Not bringing something to someone's house is a definite sign of rudeness in her eyes and the subject of hushed fodder once all the guests leave.

Ammi opens the bag. "Oh wow. Where did you get these?" A few bottles of Sri Lankan condiments sit in the bottom of the bag like precious treasures. Chili paste with dried shrimp, onions cooked down to a brown caramel hue, and spicy coconut sambol.

"My ammi brought them back when she went to Sri Lanka this year. My Sri Lankan cooking still needs a lot of work, so I thought that they would be put to better use here."

"That's so generous of you. I haven't seen this brand in years. We haven't been able to go back in quite some time," Ammi says.

Clearing my name hasn't made me forget about our other problems, just made them seem more insignificant comparatively. Somehow, I'll get us back to Sri Lanka soon.

"Well then, I'm glad they've gone to a good home," Amaya says.

"I suppose this means that you have to come over for dinner more often," Ammi replies with a warm smile. I'm grateful Ammi isn't wishing that Amaya were a cute single man, preferably a doctor, who wants to marry me. She's just happy I have another friend.

"I won't ever say no to a delicious home-cooked meal. Siri said you're the best cook."

"She flatters me, you'll have to see for yourself."

Soon all of us are gathering around the table, spooning colorful curries and rice onto our plates. Everyone is genuinely enjoying each other's company, and even Thathi seems to be doing well. My father disappears and returns with a bottle of dusty wine that he has kept for a celebratory occasion—one I'd hoped would mark my graduation or engagement. As no milestone came, the bottle sat in the dark. Getting murder charges dropped didn't fit neatly into any milestone celebration that garnered a greeting card, but it's still deserving of wine.

"We are thrilled to open this special bottle of wine today. We are so happy and thankful to Amaya"—Ammi smiles at her—"and as always to Alex, Siri's brother." Alex looks embarrassed. I know the compliment makes Alex feel even worse about his betrayal, but I feel hopeful our bond can survive this. "When Siri got arrested, we thought maybe another one of our children would leave us. It was unbearable to even think about. Thanks to you two, she is home with us again."

"And thanks to Siri herself," Amaya announces. "She is an excellent investigator."

"Uh, thank you," I respond. I guess I've gone from a very false understanding of how the criminal legal world works to having the confidence to ask questions and follow leads—things that seemed impossible only a few weeks ago. I also tackled a gun-wielding assassin. Just call me Enola Holmes.

"Any words from the woman of the hour?" Alex asks.

I'm embarrassed about all the attention, but I know I want to say something.

"I used to feel like my life was as bad as it could get, which seems crazy now. Little did I know I would end up with a dead man in my back seat and thrown in jail. Everyone has setbacks and hard days. Real life isn't an Instagram highlight reel, but I am so damn lucky." I gesture to my parents, Amaya, and even to Alex. "And this whole experience has reminded me to appreciate every second of it."

"Hear, hear!" Alex echoes. Everyone cheers and clinks their glasses.

"Your brother would be so proud of you," Ammi says, tears in her eyes.

"You've been through so much. Yet, you persevere. You go to work every day and take care of every single person around you. You work so hard at your job and do it so well. We couldn't be prouder to have you as our daughter," Thathi says, and gives me a hug.

I feel tears prick my eyes. It's not often my father is sentimental, and it feels good to hear that my parents are proud of me. Deep down inside, I think I knew this all along.

CHAPTER 46

Everyone insists on cleaning up the kitchen since Ammi has done all the work to cook a delicious meal. She finally relents, handing over the cleaning to me, Alex, and Thathi, and starts sharing embarrassing stories of my youthful indiscretions. Typical.

I look around the warm glow of the kitchen. Thathi is washing the delicate china, taken out for special occasions and not appropriate for the dishwasher, as Alex dries them. I hear Amaya laughing on the couch, no doubt at one of a million stories Ammi has up her sleeve about my brother and me. I pray the one of me pooping in my pants when I was most definitely too old to be doing so doesn't make an appearance. And for a second, I think I can almost hear my brother's voice, too, like another member of the party softly talking in the background.

"Thathi . . ." I say, turning toward my father, "are you okay?"

The case is over; I can handle the news. I want to know. Why have these past few months, even years, brought a cautious slowness to the man I've only ever known as strong and sturdy?

"I'm fine, Putha. Just old age slowing me down a bit."

"Really?" I respond, not believing my father.

"Yes, really. You worry so much about us. You always have these bad feelings, especially since your brother died. You always expect the worst. We're not going anywhere. At least for now. Old age just takes its toll; we're not the people we were when we were younger. In a few years, you'll live and die by an orthopedic pillow too." Thathi puts a hand on my shoulder. "We're so happy to have you home."

I don't want to attribute my anxiety to my parents growing closer to the end of their days, but instead to a diagnosable disease that has a cure. My parents and I don't always see eye to eye, but every time I try to imagine life without them, an unbearable ache pulls me down and threatens to submerge me completely. I have to accept that they are growing older. I also need to realize I still have time left with them, and I vow to make the most of it.

I need to make the most of my life *now.* I won't wait for tomorrow, or when I lose a little weight, or when I have the perfect job. Tonight, I won't worry about the crumbling roof, or my career, or being single. I will take in all the blessings I have had in front of me the entire time.

EPILOGUE

One Year Later

The beach is pristine. Unlike the closest beach to me in NYC, there aren't Band-Aids or other suspicious pieces of trash floating around. The water is so clear I can see not only the fish that swim by me, but also my toes wriggling through the sand on the ocean floor. The sun warms my shoulders until they are hot, and then I sit in the cool water for pleasant relief.

Back on the shore, a man offers me an ice-cold coconut, cracked open with a straw poking out. Coconut water in its freshest form and at a fraction of the cost of what's available in the new health food stores cropping up everywhere back in NYC. I accept it gratefully. My parents are lying next to me in beach chairs, looking perfectly calm, as they too take in the view. I tried to tell Ammi I didn't think Thathi should travel. And for the millionth time, Ammi assured me he was fine and quite sassily snapped at me that they are just old, not dead. And now, looking at both of them, smiling away, I know that Thathi is in fact perfectly healthy, with maybe a few more gray hairs and lower back pain that comes with aging. I've been so used to remembering my parents in their prime, I can't pretend anymore that each year doesn't bring on a spate of new ailments.

It made sense for us to get out of the house while all the extensive repairs are being done. It's amazing what a modest civil lawsuit against the police for a wrongful arrest can do. It's a life-changing amount to us, and as a result we're getting the roof replaced, new plumbing done, and a paint job. The contractor said there would be a lot of dust kicked up that would irritate Ammi's allergies, and so I happily suggested we leave for Sri Lanka, a trip years in the making. My cab is safely in Alex's state-of-the-art garage with a new crystal clear divider. No one is getting murdered or even puking in the back seat without my full knowledge.

I have my LSAT book in my lap, and I find the logic puzzles genuinely interesting, which may mean I have a personality defect. (Who likes tests?) I haven't decided whether I will apply to law school. Driving my taxi part-time and working as an investigator with Amaya is keeping me quite busy. The public defender's office needed more investigators, and Amaya put in a good word for me, and before I knew it, I was helping her with her cases in an official capacity. I like working with her, and we usually enjoy a meal together wherever the investigations takes us. I've introduced Amaya to Nepalese food, and she introduced me to a new Jamaican spot that just opened. We both love to eat, apparently a requirement for any friend of mine.

And in a particularly bittersweet moment, I moved out of my parents' place and into my own small studio. For the first time in my life, I won something—the affordable housing lottery—and the leftover money from the lawsuit helped cover the first couple of months' rent.

Alex and I are doing better, having put a lot of work into our friendship—reminding me that friendships, like many things in life, require constant thought and care. After weeks of protracted negotiations, Alex avoided a conviction and jail time in exchange for his testimony against Brett. Alex did lose his job because of all the bad press, but he's getting back on his feet.

I can say for the first time in a while that I'm happy. I'm back in Sri Lanka with my parents. I close my eyes when my phone beeps. It's a text from Amaya.

Hope you're enjoying vacation. When you're back there's an investigation I need your help with.

I pick up my phone and type back.

Can't wait.

Acknowledgments

The idea for this book originated when I got into a taxi around 1 a.m. after working a night court shift representing New Yorkers charged with everything from stealing toothpaste to unsuccessfully trying to murder someone (allegedly). I got into a cab with a driver who told me he always picked up night court fares because he loved true crime. Despite my exhaustion and initial trepidation about discussing infamous NYC murders in a locked car while hurtling across the Brooklyn Bridge, it was a moment of human connection.

New York City's taxi drivers keep this city running. My interest in their stories was born not only from marrying into a family of taxi drivers, but also because of my husband's love of the restaurant Curry in a Hurry, which stood just a block away from a taxi stand filled with drivers who looked a lot like me. As they picked up a cup of chai to fuel another late night, I wondered about the lives of these drivers who remain largely anonymous to their passengers. This novel is a true celebration of cab drivers and all the essential NYC service people who make this city special.

There are so many people who contributed, directly and indirectly, to this novel.

Common sentiment would suggest that when your agent sells your work, it's confirmation that it was the right fit all along. I knew I had gotten the best agent long before there was ever a glimmer of a hope that this novel would be published. Michelle Richter, you have had an unwavering belief in this novel and in me. You've read the manuscript so many times and had such thoughtful insights—working with you is one of the best decisions I've ever made. Thank you also to Jack McNulty, who provided wonderful edits and feedback.

Angela Kim, thank you for being such a brilliant, thoughtful editor. You've made this book so much better with your sharp and thoughtful insights. You made every part of this process such a joy, and I can't wait to do the second novel in this series guided by your keen editorial eye. I am so honored to work with you.

Thank you to Vikki Chu and Andressa Meissner for the stunning cover of my dreams. Thanks also to the rest of the Berkley team: Anna Venckus, Elisha Katz, Kaila Mundell-Hill, Jennifer Myers, Angelina Krahn—I'm so grateful for you all. Thank you also to Claire McLaughlin for your incredible work on this book.

I also need to thank my dear friends in and out of the writing world. Kellye: Thank you for being so generous with your time and knowledge. I admire you and your novels so much. Tammy and Amy: Thank you to my writing friends who gave amazing feedback on this novel and other things I've written. Amanda, Bek, Chelsey, Dara, Lauren, Lenore, Marge, Sara, and Rajvi: Thank you for being some of the best friends I could ever have. Your encouragement and unfailing support gave me the courage to write this novel. I could write another novel on how much I love you all. Thanks for being my people.

Ammi and Thathi, this novel is for you. You left Sri Lanka with no money and no resources and somehow worked insanely hard, long hours and sacrificed so much of yourselves so I could achieve my dreams. Thank you so much for always believing in me, supporting me, understanding me, and loving me unconditionally. I am where I am because of you both.

Being the mischievous, sometimes-irresponsible baby sister to two incredible big sisters has forever shaped me.

Manisha Akki, your medical advice literally kept me alive while I wrote this book and for my whole life. You've been there through medical issues large and small, life's biggest and smallest problems. Your kindness and empathy are my guiding light. Thank you for being my surrogate mom and letting me, even now, rely on you.

Eva Nangi, you've read so many versions of this novel and basically everything I've ever written for pretty much my whole life. It's with your encouragement, enormous patience, and love that I became a writer. This novel is here because of you. Somehow, even as an adult, I still want to be like you when I grow up.

I'm lucky that my sisters married two people who now feel like brothers, Ranil and Miles.

Dhyana, Sajin, Maya, Henry, and Sammy—you five are my greatest joys. The sweetest, smartest, kindest nieces and nephews. When the world feels scary, you give me hope that our future is bright, kind, and special. You've all made my life so much better in ways I couldn't have anticipated.

Adam, I'm not sure what I did to deserve you. I think I probably saved a school bus of orphans from certain death in my last life or something equivalently saintlike to have found you. You always believed I'd publish a novel, so much so that you literally told every single person you spoke to I was a novelist even when everything pointed to the contrary. This book is here because you dried every tear, convinced me to not quit writing on at least a dozen separate and harrowing occasions, and maybe most importantly because you ate at Curry in a Hurry once a week in the early years of us dating. I'm the luckiest.

What a delight to have fantastic in-laws. Debbie, Joel, Robert, and Jeannie—I adore you all so much and am so grateful for my family to have expanded in such a beautiful way. Thank you for the support, encouragement, and love.

Last but not least, thank you to my readers. It's the privilege of a lifetime to write for you all. Thank you so much for taking a chance on me and picking up this book.

THE MIDNIGHT TAXI

YOSHA GUNASEKERA

READERS GUIDE

Discussion Questions

1. *The Midnight Taxi* combines a humorous tone with serious issues in the criminal legal system, differentiating it from other crime novels. What was your take on this approach?

2. It's estimated that less than 20 percent of taxi drivers are women. Did it surprise you to see Siri driving a taxi? Why or why not?

3. Siri often feels like she's neither completely Sri Lankan nor completely American and struggles with her identity and sense of self. How does this change as the novel progresses?

4. Siri is lucky to have Amaya's phone number at a dire moment. Who would be the first person you'd call if you found a body and you knew you'd be the number one suspect?

5. Siri is obsessed with true crime, and it shapes her view of the criminal legal system. Only when she finds herself accused of murder does she realize she got a lot of it wrong. Do you

feel like the true crime content you consume shapes how you look at the criminal legal system? Has this novel made you reevaluate how you view people accused of a crime?

6. Even though they don't have much in common on the outside, Alex and Siri are best friends. Do you have any friends or connections that seem unlikely?

7. Was there anything that surprised you about how the arraignment process works?

8. Community is a huge theme in this novel. Where do you see pockets of communities where you live, and in what ways have they helped you?

9. Siri and Amaya don't even get the victim's name until they do a bunch of sleuthing themselves. Is it surprising to learn that oftentimes the defense is at a disadvantage in getting information regarding a case? How do you think that affects the way a case progresses?

10. How does Siri's relationship with her parents change from the beginning of the novel to the end?

Keep reading for an excerpt from the next book by Yosha Gunasekera

CHAPTER 1

There is blood dripping down the windshield. I punch my brakes and pull over immediately, pissing off nearly everyone who is driving behind me in this bumper-to-bumper New York City gridlock caused by protests. I hear the rhythmic chants in the near distance: "*We want JUSTICE!*" Having served as an investigator in the so-called criminal justice space for the past six months, I've discovered that actual justice is elusive. I turn my attention back toward the accident. I hope I haven't killed her. I rush out of my taxi, and there she is, lifeless. I dig my nails into my hands to stop from crying and try to see if she's still breathing. Shock makes me move on autopilot.

Dead. She's dead.

She looks peaceful in death, and were it not for the blood, someone may assume she died a quiet, nonviolent death. Goose bumps crawl up my arms as I stare at her.

"Siri! We gotta go!" Amaya shouts from the car.

I trek back, wondering who I should call.

"I killed her," I say softly as I get back into the car. The first living thing, if you don't count numerous bugs, that has died at my hand.

Amaya cranes her neck out the open window. "It's a pigeon, Siri. And it flew into your windshield. Your only crime may be keeping your taxi windshield so clear the bird couldn't see it."

"It was a rock pigeon. They mate for life and are devoted parents." Pigeons get a pretty bad rep in the city, but the fact that they are so family-oriented reminds me they're sort of like any of us trying to get by in this crazy city. I didn't grow up with this type of pigeon as a small kid and am less traumatized by them than the rest of NYC.

"Are you into birds now?" Amaya says, probably recoiling at my sentimentality. I'm sentimental when it comes to everything. Amaya seems like she's sentimental about nothing.

"Yes. It's a soothing hobby . . . and surprisingly fun." I realize I sound like I'm twenty-eight going on sixty-five right now. Maybe this is why I'm still single. My hobbies include early-morning bird-watching and *Jeopardy!* once a week with my parents. "Should I call someone to make sure she's picked up and buried?"

"Why do you assume the pigeon is a she? Flying into windows seems more like a man's work. We aren't as oblivious to our surroundings," Amaya replies with that characteristic snap in her voice I've come to love, especially when it's not directed at me. "Call the Department of Sanitation to come pick him up. If he were still alive, we could have driven him up to the Wild Bird Fund on the Upper West Side and maybe tried to save him." She emphasizes *him*, and I laugh a little.

Just when I think Amaya doesn't care. . .

"Will do," I say as I google the number. While it may appear as if the city has no system of sanitation, thanks to the rats, roaches, and outrageous smells coming from the trash in the summer, I know that without the Department of Sanitation, things would be a lot worse. After reporting the dead rock pigeon, we start navigating through the traffic again.

In Sri Lankan culture, a bird running into the windshield or a window is a bad omen. I remember the few times it happened when I was living with my parents and how spooked my normally rational Ammi would get. *It's a bad sign of things to come,* she would say ominously before going back to whatever she was doing like nothing had happened at all. A slight shiver runs down my spine before I revert to common sense and logical thinking. It was an unfortunate accident, that's all. Back in the car and still stuck in traffic, I see a group of people holding signs. "What do you think they're protesting?"

"Look at the state of the world. Could be a million things," Amaya mutters. "Fossil fuels, health insurance, the loss of due process . . ."

I keep thinking she's going to stop, but she continues to list things. Currently, I'm balancing driving my taxi part-time and serving as the Legal Services of Manhattan's newest investigator with Amaya, my former attorney turned colleague. I've been on the job for a little under two months and am still very much learning the ropes. You'd think with these jobs I'd share her outlook. Sure, I see plenty of crappy things in my cab and as an investigator, but I also see the good things people do and the resiliency they show in terrible situations. Many of them have been dealt an unfair hand. It's true there seems to be very little justice to be had in the criminal legal system with people being hauled to prison for minor crimes unless, of course, you're rich and can pay bail. Somehow, my clients remain hopeful even with the cards stacked against them.

To say I'm busy is an understatement. If you look up "chicken with its head cut off" online, I'm pretty sure a picture of me would pop up. Yet, I love it. I thought I'd be a cabdriver forever, and while there is nothing wrong with that life, a part of me has always wanted to know if I could hack it in the legal world. Once, I'd thought it would be as an attorney, but life as an investigator is close enough.

We edge closer as the traffic moves just slightly. I see someone in Native American dress and hear parts of a speech. *"Our ancient graves deserve dignity. NYC must not build over these sites . . ."*

"Oh, I think I've heard about this . . ." I don't watch Channel Five news as much as I did when I lived with my parents, but occasionally, if I'm home at 6:30 p.m., I turn it on for nostalgic value and to find out what's happening in my city. "Last night they were talking about some small protests around the city. There's reason to believe there are a lot of ancient Native American burial sites that are being exhumed by new construction. I bet it has something to do with that."

"Interesting. First, we basically steal this land that wasn't ours to begin with, and then we desecrate the graves of those same people." Refreshingly, Amaya always gets to the point.

I nod my head in agreement. It feels wrong to disturb these sites without even acknowledging their existence.

Amaya's phone buzzes.

"We've got to head to court. Criminal court arraignments are super busy today."

Amaya looks over at me, imploring me to go faster without

saying anything. We spend so much time together these days, I can usually guess what Amaya is thinking. She also wears her emotions on her face, so that helps.

With that, I make a right turn, artfully avoiding the group of tourists who are paying no attention, and head toward 100 Centre Street to meet our next client.

CHAPTER 2

I'm certainly not one to make judgments on the clothes anyone wears. I only recently started dressing nicely so as to not embarrass Amaya, because as an investigator, I'm part of her legal team, and I have to interact with real people and extract information from them. I can't hide in my taxi anymore. Besides, people are much less likely to give over valuable video footage to someone who is wearing their brother's old, oversized Knicks jersey and their Ammi's eighties harem pants. I need to look professional now, so I thrift sensible J.Crew sweaters and slacks. Amaya once joked I was copying her look. People always mistake us for sisters, and I take it as a compliment. Amaya's dark hair is always less frizzy, her smile always a little brighter, and she's just generally more put-together, so if I've tricked anyone into thinking we're similar, I'm doing something right.

I do make an effort to put my own spin on things. Today's spin is sneakers with a bright pink streak. They look like those two-hundred-dollar sneakers, but I thrifted them for ten bucks. Alex says it's gross to wear someone else's shoes, but that's probably because Alex can afford fancy new kicks. Despite the loss of his super-fancy tech job fourteen months ago, his status as a convicted criminal of fraud, and the money taken from him as a result of said criminal activity, my best friend still manages to be way richer than me.

It's with this nonjudgmental attitude—or at least me trying to have a nonjudgmental attitude—that I look at our client Lucy's criminal paperwork. Lucy is charged with stalking, which I must admit is pretty exciting. Yes, stalking is bad and scary. People shouldn't do it. But maybe Lucy didn't do it. Besides, most of the crimes Amaya picks up are gang-related shootings and garden-variety burglaries. I'd never dismiss the seriousness of these crimes and the people accused of said crimes who are facing years in prison, but they aren't always that unique. I want to investigate the cases my podcast covers. I want intrigue, mystery, and suspense, and maybe this stalking case has all those elements.

Who is she accused of stalking? A lover who turned his back? Maybe the man she's stalking is actually stalking her? All of my thoughts go out the window when I see Lucy. She's wearing a jumpsuit embellished with thousands of rhinestones, and it's certainly not what I expected. Maybe it's Lucy's rhinestone-embellished jumpsuit that's making me feel like she's less of a stalker and more of a backup dancer in a seventies disco musical.

We move toward the back of the courthouse to the dark and dusty prison cells that hold people waiting to see the judge. No matter how many times I sit back there, in the dirt and grime, I can't erase the memories of when I was on the other side as a person accused of a heinous crime that I didn't do. Only a little over a year ago, I was in Lucy's position, sitting in a cell next to other women accused of crimes. It's a reminder to never judge the people before me and to never assume that I know the truth of the matter without proper investigation. It is, after all, investigations that are one of the most important parts of criminal case—especially at the beginning when the clues are still fresh.

"Hi, my name is Amaya Fernando. I'm the attorney representing you on your case," Amaya announces warmly. Amaya is always kind to her clients. I experienced this firsthand when she represented me after I was wrongfully accused of killing my passenger. Amaya continued to investigate even when she was sure I was guilty. After all, it was just me and the dude in my locked cab. Amaya shrugs this off as "just doing her job" but I know it's more than that. She cares deeply for the people who come before her, ensnared in the legal system, devoid of a voice—literally, because they are not allowed to talk in court. They must talk through their attorney, a job Amaya takes very seriously.

"And this is Siriwathi Perera."

This is the part where I would stick out my hand for a handshake, but the metal grate that separates me and Amaya from Lucy prevents that. It's a hard way to have any conversation, let alone one that may change the trajectory of someone's life.

We both sit down and face Lucy.

"Can you tell us what happened?" Amaya asks gently.

"I didn't do it. I'm not guilty," Lucy says firmly.

And with that, the case begins.

CHAPTER 3

Determining someone's guilt or innocence is a tricky proposition. Sometimes you can find forensic or DNA evidence that can make you nearly certain someone is guilty. It is science, after all. Except, I guess, in my case, where my DNA was found on the murder weapon, making everyone fairly convinced of my guilt. For most people, that's the end of the road. I guess what I've learned in this job is that nothing is what it seems.

"Lucy, do you know why you've been arrested?" Amaya asks gently. It's quite a skill to get a stranger to spill their guts on what is undoubtedly one of the most traumatic days of their life.

Lucy is a tiny blond woman, and despite her glittering rhinestone jumpsuit that unfortunately catches the harsh overhead light, she's otherwise unremarkable.

"Just so you know, the outfit is me going undercover for a story," Lucy remarks with a thick Long Island accent.

I like her already.

I've heard a lot of outlandish things as a taxi driver, and sometimes it's hard to discern fact from fiction. Amaya reminds me to investigate cases and to not just trust my gut, because somehow my gut seems to like almost everyone we meet in this job. I need to follow the evidence and not assume the best in someone just because they're wearing a rhinestone jumpsuit to go undercover on a story and seem like they'd be a hoot at a party.

"For a story? Are you a journalist?" I ask.

"Used to be . . . I, well, it's a long story. But I'm innocent. I never stalked Diane or anyone else."

"Who's Diane?" Amaya asks.

"Diane Larsen."

I stare at Lucy impassively. I have no clue who she is talking about.

Amaya turns to me, a look on her face.

"Diane Larsen?" Lucy says, as if saying the name a second time will suddenly unearth a hidden memory for us.

"I really don't know who you're talking about." I try to cover the slight annoyance in my voice. It's my own insecurity from not always getting certain references since I didn't grow up in the States and wasn't exposed to American culture until I moved here as a kid.

"She's a socialite. Her family is big in this city. They have their own foundation. They donate millions of dollars to good causes," Lucy says slowly, pausing between each sentence as if it will ring a bell.

"She's also quite the party girl. A Page Six special," Amaya says with a little smirk.

"She's also my friend," Lucy shoots back, clearly protective.

"Oh, sorry, I didn't realize you two knew each other," Amaya says, a sheepish look covering her face.

"It's okay. To people who don't know her, she seems self-absorbed, arrogant, rich, uncaring—"

"But you know her," Amaya interrupts. She's good at keeping people on track. "So what happened?"

I'm imagining a very dramatic falling-out of this friendship. Maybe Diane stole Lucy's boyfriend and she's exacting an elaborate plan for revenge . . . Before I allow myself to daydream more nonsensical possibilities, I realize this isn't one of my podcasts. This is real life, not *Jerry Springer.*

"We're still friends," Lucy says.

"But you're charged with stalking her?" Amaya questions.

"I couldn't understand why. I'd like to see the evidence against me. Who reported me?" Lucy asks in distress.

That's going to take some time, I think to myself. They didn't give me any evidence when I was charged with a crime and fighting for my freedom. As usual, the real criminal justice system is quite different from what is portrayed on TV. Defense attorneys are usually always in an information vacuum.

"Well, we don't have much evidence against you yet. But we have some bare-bones information in the criminal complaint. The criminal complaint outlines your crimes as understood by the DA's office and NYPD at this preliminary stage," Amaya says as Lucy begins to protest. Amaya clears her throat and then, with a look of pity that I know all too well, she says, "They say that Diane claims not to know you. And that when you were arrested, you had photos from inside her house, which means it's possible they'll charge you with something much more serious, like burglary."

I cannot jump to conclusions, but a small voice in my head tells me that Lucy is very, very guilty.

Photo by Sub/Urban Photography

Yosha Gunasekera is a Sri Lankan American attorney who represents people who have spent decades in prison for crimes they did not commit. She teaches a course at Princeton University focused on wrongful conviction and exoneration. Yosha is a former Manhattan public defender and has written and spoken extensively on the criminal legal system.

VISIT THE AUTHOR ONLINE

YoshaGunasekera.com
Yosha.Gunasekera